I0824423

Blessings from Above

ISBN (Hardcover): 979-8-9945937-2-1
ISBN (Paperback): 979-8-9945937-1-4

Printed in the United States of America

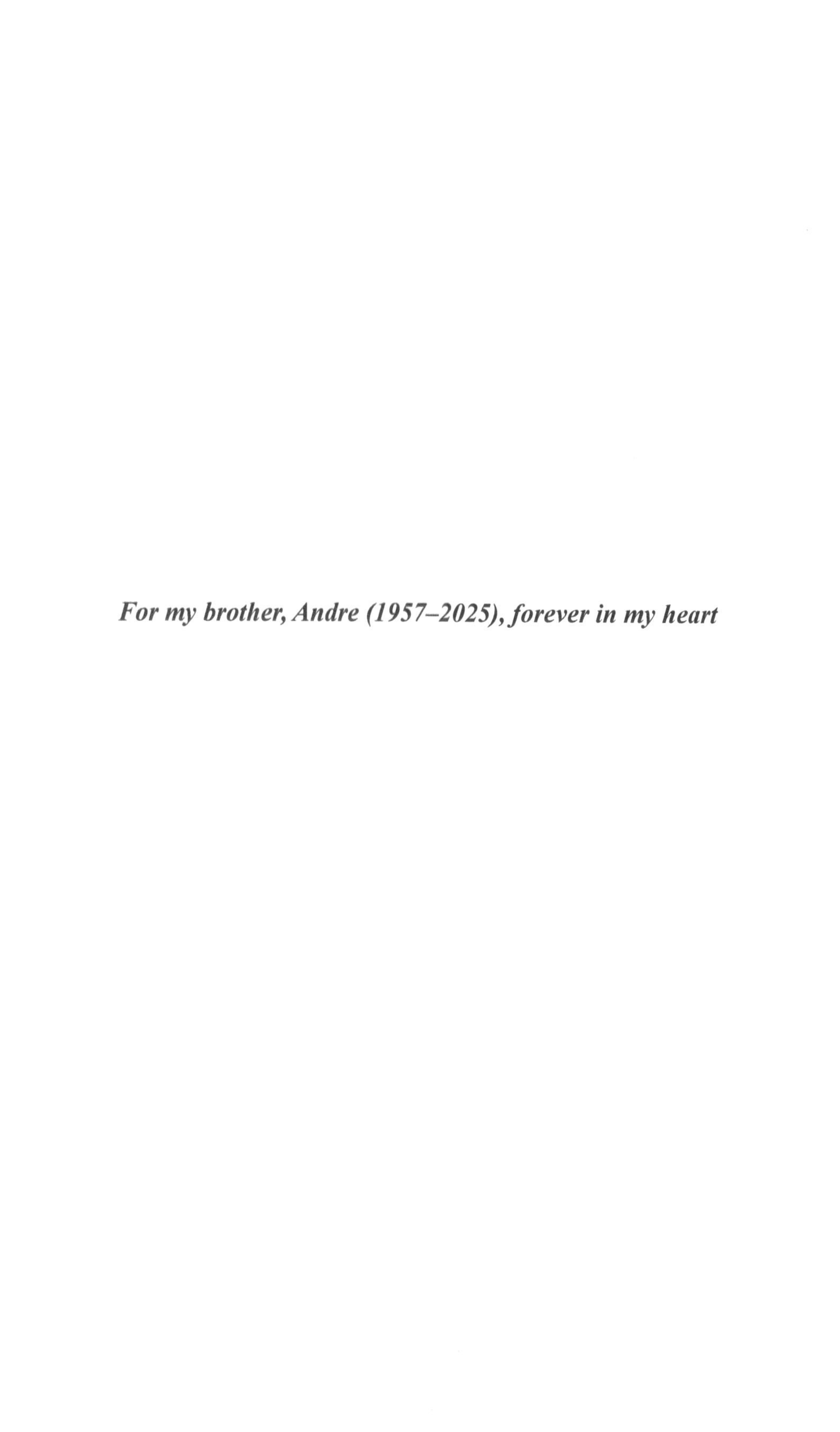

For my brother, Andre (1957–2025), forever in my heart

Author's Note

Blessings from Above was written quietly… the way many of life's most meaningful moments unfold.

This story was never meant to rush toward answers or tidy conclusions. It was born from the belief that faith often reveals itself not in grand declarations, but in small, steady moments of grace… moments of waiting, of trusting, of learning to release what we cannot control.

The characters in these pages walk through joy and sorrow much like we do in real life. They stumble. They hope. They carry burdens they don't yet have answers for. And sometimes, they simply stand still long enough to recognize that they are not walking alone.

At its heart, this is a story about community, about the strength found in shared burdens, and about a God who remains faithful even when the path forward is unclear. It is not a story about having all the answers, but about learning to trust the One who does.

When you find yourself reflected in these pages…in the waiting, the wondering, or the quiet moments of recognition, know that you are not alone. And if this story stirred something in your heart, I hope it reminds you that grace is often closer than we realize… faithfully present, even in the silence.

Thank you for reading.

Lydia

To every thing there is a season,

and a time to every purpose under the heaven.

Ecclesiastes 3:1 (KJV)

Chapter **1 Homecoming** 1
Chapter **2 Welcome Home Celebration** 16
Chapter **3 A Quiet Harbor Evening with Sam Whitaker**........35
Chapter **4 Familiar Places, Unfamiliar Feelings**....................49
Chapter **5 A Gentle Evening, A New Morning** 63
Chapter **6 New Beginnings at Harmony Grove Harbor Hospital** 83
Chapter **7 The Weight of a Promise and the Grace That Follows**...102
Chapter **8 Because of Grace** 114
Chapter **9 Echoes of a Brother's Love**...............................128
Chapter **10 The Light Over the Harbor** 144
Chapter **11 A Meeting with the Shepherd**...........................155
Chapter **12 The Bell, The Tower and Main Street** 161
Chapter **13 The Storm**..170
Chapter **14 In the Shelter of His Arms** 182
Chapter **15 The Long Night that Wakes a Gentle Tomorrow**203
Chapter **16 A Morning of Mercy** 214
Chapter **17 Reflections** 222
Epilogue 227

Chapter 1

Homecoming

The wheels touched down with a soft jolt, and the small jet airliner slowly made its way towards the terminal of Harmony Grove Harbor Regional Airport. From her window seat, Kendra Williams leaned in closer to get a glimpse of the approaching coastline. The harbor was coming into view; a whirl of activity with working and sports fishing boats heading out and returning, laden with their catch for the day.

Harmony Grove Harbor. A small city with a population of just under twenty thousand, nestled along the coastline, looks like it belongs on a postcard. Small enough that neighbors still know one another by name, yet large enough to have its own rhythm of commerce, schools, and steady tourism in the summer months. It's a place of quiet resilience where fishermen, shopkeepers, and families lean on one another like stones in a seawall.

But what sets Harmony Grove Harbor apart isn't just its postcard charm, but its spirit. Neighbors still look out for one another. Doors are held open, casseroles and bags of groceries appear on porches during hard times, and gossip travels fast but softens in the telling. People still wave at passing cars, not because they know who was inside, but because they figure they probably do. Harmony Grove Harbor is small, yes, but alive with a spirit of progress. Its streets carry the aroma of fresh-baked breads and pastry and the sound of local musicians in the square; its schools are brimmed with art and science fairs, and its officials boast about the town's historic character, continuing revitalization efforts and economic sustainability.

The nearby marina stretches along the coastline like a floating city; rows of yachts and leisure boats gleam beneath the afternoon sun, their polished hulls reflecting shards of light across the rippling water. A soft breeze carries the faint sound of laughter from the marina's clubhouse, where white awnings flutter above a terrace café overlooking the slips. Kendra could almost smell the familiar scent of grilled seafood drifting from the open deck of the Harborview Restaurant, mingling with the low clink of glasses and the distant notes of a guitar. Nearby, a boathouse stands neat and trim, its freshly painted doors open to reveal racks of life vests and the glint of brass fixtures. Every surface seems to shimmer, as if the marina itself takes pride in its reflection.

Just beyond it, the working harbor tells a quieter, humbler story. The water deepens to a darker blue where longliners, crabbers and weathered fishing boats rest side by side, their nets coiled neatly like sleeping serpents. Seagulls perch on pilings worn smooth by years of tide and wind, and the faint scent of salt and diesel lingers; a perfume of honest labor. Rust-flecked cranes stand at attention along the docks, and old wooden signs bearing names like *Faithful Star* and *Martha Jane* rock gently with the tide. It is utilitarian, yes, but not without grace; there's a rhythm to it, a kind of nostalgia that speaks of endurance and pride.

Together, the marina and harbor mirror the soul of Harmony Grove Harbor itself. Refined but hard-working, modern but still touched by memory. Sunlight danced across the entire bay, scattering into a thousand tiny prisms that seem to bless the waterfront and everything it touched.

Kendra momentarily took a deep breath and closed her eyes, and just above a whisper, said, "*Home*."

Seated next to her was Charlene Matthews letting out a dramatic sigh. "Land! Bless-ed, beautiful land!" She slapped her palms together excitedly and tapped the floor with her military desert boots. "And not a speck of desert sand in sight. God is good!"

Kendra smiled faintly. "You're awful."

"Yes, and ridiculously thankful," Charlene adjusted her curly ponytail as her large brown eyes danced with mischief. "Come on, admit it, you prayed as hard as I did for this day. And now,", nudging Kendra playfully, "prayer is about to carry us into an ocean-kissed, small-town with air that smells of fresh sea and fried shrimp."

Kendra's laugh bubbled out, light and unexpected. Charlene's humor was contagious.

Charlene leaned in closer to the window and motioned for Kendra to follow her gaze. In the distance, a gleaming glass building caught both of their eyes. Their gaze followed the curve of the bay until it rested on a new landmark, one that caught the sunlight through its beckoning glass façade; the new hospital, rising on a hill just beyond town. Its huge glass windows shimmered with promise,

"Geez, Kendra. That must be the new hospital."

"Wow, that's really impressive," Kendra said with a low whistle. "And to think, we'll be working there in just a few days."

The new hospital was a reminder of one of the main reasons why she'd come back, though part of her still wondered if she was ready. Gratitude and unease tangled quietly inside her. So much looked and felt different, yet somehow it all felt like it was supposed to. Shining brighter than she remembered, waiting to welcome her back.

For a long moment, Kendra didn't look away. In the distance, Harmony Grove Harbor spread out like a memory brought back to life; familiar and yet somehow, strangely different. Her heart lifted at the sight of it, that soft curve of coastline she'd once taken for granted now gleaming under the afternoon sun. A warmth engulfed her, a part that felt like happiness, and a part that felt like sadness, but overall, she felt the embrace of the peace and the joy of being *Home.*

Kendra released a long, grateful sigh. Her legs and back were slightly stiffening from the effects of a long journey that had seemed to go on for days, but her mind wandered momentarily back to a place where the stress and strain of a decision to save a life... or a limb…was the norm. She instinctively grabbed her dog tag and glanced down at the front of her camouflage uniform jacket and sleeves, brushing away faint creases that refused to disappear. The silver insignia on her collar caught the sunlight and glinted briefly, a quiet reminder of the life she was leaving behind, the long nights, the medical field tents, the endless rhythm of duty and loss. She straightened her shoulders out of habit, then realized there was no incoming call, no shouted warnings…only the simple grace of calm.

A small, almost shy smile tugged at her lips. "*I am home now",* she thought.

Her hands came together loosely in her lap, fingers intertwining as she bowed her head. The gesture was natural, humble. Her eyes drifted closed, and a soft prayer rose within her; part thanksgiving, part plea for whatever came next.

Thank You, Lord... for getting us here. For this day, this town, this sky, this light, this harbor. But... her throat ached, *why me? Why us?*

Behind her closed eyes she fought to restrain the memories that now seemed to flood in: memories of another sky that burned orange over a desert, medical choppers beating the air, dust curling around tents marked with red crosses. She saw flashes of faces… the young corporal who'd squeezed her hand and whispered for his mother, the soldier who'd joked through his pain until he couldn't.

The plane turned slightly, and the view grounded her again. The blue water sparkled clean and pure, the shoreline dotted with pastel rooftops and the distant church spire that had always pointed her home. A thin veil of tears blurred the colors, turning the scene into a watercolor of mercy and ache.

Help me, oh Lord, she whispered inwardly. *Help me live in a way that honors them. Help me find strength here to help those who are in need of healing, and the peace to live, not just to survive.*

Charlene nudged her elbow, pulling her gently back to the present. "You okay?"

Kendra blinked, managing a small smile. "Yeah. Just taking it all in."

Charlene glanced sideways, studying her friend's reflection in the airplane window. "Okay," she said softly, nudging her elbow. "What's really on your mind? I know that look."

Kendra hesitated; her gaze still fixed on the harbor below. "Just… thinking how different it feels to be home again."

Charlene tilted her head, unconvinced. "That's not all."

Kendra smiled faintly, the kind that tried to hide what her heart hadn't yet settled. "You caught me," she murmured. "It's nothing bad, just… a lot of memories all at once. Let's talk about it later, though. I don't want to spoil this moment."

Charlene's expression softened. She gave Kendra's hand a quick squeeze. "Alright. Later it is."

Kendra nodded, blinking back the emotion welling inside her. Before either could say more, the intercom crackled and the co-pilot's voice, velvety and smooth, coupled with confidence filled the cabin

"Ladies and gentlemen, this is your first officer speaking. I'd like to extend a warm welcome to Harmony Grove Harbor. The local time is 2:30 p.m., and the weather outside is a clear seventy-two degrees. We thank you for flying with us today."

There was a brief pause, and then the first officer's voice softened warmly.

"We'd also like to extend a very special welcome home to two of our passengers traveling in uniform. On behalf of the crew and everyone aboard, thank you for your service, and welcome home."

Enthusiastic applause rippled through the cabin, some passengers craning their necks to see where the soldiers sat. Charlene flashed a cheerful grin and gave a little wave, while Kendra lowered her head, smiling shyly, a lump in her throat threatening to turn into tears. They had completed the work they were assigned to do. Now, they were being led somewhere quieter…back to the place that first shaped them… to continue the work they were called to do.

The aircraft made a slight jolt as it parked by the new jet bridge, and the cabin doors opened. Kendra and Charlene made their way down the narrow aisle, their uniforms drawing nods and quiet smiles of approval and appreciation from fellow passengers.

The Harmony Grove Harbor airport was as modest as they remembered; one terminal, five gates, and floors that shone with the polish of small-town pride rather than big-city gloss. The rattling and whirring of luggage carts and the occasional announcement over the loudspeakers echoed in the airy space as the women made their way toward baggage claim.

Kendra felt her heart pound faster with each step. She imagined her father's gentle smile and her mother's familiar perfume, waiting just beyond the carousel. Beside her, Charlene was practically bouncing, straining her neck for any glimpse of her parents.

The air inside the terminal was cool and faintly scented with coffee and cinnamon buns. Their footsteps echoed softly against the tile as they followed the stream of passengers toward baggage claim.

Charlene rolled her shoulders and sighed. “I still can’t believe we’re actually back. Almost feels like a dream, doesn’t it?”

Kendra smiled faintly. “Yeah, a good dream.”

Charlene glanced at her, catching the distant look in her friend’s eyes. “Okay, talk to me. What’s really going on in that head of yours? I noticed that look on the plane.”

Kendra hesitated. “It’s nothing, really. Just… I feel kinda guilty. Everyone’s going to be so glad that we’re back home, and I am too, but part of me…” She trailed off, searching for words. “Part of me still feels like I left something unfinished over there.”

Charlene slowed her pace, her voice gentle now. “You know we gave it our best, Kendra. We both gave all that we had to give.”

“I know,” Kendra said quietly. “But sometimes knowing doesn’t make it easier.” She gave a small, almost apologetic smile. “Sorry. I don’t want to drag us down. Let’s just enjoy being back home.”

Charlene touched her shoulder. “Hey, it’s not dragging us down. It’s being human.”

Kendra managed a grateful nod, and they walked. The buzz of conversations swelled around them; the clatter of luggage wheels, the muted laughter of families reunited. These sounds drew Kendra’s focus outward again, comforting her.

As they approached the baggage claim area, they surprisingly noticed how different it looked from what they remembered; sleek, bright, and spacious, with those polished floors gleaming beneath soft recessed lights. New wide windows let in generous sunlight, and the air carried a faint, comforting trace of fresh baked pastries and cocoa from a nearby café. The faithful churn of the carousel was now replaced by a low, smooth whir, and its chrome surface gleamed like new.

Charlene gave a low familiar whistle. “Well, would you look at this? Looks like our little airport has gotten something of a facelift. We’re fancy now!”

Kendra smiled, shifting her tote higher on her shoulder. “Looks like our little airport earned itself quite the promotion while we were gone.”

Then, just ahead, she spotted a cluster of familiar faces waving handmade signs. It wasn’t their families who stood waiting. Instead, neighbors and friends waved and shouted their names enthusiastically. The younger ones were jumping up and down as soon as they spotted Kendra’s and Charlene’s uniforms holding homemade signs with “*Welcome Home Kendra* and *Charlene, We Missed You!”*, scrawled in colorful markers. Kendra caught her breath, then flashed the broadest smile she’d had in months. The heaviness she had experienced earlier left her and now the two of them were surrounded by an outpouring of love and appreciation. Both of them welcomed the hugs, handshakes and sometimes embraces that lasted a little too long.

Kendra blinked in surprise, then let out a laugh as recognition dawned. “Those are the Mitchell kids,” she whispered, pointing at two teenagers grinning ear to ear. “And Mrs. Porter from down the block.”

Charlene’s mouth opened wide with delight. “Would you look at this! I was expecting Mom’s bear hug, not a fan club!”

One of the neighbors, a cheerful man in his fifties, pushed forward. “Your folks wanted to be here, but we talked them into letting us come first. There’s just a ‘little’ welcome home reception planned for you both. Nothing fancy.” His eyes twinkled, giving away the truth.

Kendra's throat tightened again, though this time she couldn't stop little chuckle. "A 'little' reception,' huh?" she said softly.

Charlene slung an arm around her shoulders with a big grin. "Guess this is their version of 'little'. I can't wait to see what 'big' looks like."

Kendra glanced at Charlene, her heart fluttering with both nerves and warmth. Instead of the quiet reunion she'd imagined, their homecoming was already turning into something bigger; something unmistakably Harmony Grove Harbor.

The cheering crowd appeared to part slightly as they spotted someone pushing their way towards them waving and calling out above all the others, "Kendra! Charlene!"

Before they could react, Sheryl Robbins stood right in front of them, slipping her braided hair behind a shoulder and opening outstretched arms and a big smile that was impossible to resist. Laughing through tears and throwing her arms around both women in a fierce hug that spoke louder than words.

"Welcome home, you two," she said, stepping back but keeping her hands on their shoulders. "We've got a lot of catching up to do."

Kendra smiled, touched. "Sheryl Robbins; still the first one to get to the front of the crowd."

"You know it," Sheryl said with a grin. Then she gestured toward the glass doors leading to the curbside pickup. "Come on, Raymond is outside; he will be driving you to the reception. Everyone's waiting. You do remember Raymond… don't you?"

Charlene froze mid-step, then tried to play it cool, though a faint blush betrayed her. "Oh, I remember," she said lightly, glancing toward the doors as if that might somehow prepare her.

Kendra bit back a grin. "How could anyone forget?"

Just then, Raymond Carter appeared in the doorway; late thirties, handsome in that effortless kind of way, his matching black chauffeur's cap and crisp shirt both bearing the embroidered insignia of *Carter Executive Transport*. The short sleeves stopped just beyond his biceps, perfectly suited to the warm autumn day in Harmony Grove Harbor, and the tailored fit did little to hide a frame that looked more at home weightlifting at the athletic club than steering a car. His smile carried an easy warmth, but it was his eyes; dark, clear, and quietly self-assured that caught attention first. His hair was neatly trimmed, his posture confident without arrogance, the picture of a man comfortable in his own skin. Just the sight of him was enough to make Charlene blink twice before she remembered to breathe.

He gave a friendly wave. "Afternoon, ladies. I hope you still remember me from church."

Charlene straightened a little too quickly. "Of course we do!" she blurted, then immediately laughed to cover it. "I mean, how could anyone forget *you*, Raymond?"

Raymond chuckled, the sound warm and unassuming. "Good to know I made a lasting impression. And today, I've got the honor and pleasure of driving two beautiful hometown heroes."

Charlene opened her mouth to reply, but nothing came out. Her mind supplied the words instead; "*oh, I assure you, the pleasure is all mine*" and she quickly settled for a smile that didn't fool Kendra one bit, giving her a playful nudge.

Raymond tipped his cap. "Then let's get those bags and make it official." Just then, their duffel bags appeared on the carousel; scuffed, but still sturdy, and speckled with the faded dust of a faraway place.

Sheryl tried, and failed, to hide her amusement as she watched the exchange. The corners of her mouth twitched with a knowing smile while Charlene fussed with the straps of her duffel bag, before Raymond relieved her of it, pretending to be completely unfazed. Kendra shot Sheryl a quick, conspiratorial look that said *some things never change*, and the two women shared a quiet laugh as Raymond reached for the luggage cart.

Kendra laughed as she reached for her duffel, but Raymond was too quick. With an easy, practiced motion, he lifted the heavy bag as if it weighed nothing and set it neatly into the luggage cart beside Charlene's.

He gave a low whistle and glanced between them with a smile. "I don't know what they're feeding you two in the service, but these bags feel like they've been through a tour of duty themselves. You carried all this on your own?"

Charlene grinned, folding her arms. "We've carried a lot heavier, trust me."

Kendra smiled faintly, her eyes pausing on the solid lines of his forearms before she caught herself. "Guess we got used to managing without much help."

Raymond's grin softened. "Well, you've done your share of carrying. Let someone else take it from here."

Kendra and Charlene exchanged a knowing glance; the kind that carried unspoken memories and quiet understanding. Then, almost in unison, they smiled. "Thank you," they said softly.

Kendra adjusted the straps of her tote across her shoulder and glanced around the renovated baggage claim area. The bright signage, the clean lines, even the art on the walls; everything looked renewed, as if the place itself had been waiting to welcome them back.

"It's nice to see home looking so fresh," she said softly.

Raymond led the way in front of them, steering the luggage cart with an easy rhythm as they made their way toward the sliding glass doors and the afternoon light beyond. The welcome home committee followed closely behind them; some chanting their names more softly now, but not with less exuberance. The cheerful chatter of the small crowd faded just a little as the group reached the baggage claim exit and the waiting sun.

Charlene nudged her with an elbow. "Come on, soldier. Let's see what else they've fixed up while we were gone."

Outside the terminal, the afternoon stretched clear and bright, the kind of day when the sky looked freshly washed and the air carried a whisper of ocean breeze. As they walked onto the curb, they paused briefly letting their eyes wander over every familiar and unfamiliar detail. The airport's exterior had been refreshed too, sporting a fresh coat of a bold but welcoming paint color, the modernized and larger windows making for an even more impressive view from the outside; geometric stone planters filled with in season flowers bursting with color. A new airport sign above the main entrance gleamed as if it, too, shared in the town's pride.

Charlene grinned and motioned toward the new awning. "Would you look at this place? This little airport is really coming up!"

Kendra smiled, her eyes tracing the cheerful faces around her. "It sure is," she said softly. "Guess we picked a good time to come home."

At the curb, a white Lexus SUV limo with a black roof gleamed beneath the autumn sun, awaiting their arrival. It was the newest member of Raymond's luxury line fleet; a mix of custom sedans, SUVs, and sprinter vans that secured *Carter Executive Transport's* place as Harmony Grove Harbor's preferred service for both special occasions and professional travel alike. The doors were dressed with banners reading "Welcome Home, Kendra and Charlene!" Red, white, and blue ribbons streamed from the mirrors, catching the light breeze as they swayed.

Charlene opened her mouth, ready with one of her usual quick-witted comments, but nothing coherent came out. All she managed was a breathy, "Whoa… nice!" as she nudged Kendra with her elbow.

Kendra just shook her head, fighting a smile. Charlene straightened, pretending she hadn't just lost her verbal footing over a limo, or the man who owned it.

The late afternoon sun cast soft reflections across the limo's polished surface. Raymond guided the luggage cart to the rear of the vehicle and, with a press of a button, started the engine remotely. He turned back toward Kendra and Charlene.

"Here, let me take those," he said, reaching for their tote bags before either could protest. He placed them carefully on the cart, then walked ahead to open the passenger doors, motioning them inside with easy courtesy.

"Go ahead and get comfortable," he said with a warm smile. "I'll get these bags loaded in the back. You might want to call your folks and let them know you've landed safe and sound. I'm sure they'll be glad to hear your voices."

Kendra smiled, touched by his thoughtfulness. "That's a good idea. Mom's probably already pacing by now."

Charlene laughed, nodding in agreement. "Same here. And my dad's probably trying to calm Mom down before she wears a hole in the floor."

Both women exchanged a knowing grin; different mothers, same nervous energy, and the sound of their shared laughter mingled softly with the bustle of the airport.

Raymond chuckled as he loaded the duffel and tote bags into the rear hatch, closing it with a quiet thud before climbing into the driver's seat. "Guess I'd better get you both to the church before there's a family search party on our hands. We've been planning this ever since your return was announced at church a few Sundays ago."

Both women replied in unison, voices full of playful exaggeration, "When Main Street Baptist Church knows, the whole town knows!"

They burst into playful laughter, deep, genuine, and contagious, until even Raymond joined in, shaking his head with a grin.

Kendra's mood felt lighter now, lifted by all the love and cheerful excitement surrounding them. But then her expression shifted, and she turned to the window in quiet thought. For a heartbeat, everything around her faded into a hush. She tilted her face toward the sky, eyes closed, drawing in a long, deep breath, as if she could absorb every bit of salt, sunlight, and small-town air her soul had missed.

Charlene smiled softly, turning to look out the window on her side of the limo. The familiar landscape stretched out before her; the tall palms and pines, the glimmer of the harbor in the distance, the sunlight dancing off the water. She glanced toward Kendra, noticing the peaceful expression on her friend's face, and her own smile deepened.

"Oh, it's real, all right," she said, her voice full of gratitude. "We're home, Kendra. We *actually* made it home." Kendra opened her eyes, still smiling, but a tear catching the light before she brushed it away with a quiet smile. "Yeah," she said softly. "We did."

Raymond smiled thoughtfully, finally closing the front door. "Welcome home, ladies."

As they slowly pulled away from the airport, the crowd that had greeted them in baggage claim had already filed into their cars, and now followed closely behind while continuing to wave, snap pictures, and honk their horns; each vehicle decorated in its own way to welcome the two women home.

Kendra looked out the window one last time at the harbor gleaming beyond the runways, gulls circling above like blessings on the breeze. For the first time since she'd landed, her shoulders loosened, and gentle peace settled over her.

Charlene nudged her. "Now *this*," she said with a grin, "feels like coming *home*."

Kendra's smile deepened. "It really does."

Chapter 2

Welcome Home Celebration

The short drive from the airport to Main Street Baptist Church felt almost like a parade. The small convoy wound through tree-lined streets that shimmered in the soft glow of late afternoon, sunlight flashing off car hoods and windows like sparks of celebration. On both sides of the road, people gathered; neighbors leaning over porch rails, couples standing arm in arm on front lawns, and children racing barefoot along the sidewalks waving small flags.

On the older part of town, where the houses sat close together, porches were dressed in bunting and flags that fluttered gently in the sea breezes. Elderly couples waved from their porches in rocking chairs, their smiles deepening the lines that told a lifetime of stories. A retired fisherman in a faded cap stood at the end of his driveway, one hand shading his eyes as the cars passed, his dog wagging eagerly beside him. Farther along, a few folks paused from their yardwork: one man resting his rake against a tree, another waving with his gardening gloves using both hands. Faces glowed with the kind of love that small towns are built on; joy and pride for their own, returning home.

A cluster of teenagers stood near the corner store, holding homemade posters painted in bright pastel colors: *Welcome Home, Kendra and Charlene!* and *Our Heroes Are Back!* A little boy on a scooter waved a toy airplane in the air as if to guide their path, while his sister ran beside him, her laughter tumbling ahead of her like music.

As the convoy turned toward downtown, the scenery changed. The narrow neighborhood streets opened into a wide stretch of colorful coastal cottages giving way to stately old homes with broad verandas and ivy climbing their brick walls. Gas-style lanterns lined the curbs, ready to glow when dusk fell, their glass panes already catching glints of gold from the sinking sun.

Downtown bustled with life. Storefronts displayed ribbons and flags; the scent of coffee, sugar, and sea air mingled in the breeze. At the corner stood Henderson's Bakery, its wide windows fogged faintly from the heat inside. The owner, Mr. Walter Henderson, stood in the doorway, flour dusting his forearms, his white apron smudged with the proof of an already long day's work. He waved with a beaming smile; the same one he'd offered to nearly every resident for more than forty years. His father had opened the bakery after returning from the Navy, and Walter had carried it on faithfully; rolling dough every morning before sunrise, arthritis or not, because "the town runs better when it smells like bread."

He too waves his hands in greeting as the caravan passed, and the scent of his signature cinnamon loaves drifted into the street, sweet and warm and unmistakably home.

The convoy slowed as the view began to widen. The buildings thinned out, replaced by glimpses of glinting masts and rippling water. The harbor shimmered ahead, calm and inviting, and there, just a few blocks from the waterfront stood Main Street Baptist Church flanked between two immense old oaks and azaleas that bloom faithfully each Spring with hearty blossoms.

Built more than a century ago by the hands of local craftsmen and sailors who hauled timber from the very forests that once bordered the bay, the church had stood through hurricanes, and the slow tides of time. Its brick walls bore the softened scars of salt and weather, and its arched windows, framed in white, caught the light like gentle eyes watching over the town. Within those arches, panels of stained glass told the story of faith and endurance; vibrant scenes of shepherds and fishermen, of doves in flight and hands lifted in prayer. In the morning, sunlight streamed through them in ribbons of color, amber, sapphire, and rose; casting a quiet kaleidoscope across the wooden pews. At dusk, the glow from within turned the windows into living lanterns, as if the heart of the church itself was shining outward. The steeple, once the tallest structure for miles, rose sure and symbolic against the horizon, crowned with a weathered bronze cross that still gleamed and stretched heavenward with quiet dignity, glowing softly in the sunlight.

The bell, however, beneath it had fallen silent not long after Kendra and Charlene left for active duty. A powerful coastal storm, more than five years ago, had cracked its mount and stilled its voice. Townsfolk would still glance up toward the belfry and say they could almost hear it in the wind; echoes of Sundays past, of weddings and homecomings, of moments when joy overflowed…and moments when grief gathered families close. Its silence was more than an absence; it was a kind of waiting, a promise, a hope that someday, when the town was ready, its voice would rcturn.

Yet even without its bell, the church still *spoke.* Its front doors, gently worn, but maintained immaculately by generations, seemed to speak with the graciousness of every welcome ever offered. The white-painted railings wrapped around the sanctuary entrance like open arms, and the stained-glass cross above the entry caught the fading light, scattering soft color over the steps below. There was a quiet dignity to it; a faithfulness that mirrored the people it served.

Though time had weathered its edges, every detail, from the arched stained-glass windows to the neatly kept hedges and lawn, spoke of reverence and care.

As the convoy approached, the sun caught the steeple's cross, gilding it for a fleeting moment in gold. The scene seemed to whisper of endurance, of grace, and of all the unseen prayers that still rise from within its sacred walls.

Today, the normally quiet grounds of the church carried a rare liveliness and an atmosphere of excitement and expectation. The lighted marquee sign in front of the old church displayed bold orange letters that read "Welcome Home, Kendra Williams and Charlene Matthews – To God Be the Glory." The fellowship hall was just beyond the sanctuary, through a generous hallway. The final placement of dinnerware, silverware and drinking cups were being set out in buffet style in neat rows. White tablecloths stretched across round banquet hall tables, and serving tables were filled with deviled eggs, homemade casseroles, and baskets of rolls, pastries and fresh baked breads. The air was rich with the fragrance of fried chicken, and peach and apple cobblers still steaming from the oven. That aroma alone spoke of love and hospitality. Mason jars of sweet tea caught the glow of light as children darted between tables, their laughter mingling with the sound of chatter.

At the far end of the hall, a hand-painted banner stretched across the wall. The uneven letters, brushed in navy and gold by the children's Sunday school class, only made the message more heartfelt. Church friends and members gathered, ready to welcome them back.

Evelyn Williams checked her watch for what had to be the fifth time in ten minutes. "They should be here by now," she murmured, glancing down the street through a large fellowship hall window as if sheer will would make the caravan appear sooner.

Beside her, Thomas Williams smiled patiently. “They just left the airport a little while ago, honey. You know how traffic can get, especially when everyone’s trying to welcome them home at once.”

Evelyn folded her arms but couldn’t keep from smiling. “I know, but it’s been so long, Thomas. So much has happened since she’s been gone.”

Thomas reached over, giving her hand a squeeze. “She’s home now. That’s what matters. Let’s let her see that smile when she walks through those doors, alright?”

A few steps away, Margaret Matthews had stepped outside and was pacing along the fellowship hall walkway, her steps carrying her closer to the edge of the parking lot before turning back again. Her restlessness was quiet but unmistakable. Harold leaned casually against the railing, watching her with gentle amusement. When she passed him once more, he reached for her hand and guided her back inside, settling her into a comfortable chair in the fellowship hall.

“Margaret,” he said gently, “sit a minute… you’re going to wear yourself out before they even get here.

She let out a huffed breath and glanced up at him. “I can’t help it. I just keep wondering if we should’ve gone to the airport instead. I don’t know how I let them talk me into waiting for them here.”

Harold chuckled softly. “Just a few more minutes, honey. Besides, you know half of the church and God knows how many from the neighborhood showed up to greet them at the airport. I figured they’d enjoy all the attention and love they’d get there and save the best for last… *here*!” Harold had obviously passed on his sense of humor to his daughter.

Margaret smiled at that, her eyes softening. "You're probably right. Still, I just… wanted her to see us first. To know we've been waiting all this time."

Harold wrapped an arm around her shoulders. "She'll know. Trust me, the moment she steps out of that car and sees you, nothing else will matter." Their laughter mingled with the chatter and the gentle clinking of plates and glasses as they were being set on the banquet tables.

The Matthews and the Williamses stood together in anxious silence for a moment before Thomas tugged his ear slightly, a smile spreading across his face. "You hear that?" he said. "Sounds like car horns. I think they're finally here." Both couples exchanged glances… half laughter, half relief… as their gaze shifted toward the windows. Evelyn smoothed her hair and pressed a hand over her heart. Margaret reached for Harold's hand. For the first time that afternoon, neither of them checked their watches.

The chatter of conversation inside the fellowship hall faded into an expectant hush as the sound of car horns entering the parking lot announced their arrival. A couple of deacons hurriedly opened the wide double doors, allowing the afternoon sun to spill through the entryway like a blessing being poured out.

The once-quiet parking lot brimmed with excitement as the small caravan entered. The white limo, carrying its honored heroes, pulled in first and was carefully positioned in a space closest to the fellowship hall walkway. The tires had barely stopped moving before the rear doors swung open and two pairs of sand-colored military boots met the pavement. Their arrival was now official. Anxious, longing parents were already outside, waiting for the moment they could finally embrace their daughters.

"Mom! Dad!"

The words came out almost at the same time, tangled with laughter and tears. Kendra's face lit as she broke into a run straight for her parents. Starting out behind her, Charlene sprinted past

Kendra and, in her haste, left the limo door swinging open behind her. Raymond, discreetly wiping a tear from the corner of his eye, smiled and shook his head, realizing the two women hadn't even waited for him to open the doors for them.

Evelyn Williams was the first to reach her daughter. She gathered Kendra into her arms with a sob that was a mix of unbelievable joy and relief… this time without the shadow of another goodbye hanging over them. Thomas was there an instant later, wrapping them both in an embrace so tight it seemed to fold the years of worry and distance into nothing.

Kendra pressed her face into her mother's shoulder, breathing in the familiar scent of lilac and home. "I missed you so much," she whispered, her voice trembling.

"We missed you more," Evelyn said through tears, her arms tightening around Kendra as if to assure herself she was real.

Just a few steps away, Margaret, Harold, and Charlene Matthews hugged each other so tightly they nearly missed a breath, almost in unison. Charlene laughed and cried all at once, holding her mother as if she would never let her go.

"Easy, soldier!" Harold said with a grin that barely hid the tremble in his voice. "You break your mama's ribs and you're buying her dinner for a week!"

Charlene sniffled, laughing through the tears. "Deal, long as you're cooking, Dad."

Margaret swatted lightly at her daughter's arm, still smiling through tears. "Oh, you two hush and let me cry in peace."

Harold chuckled and wrapped both arms around them. "Ya'll go ahead and cry. Just don't drown us before we get inside." They all burst into laughter again, and the joy of the moment felt like rays of sunshine beaming down on an unclouded day.

Everyone else in the fellowship hall seemed to pause, instinctively giving the Williamses and the Matthews a moment of privacy to welcome their daughters home. It was almost as if the room itself held its breath. They watched with glistening eyes, waiting patiently for the families to gather themselves before moving on. Someone sniffled softly; another whispered, "Praise the Lord." Mothers held their small children's hands a little tighter. Even the children seemed to sense the weight of the moment… their frolicking softening into quiet, attentive smiles.

Kendra finally pulled back just enough to look at her parents. "I can't believe I'm really here," she said, her voice barely a breath.

Thomas touched her cheek. "You are, sweetheart. You made it home."

Behind them, Raymond discreetly brushed away another tear and paused before following them inside. The sight of the two families reunited, laughter tangled with tears, arms wrapped tight was more moving than any parade or welcome sign could ever be.

A few moments later, he opened the rear hatch and reached for their totes and duffel bags. The weight this time made him grunt slightly, followed by a quiet chuckle. *Mercy, these two packed for a lifetime,* he thought to himself. Before he could attempt to manage all four bags, Deacon Eric Bennett hurried over from the fellowship hall doorway.

"Here, brother…let me help you with those."

Together, they carried the bags inside and set them neatly near a coat rack just off the entryway.

Once inside the fellowship hall, a few began to clap, slowly at first, then others joined in until the sound swelled and rolled like gentle thunder. The applause wasn't just for the homecoming heroes, but for the answered prayers standing before them; flesh and blood reminders of grace and mercy.

Charlene turned toward Kendra, their eyes meeting across the small space between their families. Both were crying, both laughing, and for a moment neither said a word. Kendra reached out; Charlene met her and took her hand.

Home. Finally, home.

As friends and church members gathered around them, Charlene, true to her nature, couldn't resist. Standing on her tiptoes to address the group, she chimed in with a grin, "I see y'all hung the banner straight… eventually," drawing a ripple of laughter. Friends and neighbors joined in a continuous stream of handshakes, embraces, and words spoken from the heart: "It's good to see you back."

"Been praying for you every day."

"Bless you, child, you made it home."

"Thank God for keeping you safe."

Each blessing, each touch of a hand, felt like a thread binding them once again to the place they had missed so deeply.

And then, across the room, Kendra's gaze caught on someone just entering the fellowship hall. Someone she hadn't expected… but someone she had thought about… often.

There *he* was, standing near the back of the fellowship hall, half-turned from a conversation, his eyes meeting hers just as she looked up. For a single heartbeat, the world around them seemed to fade away.

Samuel Whitaker. But everyone called him Sam.

The same, kind eyes. That easy, elegant posture. His dark hair was a little shorter now, his shoulders broader, and the faint smile that tugged at his mouth was one she remembered, but deeper somehow, more assured. For an instant, their eyes met.

Neither moved, but something unspoken passed between them; an immediate recognition, a rekindling that awakened something she had kept hidden… something that made the room feel smaller, as if the years hadn't dimmed the pull between them at all.

Across the room, Sam started moving toward her. His shoulders squared, his smile growing as he navigated his way through tables, chairs, and narrow aisles. He greeted a few church members and friends as he passed, shaking hands and nodding politely, his gaze never straying far from Kendra.

Charlene noticed him and leaned toward Kendra with a mischievous grin, her eyes narrowing with playful curiosity. “Wait a second… is that who I think it is?”

Kendra’s gaze was already fixed ahead, her breathing just a little heavier. “Uh-huh,” she murmured, not taking her eyes off Sam. Sam was smiling now, his gaze locked on hers.

Charlene’s grin widened, but her voice softened. “Well, I’ll be. Some things get better with time, huh?”

Kendra blinked, still watching as he drew closer. “Uh-huh.”

Charlene gave her a gentle nudge. “I knew he was going to show up.”

Kendra blinked again, startled as he closed the distance between them, and then he was there, right in front of her. That familiar, easy smile was aimed right at her.

When he finally stopped before them, he hesitated just a fraction, then said, in a voice much richer and deeper than she remembered, “Welcome home, Kendra.”

Her name, spoken by him, stirred an unfamiliar flutter in her heart… one she found herself welcoming.

He turned to Charlene with equal sincerity. “And welcome home to you too, Charlene. I think the whole town’s been waiting for this day.”

Charlene grinned. “Feels good to be back. And thank you, Sam, it’s nice to see you again too.”

As she shifted aside to greet an old church friend, Kendra found herself face-to-face with him again.

“Wasn’t sure you’d remember me,” he said, his eyes bright with a teasing glint.

“There’s no way I could forget you, Sam,” she replied softly, her voice caught somewhere between a laugh and a whisper. “You’ve changed, though. Maybe taller. And I’m sure… wiser.”

Sam chuckled. "You've changed too. But somehow… just how I remember you."

Her cheeks warmed under his gaze, and for a moment, neither seemed to know what to say next. The sounds of laughter, music, and the tinkling of silverware and glasses filled the pause.

Finally, Sam nodded, his expression softening. "It's really good to see you again, Kendra. Welcome home."

"Thank you, Sam," she said quietly. "It's…", she paused to take in a quick breath, "really good to be home."

He moved on to greet others, Charlene slid back over, eyes dancing. "You two were practically glowing," she teased. "Should I warn the church ladies to start planning a wedding, or let this simmer a while?"

Kendra tried to laugh, shaking her head as she tried…and failed to hide the warmth rising in her cheeks. The moment lingered between them for just a heartbeat before giving way to the warmth of the room itself.

From the side doors leading in from the sanctuary, Pastor Nathaniel Thompson, senior pastor of Main Street Baptist Church, had made his way into the fellowship hall, his familiar smile and presence filling the room. As he mingled his way through familiar faces, he paused to shake hands, share brief embraces, and exchange a few kind words with longtime members and visiting neighbors alike. When he reached Kendra and Charlene, he welcomed them home and hugged them both warmly, his voice carrying that gentle strength that everyone knows so well.

"Welcome home, Kendra and Charlene," he said, his eyes and tone filled with gratitude and pride shared by everyone gathered. "Praise God for your safe return!"

He reached out, clasping each of their hands in turn. "You've both made this church, and this town, so proud. We prayed for you every Sunday while you were away. I can't tell you how good it is to see you standing here, safe and sound again."

Charlene smiled, her voice soft but somewhat shaky. "It means a lot to be back, Pastor. We felt those prayers more than you know."

"And we sure needed them," Kendra added with a quiet laugh, her eyes glimmering with emotion.

Pastor Thompson chuckled gently. "Well, the Lord surely heard every one of them." With a final pat on Kendra's shoulder, he straightened and began making his way toward the front of the fellowship hall. When he reached the podium, he lifted a small glass and gave it a gentle tap, calling for the room's attention.

"Welcome and thanks to all for your presence as we celebrate this joyous occasion," he said, his voice strong and resonant. "I would like to ask everyone now to please be seated. Kendra and Charlene, I understand that guest-of-honor tables have been specially prepared for you. All others, please feel free to take any available seat."

Pastor Thompson stood at podium at the front of the fellowship hall, his tall frame carrying both quiet strength and gentle humility. Though time had silvered his hair and softened the lines of his face, his shoulders remained broad, and his presence was like the kind of calm that comes from walking beside one's flock through both joy and sorrow. As he adjusted the microphone and offered a few more words of welcome and opening remarks, his wife, Leah, made her way through the tables with a graceful ease that matched her radiant smile.

Leah, whose kind spirit had long been a source of comfort within the church, paused at the Williamses' table, resting a gentle hand on Kendra's shoulder. "Welcome home, dear," she said softly, her eyes glistening with affection. "We've all been praying for this day." She turned to greet Charlene and her family with the same heartfelt energy before taking her seat nearby, her presence a quiet reflection of grace and community.

Together, Pastor Thompson and Leah embodied the compassionate heart of Main Street Baptist Church; two souls whose faith and love had shaped the congregation for more than three decades.

To Kendra and Charlene, Pastor Thompson had been more than a spiritual leader; he'd been a mentor, a counselor, and, in many ways, a second father. His sermons had carried them through heartbreaks and doubts, and his gentle wisdom had helped shape their faith long before they'd ever left home. Seeing him there now, smiling, proud, and misty-eyed, made the moment of their return all the more heartfelt and memorable.

Kendra and Charlene were seated at the two front tables with their parents. A few seats away, Sam had chosen a place with his parents near the end of the same row. Every so often, Sam and Kendra exchanged brief, but unguarded glances. Each time their eyes met, she felt that same subtle pull, a spark both welcome and oddly reassuring, as if the Lord Himself had woven a quiet thread between them.

From the podium, Pastor Thompson's gaze moved toward Charlene and Kendra as he prepared to speak.

"Brothers and sisters," he began, a smile warming his face, "tonight we have gathered for one of those rare moments when joy and gratitude overflow together. We're here to welcome back home two of Harmony Grove Harbor's own, two brave young women who answered the call to serve not just their country, but humanity itself. They left us to serve others in a time of great need, carrying both skill, passion, and faith into places where the world around them may have seemed to be falling apart. But by God's grace and mercy, they have returned to us safely. This evening, we celebrate not only their return, but the faithfulness of the God who brought them back to us."

A wave of "Amens" swept through the hall, followed by soft applause.

"Charlene Matthews and Kendra Williams," the pastor continued, turning toward their table, "you have come through some tough times from the other side of this world, and yet, you have come home with a spirit of humility and gratitude. And that spirit reminds us of the grace and mercy of God."

Kendra lowered her head modestly as the crowd applauded again, her heart tightening with humble emotion. Charlene beamed beside her, mouthing a quiet, "Amen."

Pastor Thompson went on, his tone reverent yet warm. "Many of us here prayed for you daily, not only for your safety, but for your strength and endurance. And tonight, we give thanks that God has answered our prayers. For your return, for your courage, and for the Deliverer that carried you both through."

He bowed his head, and the room followed suit.

"Heavenly Father, we thank You for bringing our daughters home. May their gifts continue to shine here in Harmony Grove Harbor, and let this new season be filled with peace, purpose, and the touch of Your hand upon their paths. In Jesus' name, Amen."

"Now," he said, smiling, "I believe Sister McCall has prepared her famous apple pie, and that's a blessing in itself. But before we eat, let's give our guests of honor an opportunity to share a few words, if they are willing."

The room responded with cheerful laughter and applause. Charlene immediately nudged Kendra. "You first, Captain."

Rising slowly and somewhat hesitantly, her eyes met Sam's as she stood. He gave her a quiet, encouraging smile, and somehow, that tiny gesture calmed her heart more than she expected. Her voice was confident and reverent. Kendra lifted her eyes heavenward before she spoke.

"I know… that God was with me every step of the way. And I learned to lean on the Lord even more than I ever had before. It was His hand that guided me in caring for my wounded comrades. When fear threatened to overtake me, it was His peace that surrounded me. I was in a place where sometimes hope seemed beyond hope, but because of your prayers and God's faithfulness, I can declare that He is a very present help in the time of trouble. I'm grateful and blessed to be home, and I pray I can serve this community as faithfully as you all have supported and loved me."

Then Charlene stood, her eyes twinkling, her thoughts briefly flashing back to the heaviness of what they had come through.

"You all know me," she began with a light laugh. "I can't go five minutes without cracking a joke. But out there, in the middle of indescribable pain and suffering, I didn't have much to joke about."

She paused, then smiled softly.

"Even so, God gave me a lightness…and just enough humor to be a small light in the darkness. Sometimes faith takes the form of a prayer whispered in silence, and sometimes it's a bit of laughter that helps a wounded and weary soldier make it through the night." I don't know how to thank you all enough for the prayers and support. I felt them. I carried Harmony Grove Harbor in my heart every single day. It was those prayers and that love that kept me going, and being home is just one more reminder of how faithful God truly is."

A hush lingered for a few precious seconds after Charlene's and Kendra's shared words. It was the kind of silence that held both respect and appreciation. Then, starting from the front of the room, the parents stood and applauded their daughters, and within moments the entire fellowship hall was on its feet, applause swelling until it filled the hall. Even Pastor Thompson stepped aside from the podium and joined the room in applause.

For more than five minutes, the whole room seemed to pulse with a shared sentiment. Gratitude, not only for Kendra's and

Charlene's safe return, but for the faith that had carried them through it all.

Pastor Thompson raised both hands in humble praise before he spoke. "Praise God for both peace and joy, for both calm and laughter. And praise Him for bringing our daughters safely back to us. Amen."

The two women had been celebrated and welcomed home with such enthusiasm, grace and love that their hearts were full beyond anything that they had felt before

By the time the last "amen" was spoken and the final slice of apple pie passed around, the joy of the evening had settled into every corner of the fellowship hall. Kendra and Charlene sat surrounded by their parents and neighbors church friends, answering questions, accepting hugs, and smiling until their cheeks ached.

"You'd think we were celebrities," Charlene whispered, leaning toward Kendra with a grin.

Kendra laughed softly. "In Harmony Grove Harbor, we kind of are."

Charlene chuckled. "Then I'm asking for an autograph from Sister McCall for her pie. That thing was divine."

They shared a laugh, their hearts full, as the celebration slowly began to wind down. People waved across tables and began saying their goodbyes. Charlene and Kendra's parents shared genuine hugs before the Matthews prepared to leave as well.

"Everybody get some much-needed rest tonight. It's been a long but happy day."

Charlene leaned down to hug Kendra tightly. "Get some rest tonight, okay. I'll talk to you tomorrow…and don't stay out too late."

She gave Kendra a discreet wink as she straightened up.

"I won't," Kendra winked back with a smile. "Goodnight, Char."

"Goodnight, sis."

And with that, Charlene and her parents made their way out, stopping by the coat rack near the entryway. Her tote and duffel bags waited just where Raymond and Deacon Eric Bennett had left them earlier. Mr. Matthews easily lifted the heavier one while Charlene slung the tote over her shoulder.

"Got everything, sweetheart?" her mother asked.

Charlene smiled, a trace of weariness in her eyes but warmth in her voice. "Yeah, thanks, Dad," she replied.

Charlene walked out with her parents into the cool night air, the sound of laughter still drifting softly from the fellowship hall behind them.

Kendra remained at the table with her parents, who were finishing the last of their coffee and chatting with another couple from church. As she turned toward the door, she spotted Sam near the hallway, speaking with Pastor Thompson. He must have felt her gaze, because he looked up at that exact moment. Their eyes met once more, and this time, they held.

Sam made his way toward her, his movements confident but relaxed, his steps deliberate and directed, all the while keeping his gaze on Kendra.

"Evening again," he said as he reached her table. "We didn't get much of a chance to talk earlier."

Her father looked up, recognizing him immediately. "Sam Whitaker, isn't it?"

"Yes, sir," Sam said warmly, shaking his hand. "Good to see you again, Mr. Williams. It's been a while."

Her father smiled. "It sure has. You've grown up a bit since those high school baseball days."

Sam chuckled, rubbing the back of his neck. "I'd like to think so." He turned to Mrs. Williams with a polite nod. "Mrs. Williams, it's wonderful to see you again

"Oh, Sam, it's wonderful to see you, too," she said kindly. "You remember our Kendra, don't you?"

Sam turned slightly to Kendra, his eyes soft and thoughtful. "I certainly do," he said quietly. "She's impossible to forget."

Kendra felt the heat rise in her cheeks again, and her father cleared his throat with an approving smile.

Sam straightened a little. "If it's alright with you, Mr. Williams, and Kendra, I would like to take Kendra home, maybe stop by the waterfront for a bit. I know that's one of her favorite spots in town. I'll make sure she gets home safe. I live just a few streets over."

Kendra was readying herself to stand when Sam offered a hand to help her up. Mr. Williams glanced at his daughter, who was now giving him that "*You better say yes*" look.

"That sounds fine by me. Thank you, son."

Sam nodded respectfully. "Don't worry; I'll take good care of her."

Mrs. Williams smiled, clearly impressed by his thoughtfulness.

Kendra tried to curb her excitement but failed. "It'll be great to catch up… it's been awhile!"

He smiled, easy and sure. "It has been. And now that you're back… it feels like the perfect time to start."

"Well then," Mr. Williams said, standing and gathering his jacket, "we'll see you at home, sweetheart." He gave Sam a friendly pat on the shoulder before leading his wife toward the door.

As they left, the hall grew quieter. Only a few church volunteers remained, tidying tables and folding chairs. Sam offered his hand toward the door.

"Ready when you are," he said with a playful glint in his eye.

Kendra laughed softly as she moved a little closer to him. "I'm as ready as I'll ever be."

He chuckled, his smile widening. "That's exactly what I needed to hear."

They walked toward the entryway, where Kendra's tote and duffel bag were still waiting near the coat rack. Sam reached for the duffel without a word, lifting it easily while Kendra picked up the tote. "Thanks," she said, smiling up at him.

"Least I can do," he replied, holding the door open for her.

And together, they went out into the cool, starlit night, the sound of the harbor in the distance and the soft whisper of the waves carrying the promise of something new.

Chapter 3

A Quiet Harbor Evening with Sam Whitaker

The night air was cool, the ocean breeze gentle, carrying with it the promise of calm after a long, full day as Kendra and Sam walked out of the fellowship hall. The sound of laughter still spilling faintly through the church doors, wrapped in the quiet chorus of crickets and the distant hush of the tide. The glow from the lampposts cast a golden shimmer on the sidewalk, painting long shadows that stretched towards the parking lot.

Kendra breathed in the cool salt air, her heart still full of the evening's joy. "I'd almost forgotten how good it feels to be back at Main Street Baptist," she said. "And I'm glad we finally get a chance to reconnect. It's really good to see you again. I feel like I missed so much while I was deployed."

Sam smiled as they walked beside each other. "Yeah… the few times we managed to talk were sporadic at best. Virtual calls are better than nothing, I guess," he said lightly. "But nothing beats having you here in person again."

She glanced up at him, catching that easy smile she remembered so well. "The last time we talked, you were thinking about moving away," she said. "Is that still something you're still considering?"

He shook his head, lowering his eyes for a moment. "I thought about it," he admitted. "But after Joseph was killed overseas… Mom and Dad needed me. And I didn't want to leave them."

Kendra slowed beside him, her voice softening under the weight of his words. "I remember how hard it was trying to reach you," she said gently. "Sam… I'm so sorry. I really wanted to be here for you, but I couldn't get leave." She paused. "Losing someone, especially in war leaves a hole in your heart… one that never really goes away. I know how close you were to your brother."

For a moment, Sam didn't answer. The breeze carried only the sound of waves brushing the shoreline. Then he nodded, a quiet warmth flickering behind his eyes. "Thank you, Kendra," he said, his voice low. "That… means more than you know. And you're right. It never really goes away."

For a time, neither spoke. Their footsteps echoed softly over the pavement as they followed the walkway that wound past the church's main sanctuary. Light from its windows glowed against the night, and fireflies hovered along the hedges; small, flickering companions to a silence that breathed peace.

Sam turned his head toward her, his voice light again. "You know, you and Charlene gave quite the speeches in there. Folks will probably be talking about that for a while."

Kendra laughed softly. "Charlene's good with public speaking and people. Always has been. Me, I just tried not to cry halfway through mine."

"You did great," he said sincerely. "You both spoke from the heart. That's what people will remember."

She met his eyes for a moment, unwavering, sincere, and kind. There was something different about the way he looked at her, something different about how she felt when he looked at her. There was something different about the way they looked at each other.

They reached his old red pickup parked near the edge of the lot. The headlights gleamed faintly under the streetlamp. He opened the tailgate and, with a slight grunt, lifted the duffel bag into the cargo bed, and she tossed her old tote bag next to it.

"You still drive this old thing?" Kendra teased, smiling as she brushed her hand over the lip of the bed.

"Still runs," he said with a grin. "Can't part with her yet. Too many memories."

"Like when you and David Malone tried to jump that dirt hill behind the football field?"

Sam groaned, laughing. "Oh no, don't remind me. I thought the truck would come apart before we hit the ground.

Come to think of it, David never rode with me again…anywhere. And mom banned me from driving for two weeks after she heard about that."

Kendra grinned. "We were fearless, or foolish, depending on who you ask. Either way, those teen years kept us busy finding new ways to get into trouble and get grounded. We felt invincible back then."

"Maybe. But I've learned a few things since those invincible years."

She paused before getting in, her heart fluttering in that uncertain, nostalgic way. "Like what?"

"Like learning how to wait for something or someone, worth waiting for."

Kendra's smile faltered just a little, catching her breath as their eyes met in the dim glow of the lamplight.

He nodded toward the seat. "Come on. Let's take that drive."

Kendra rounded the front of the truck toward the passenger side, reaching for the handle, only for Sam to step beside and slightly behind her to open the door. His grin was quiet but knowing, the kind that warmed more than the cool night air.

"Easy there, soldier," he said softly, his voice threaded with teasing warmth. "Some of us still remember how to be gentlemen."

Kendra smiled, a hint of amusement in her eyes. "Well, I'd hate to stand in the way of that."

He chuckled, holding the door as she climbed in and slid into the passenger seat. When he circled to the driver's side and slid behind the wheel, a soft quiet settled between them. For a heartbeat, their eyes met, just long enough for something unspoken to pass between them, something tender but cautious, the echo of a friendship that once was and the hint of maybe something more that could be. A brief quiet moment saying more than words ever could.

He turned the key, and the old pickup rumbled to life with a low, familiar purr that seemed to echo in the stillness of the parking lot. Headlights cut through the deepening dusk as he shifted into gear, and the warm glow of Main Street Baptist Church faded from view as the old truck quietly made its way toward Main Street.

The steeple cast a long shadow across the quiet road, the last shimmer of stained-glass light glancing off the windows before vanishing into the dark. The laughter and music that had spilled from its fellowship hall only moments ago faded into memory, leaving the hush of night and the rhythmic hum of the engine to fill the silence.

They rode on, Harbor Road was just as picturesque as she remembered it: peaceful and still as the evening, the kind of stillness only a coastal town could hold. Porch lights glimmered from tidy clapboard houses set back beneath sweeping oaks. The scent of magnolia and ocean-kissed air drifted by, and now and then the soft call of a night gull echoed in the stillness.

"It just feels so good, being back," Kendra said softly, her voice low and a little worn, carrying the weariness of a long day. "It just feels like a dream that I'm hoping won't end."

Sam nodded, his eyes on the road but managed to reach for her hand and held it. "It's not a dream Kendra, you're home and that's not going to end. We're not going to end. And just so you know, I wouldn't have missed a chance to see you again for anything."

Kendra gently squeezed his hand a little tighter. "Well, I guess I know now." But she thought, "*this is definitely not the same Sam Whitaker that I remember.*"

Kendra leaned against the window, watching familiar landmarks slip by; the bait shop her father still liked to visit on Saturday mornings, the lighthouse blinking its faithful rhythm out toward the dark horizon. The road finally opened toward the waterfront where twilight had softened the water into shades of silver and indigo. Lanterns along the boardwalk flickered to life, their reflections trembling gently across the tide. Rows of boats moored at the marina rocked with the waves and their sails swayed with the evening breeze. The scene was calm now; peaceful and inviting, so different from the bright bustle of the afternoon.

"It's strange," she said softly, breaking the quiet. "Everything looks just the same… but it feels different somehow."

Sam glanced over with a small smile. "Maybe it's you that's different."

She returned his smile, thoughtful. "Maybe."

When they reached the riverwalk, Sam parked the truck and turned off the engine. The world around them settled into a hush, broken only by the rhythmic lapping of the ocean beneath the wooden planks. Lanterns along the dock cast a soft amber glow that shimmered on the surface of the water.

"Come on," he said, opening his door. "It's too pretty an evening to just sit in this truck."

They began walking slowly down the boardwalk. The boards creaked softly under their feet. They paused for moments to enjoy the cool ocean breeze and let the sounds of the ocean soothe them. They reminisced over moments that only the two of them shared. Laughter accompanied those looks that said *I can't believe we did that...* quietly folding what time had done to separate them. Without noticing when it happened, they found themselves walking a little closer, his arm occasionally brushing hers. The silences between them felt easy and unhurried, carrying as much meaning as the words they didn't need to say.

Then Sam chuckling and breaking the silence said. "You remember that time you and Charlene tried to bake cookies for the senior fundraiser?"

Kendra groaned. "Oh no, not that story again."

"Oh yes," he said with mock seriousness. "Those things could've doubled as paperweights. I bought three bags; thought it only fair to honor the effort."

She laughed, nudging him playfully with her shoulder. "You did not!"

"I did," he said, grinning. "Didn't eat a single one, but I figured it was the right thing to do."

Her laughter softened into a smile that stayed. "I always wondered who kept buying those."

He chuckled, then added more quietly, "Truth is, I had a bit of a crush on you back then. Everyone probably knew but you."

Kendra blinked, taken aback. "You... did?"

She smiled, a now familiar flutter blooming in her heart. "I never knew." She shook her head lightly, a soft laugh escaping her. "Truth is, I had a crush on you too, but I didn't want to risk losing a good friend. You are too important to me for that."

"I guess I didn't want to risk losing you either," he said softly. "But maybe time has made this all the better for waiting."

"Can't argue with that," she replied.

They walked on for a few steps in easy silence, the water moving softly beneath them. Kendra sighed softly. "You know this place always feels like it lets truth breathe. I used to come here all the time before I enlisted. It's where I'd go to think, or pray when I needed quiet and calm."

Sam smiled, but his gaze drifted toward the water. Thoughts of his brother surfaced briefly before he spoke again. "I did too. This place helped when things felt too noisy inside."

She looked at him, surprised. "Guess we both needed the same thing without knowing it."

The air between them shifted; quiet, warm, and cozy, edged with something unspoken. Sam reached out, brushing his thumb along the railing, then looked back at her.

"I'm really glad you're home, Kendra."

She met his gaze, her heart catching. "So am I, Sam. More than I can say."

Sam reached out and gently took her hand into his. "I used to imagine moments like this," he said softly, "but never thought I'd actually get one."

Kendra felt her heart tremble. "Now that I am back… maybe we can have more than just this one moment, Sam."

He smiled, stepping a little closer. "I think I would like that, Kendra."

He hesitated; just long enough for her to notice the thought in his eyes, then leaned in and pressed a tender kiss to her cheek. The touch lingered just long enough to make her heart flutter.

When he drew back, he reached for her hand. She reached for his, and they stayed that way for a moment before continuing their walk up the waterfront. When Sam noticed the tiredness in her eyes ebbing in, he reluctantly said, "I better get you home.

You've had a long day, and I promised your folks that I would take good care of you."

Their steps were a little slower walking back to Sam's truck, the boards almost groaning as if echoing Kendra's unwanted fatigue.

When they reached the truck, Sam helped her in, closing the door gently before circling to his side. As they pulled away, the harbor lights shimmered behind them like distant stars, fading little by little as the road curved toward the quiet streets of Harmony Grove Harbor.

The town had settled into sleep. Storefront windows along Main Street reflected the soft amber of streetlamps, and the old clock tower near the courthouse chimed ten times, its echo carrying across the still night.

Kendra leaned back in her seat. "It's so peaceful," she said softly. "Thank you, Sam, for helping me remember what peace and calm feels like again."

Sam nodded, glancing at her. "Peace can feel a little strange after what you've been through. But you will get used to it again… if you let yourself receive it."

She smiled faintly, her heart touched by his gentle calm. "You've gotten wise over the years."

He chuckled. "Maybe a little. Or maybe I just had some time to think."

The spell of the water lingered as they left, like salt clinging to the air. As they got closer to Kendra's home, the more Kendra felt that strange mix of comfort and uncertainty, the kind that comes when one chapter ends and another begins. When Sam pulled into the Williamses' driveway, he noticed that the porch light was still glowing, spilling a soft golden circle onto the walkway. He got out first and came around to open her door, just as he had after the ceremony.

"You've got a welcoming committee," he said, nodding toward the light.

Kendra laughed softly. "My mom probably peeked through the curtains three times already."

"I wouldn't doubt it."

They both came to the back of the truck, and he lowered the tailgate. Kendra tried to hide a yawn, but Sam noticed anyway, a quiet chuckle escaping him.

"Looks like I got you home just in time," he said softly. "Get some rest. I'll call you in the morning."

She gave a quiet laugh. "Guess I'm not as tough or as young as I used to be."

He shook his head, still smiling. "Tougher, maybe, but still human. Maybe we can grab coffee or take another walk. something easy."

"I'd like that," she said, her voice warm but tired.

"Then it's a plan."

Sam reached for her tote and handed it to her. Then he grabbed the duffel bag and released it to the ground before firmly closing the tailgate.

He held onto the tailgate for a few seconds and gently stroked the top of it.

"This old girl has been faithful and dependable for me over the years, so I treat her gently and with respect.

Kendra smiled knowingly, sensing that he was speaking about more than just about his *old* truck.

They walked together up the driveway, their steps slowing as they neared the porch. At the door, Sam quietly set the bag just inside before stepping back.

For a moment, neither moved. Both seemed reluctant to let the night end.

"Thank you for everything," Kendra said quietly.

Sam's expression softened. "Wouldn't have it any other way. And… I meant what I said earlier. Don't worry. I'll take good care of you."

Her smile trembled just slightly. "You always did."

He hesitated, then moved a little closer and placed his hand gently on her arm. "I'm really glad you're back, Kendra. I can't say that enough."

She nodded, feeling her heart lift. "I'm glad I'm back too, Sam."

He hesitated for a moment, as though weighing his next move. Then, without a word, he moved one step closer to her and wrapped his arms around her; a strong embrace that felt safe, and full of things neither of them were ready to say aloud.

Kendra closed her eyes briefly, feeling his warmth and the calm strength in his touch. For the first time in a long while, she felt truly safe and at peace.

When he released her, it was slow and reluctant, his hands lingering lightly at her shoulders. "Goodnight, Kendra."

She smiled softly. "Goodnight, Sam."

He started down the walk, his footsteps echoing against the driveway. She stood on the porch, watching him until his taillights disappeared down the street. The night air felt cool against her skin, still touched with the scent of salt and magnolia.

Kendra lifted her fingers to her cheek where his gentle kiss had brushed earlier, and her smile deepened. Tilting her eyes toward the sky, she whispered, "Thank You, God… for bringing me home, and maybe, for something new beginning."

The breeze stirred lightly around her, rustling the leaves and carrying a quiet peace that felt like an answer.

Kendra smiled again, then turned and went inside; her heart full, her spirit calm, and her faith quietly blooming anew.

Sam Whitaker started the short drive to his own condo, each turn of the wheel carrying a mix of anticipation and apprehension. As he drove through the now-quiet streets of Harmony Grove Harbor, the distant sounds of the marina seemed to echo his own restless thoughts. Underneath that smile, a flicker of unease stirred. He was drawn to her in a way he hadn't expected; vibrant, steadfast, and alive in a world that often felt fickle. Yet alongside that excitement, a shadow lingered: the memory of his brother, the weight of grief he hadn't shared with anyone, and the gnawing uncertainty of whether he was ready to open his heart again.

Approaching the entrance to his condo community, Sam felt a faint smile tug at his lips; one that came not from habit, but from the quiet contentment still echoing from the night. On the surface, he felt a lightness he hadn't experienced in months, a spark of excitement after seeing Kendra again. But beneath it, a storm churned: a tangle of longing, grief, and hesitation he couldn't shake.

He eased the truck into his usual parking space and cut the engine, the soft rumble fading into the night. For a moment, he just sat there, hands resting on the steering wheel, feeling lighter now than he had that morning; yet somewhere beneath that lightness, something stirred. A quiet conflict, living somewhere between happiness and heartache.

Stepping out, he closed the door gently and breathed in the cool night air. With each step, the echo of Kendra's laughter seemed to follow him, mingling with memories he hadn't let surface. When he reached the landing, he fumbled with his keys for a moment before unlocking the door and stepping inside.

Warm lighting greeted him, offering a sense of comfort. Beyond the large window, the waterfront spread wide, boats swaying gently on the tide. The water caught the moonlight, reflecting silver and white that rippled with the motion of the waves. Lights from the marina glimmered like scattered stars across the surface, calm yet alive, reminding him that life went on even when he felt stuck.

His condo was thoughtfully arranged, understated yet refined, each piece chosen with quiet intention. A modern built-in bookshelf lined one wall, its shelves filled with lesser-known novels and a handful of carefully chosen artifacts. A family heirloom guitar, priceless to Sam, rested in the corner, and framed photographs captured moments of family, friends, and adventures now past. It felt warm and lived-in, comfortable without being extravagant; a space shaped for living well and for sharing.

His eyes fell on a photograph on the bookshelf. He'd placed it there, because the frame always caught the morning light. His brother, Joseph, frozen in time, smiling wide in fatigues, captured in a moment of joy now achingly distant. Sam picked it up gently, as if the frame itself held a memory he could cradle.

"Hey," he murmured, almost laughing at himself for speaking aloud to the empty room. "I saw her today."

The imagined voice of his brother echoed, sharp and familiar. "Saw who?"

"Kendra," Sam admitted, voice low. "She's strong... Confident. Makes me feel…" He hesitated, words catching in his throat. "Like I could have something real. Something more than before… more than pretending I'm okay."

"And you think you can have that without giving of yourself?" the imagined voice prodded.

Sam's gaze softened as his mind drifted back to that terrible day. The knock came just after breakfast, sharp and formal against the screen door. He'd been the one to answer it.

His mother, still in the kitchen, called out, "Is that Mrs. Jones waiting for the sugar she asked for?" She made her way hurriedly to the front door, still holding a bowl of sugar.

Sam swallowed hard as he looked at the two uniformed officers standing on the porch, their faces solemn, their eyes already carrying the weight of what they had come to say. "No," he said quietly, his voice cracking under the strain, his eyes daring himself not to blink. "It's not Mrs. Jones."

His mother came to a stop beside him in the doorway, the ceramic bowl still in her hand. The moment she saw the officers, the color drained from her face. The bowl slipped from her grasp, spilling sugar across the floor in a soft white cloud.

His father hurried in from the den at the sound, his face frozen, lips parting but no words coming; he already understood. No explanation was needed; the sight alone told the story.

The officers spoke gently, their rehearsed words breaking through suffocating silence. "Killed in service overseas." The phrase barely registered. It couldn't be real.

"There's got to be some mistake," Sam had said, his voice breaking as he looked from one to the other, desperate for denial. But the truth was written in their eyes.

His mother's sob came soft and raw, his father's trembling hand reaching for her as though he could hold back the weight of it all. The steady tick of the clock filled the quiet. Cruel in its normalcy, Sam stood frozen in a world that suddenly felt heavier, emptier, and unbearably still.

The military funeral followed, precise and reverent: the flag-draped casket, the rifle salute, the bugler playing taps, the folded flag handed to his parents; every detail etched itself into him. He had stood rigid, forcing composure for the assembled mourners, the tears that begged to come were held at bay by sheer force of will. Between ceremony and final salute, his world stopped, suspended in time. The weight of that day, the scent of flowers, the crisp air, the distant roll of the drums had never left him.

He set the photo down, closing his eyes, and let the imagined conversation continue.

"You think you can't love again because I'm gone?", the voice asked gently.

"I don't know," Sam admitted. "I don't want her to see, to know my pain, the heaviness of my grief. I have kept that part of myself hidden. I don't want her to think that I am weak."

"The best way that you can remember and honor me is by living, by freeing yourself and allowing yourself to love again," the imagined voice reminded him. "Don't hide behind the pain. Don't let it keep you from living life again."

Sam exhaled slowly, the words sinking in, a small warmth relieving the tightness he held in his heart.

"She deserves someone whole, not someone still trying to stitch himself together," he murmured. "And maybe… maybe I need a little more faith in something. Faith, hope, trust. Faith that God is leading me to the someone He meant for me. I've been drawn to her for as long as I can remember."

He moved back to the window, letting the cool glass press against his palms. The harbor lights danced across the water, flickering in rhythm with the gentle sway of the boats. The scene grounded him to the present while reminding him of everything he'd lost; everything he still wanted to protect, and what he wasn't ready to receive.

Eventually, Sam retired to his bedroom, closing the door softly behind him. He lay down, the pillow cool against his cheek, but sleep eluded him. Thoughts of Kendra, of his brother, of all the choices he hadn't yet made, churned like the tide. Outside, the harbor shimmered quietly, indifferent to his turmoil. And Sam knew that, for now, the answers wouldn't come tonight.

Chapter 4

Familiar Places, Unfamiliar Feelings

Morning sun gently awakened Kendra, spreading thin ribbons of light through the curtains and across her bed. She stirred, blinking as her eyes adjusted to the soft glow. Beyond her window, the calm water of the small lake shimmered like glass, disturbed only by faint ripples where a heron waded along the reeds. Somewhere in the distance, a small boat motor purred to life, blending with the soft chorus of early-morning cicadas.

For a moment, she simply lay there, absorbed in the peace. Her heart still felt light from the night before…the quiet conversation, the shared laughter, the way Sam had looked at her beneath the moonlight. But beneath that warmth lingered a flutter of caution, an old instinct reminding her not to wade too far, too fast. It had been years since she'd felt this kind of closeness with him and for him…alone.

They'd all been friends once; she, Charlene, and Sam, the inseparable trio back in high school. Life, distance, and war had scattered them…and changed them. Yet, here they were, together again, trying to figure out where the pieces fit now.

Her phone vibrated softly against the nightstand, pulling her from her thoughts. She glanced at the screen before picking up and smiled…Sam.

"Good morning," he said, "Hope I didn't wake you."

She smiled despite herself. "Good morning, and no you didn't wake me, and it's good to hear your voice before I start my day."

Something about hearing her say that made him smile. "I think you just made my day! Not going to hold you but just wanted you to know that I am a man of my word."

They talked and laughed together for a few minutes more, both of them surprised at how natural and easy it felt. When the call ended, Kendra sat quietly for a moment after placing the phone back on the nightstand. Between them nothing was rushed or forced…just familiar. Comfortable. Like something gently finding its place again.

A familiar scent met her next…the unmistakable aroma of bacon and biscuits, and freshly brewed coffee wafting down the hallway. Her stomach answered before her feet hit the floor. She slid into her favorite bunny slippers and made her way down the short hallway toward the kitchen aromas calling her.

In the kitchen, her mother stood at the stove, humming softly as she flipped bacon in the skillet. Sunlight danced across the countertops, catching the steam rising from a pot of grits.

"Well, good morning, sweetheart," her mother said with a teasing smile. "You and Sam were out a little while last night."

Kendra grinned as she took a seat at the table. "Good morning, Mom. So…you were timing us?" she said, returning the smile. Then she noticed the steaming pot on the stove. "Oh, my favorite…grits," she added, her tone jokingly sarcastic.

Her mother chuckled, shaking her head. "Well, your dad loves them."

They shared a laugh, and the familiar warmth of home settled around them.

"It was really nice last night, Mom," Kendra said, her tone softening. "I really enjoyed spending a little quiet time with Sam. We just walked along the waterfront for a while and talked. It's been a long time since we've had a chance to really talk like that. And… I think I feel something different for him now."

Her mother turned from the stove, one eyebrow raised with that knowing, motherly look. "And what are you feeling for him now?"

Kendra hesitated, tracing her fingertip along the rim of one of the coffee mugs her mom had placed on the table earlier. "I'm not sure yet. Part of me wants to let it be what it was…just friendship. But another part, a much stronger part…" She paused. "I just don't know if I'm really ready for something more."

Her mother poured two cups of coffee into the mugs and joined her at the table. "Sometimes the heart doesn't ask for permission, honey. But you don't have to rush it. The Lord's timing has a way of being just right…even when it takes its sweet time."

Kendra smiled faintly. "Thanks, Mom. You always help me see things the way I need to."

Before her mother could reply, the back door creaked open and her father walked in, a towel draped over his shoulder, the fresh lake breeze following him inside.

"Well, good morning, girls," he said cheerfully. "Oh, I see we're having Kendra's favorite this morning…grits!"

Kendra laughed, rolling her eyes. "You two planned that, didn't you?"

Her parents both chuckled, and her mother shook her head, still smiling. "I missed this," she said softly. "Nothing like starting your day with a good laugh with my two favorite people."

Her father poured himself coffee, then sat down at the table, his eyes warm but thoughtful. "Laughter's good medicine. And while we're at it, baby girl, a little advice…don't feel guilty about enjoying life a little again. After all you and Charlene have been through, you deserve it."

Kendra reached for his hand and gave it a gentle squeeze. "Thanks, Dad. I really needed that."

Leaning back in her chair, she felt calmness settle over her…a tender calm that reached someplace deep inside. It was the kind of peace that only home could give, wrapped in love and the quiet assurance that she was right where she belonged. A smile and a tear rose together before she could stop them.

Bowing her head, she whispered a soft, heartfelt, "Thank You, Lord." Then, lifting her cup, she took a slow sip of coffee, trying to hide the little sniffle that escaped anyway.

The three of them lingered over breakfast, laughter weaving easily between bites of bacon and buttery biscuits. Her father told one of his familiar fishing stories…the kind that grew a little more dramatic every time he told it, while her mother rolled her eyes and teased him about the one that got away.

After breakfast, the house settled into its familiar morning rhythm…the sound of her father's radio drifting old-school tunes from the back porch, her mother tidying the kitchen while humming an old hymn, and the faint whisper of a breeze slipping through the open window.

When the plates were cleared, her mother wiped her hands on a towel. "I need to call Ruth before she heads to the community center," she said, reaching for the phone on the counter. "We're finalizing the committee plans for the fall luncheon."

Her father rose from the table, stretching his arms. "And I'll be on the porch if anybody needs me. That lake and hammock are calling my name."

Kendra laughed softly. "Tell them I said good morning."

Her parents smiled. Evelyn was already dialing, and Thomas stepped back out onto the quiet, sunlit porch. Kendra lingered a moment longer, watching the light dance on the water. The gentle sounds of home spoke of normalcy…of gentleness and of love. Even the walls seemed to whisper the quiet reassurance that there was still a place where healing and renewal abided in abundance.

Kendra carried her coffee to her room, pausing by the window for one more look at the little lake. Sunlight danced across the surface like scattered silver. It reminded her that healing didn't always come in earth-shattering moments…that sometimes it arrived quietly, in the calm of an ordinary morning.

She smiled faintly and set her mug on the dresser before opening her closet. Jeans, a soft white blouse, and her favorite light-blue cardigan…something simple, but nice. But first, a shower. The steam and warm water felt like a small renewal in itself, washing away the last traces of the long journey back home. A few minutes later, wrapped in a towel and surrounded by the familiar scent of lavender soap, she felt ready to face the day.

She dressed slowly, adjusting her hair before the mirror. For a moment, her reflection caught her off guard. Sam's face drifted into her thoughts, the warmth in his voice, the way his laugh still held that same unforgettable spark.

"Don't get ahead of yourself.", she murmured to herself fidgeting with a loose strand behind her ear. "It was just a walk."

Still, her pulse quickened as she reached for her phone on the nightstand. She slipped it into her purse before she could second-guess the thought.

"Mom, I'm going to hang out with Charlene for a bit today!" she called toward the kitchen.

"Tell Charlene I said hello. And you two behave yourselves!" her mother answered with a playful lilt.

Kendra laughed. "No promises!"

The soft late-morning air met her as she stepped into the garage. The scent of pine and distant sea salt mingled together…the unmistakable fragrance of Harmony Grove Harbor. In the garage sat her old silver Honda Civic, the one her parents had surprised her with back in high school. It wasn't much to brag about, but it had carried her through college, cross-country drives, and countless late-night coffee runs. Her dad had kept it spotless while she was away, right down to the shine on the tires.

She smiled, running her hand along the cool hood before sliding behind the wheel. It still smelled faintly of vanilla air freshener and memories. Tomorrow, she'd be picking up her new car, but for now, she knew this one would get her wherever she needed to go.

As the engine turned over, the car stereo picked up where it had left off…Whitney Houston's voice soaring from a homemade soundtrack of songs from *The Preacher's Wife*. Kendra couldn't help but smile. Before she even backed out of the driveway, she was already singing along, her voice soft at first, then growing with the music. The joy in Whitney's gospel tones filled the car like sunlight, warming every corner of her heart.

She eased down the driveway and slowed near the end, taking a long look at the neighborhood she'd missed. Some of the houses had been freshly painted, with new porches and backyard decks added, flowerbeds bright with marigolds and lilies. Farther down, a brand-new brick mailbox stood where Mr. Martin's old wooden one had once leaned. Just beyond the next turn, closer to the marina, she noticcd a small condo community that hadn't been there before…modern, tidy, with white railings and balconies that caught the light.

"Now that might be worth a look," she murmured with a grin.

She didn't realize that the condo community she was admiring was Sam's.

The street wound past the lake and towards town, sunlight flickering through the trees like rhythmic blessings. She rolled down the window, letting the soft salt-and-pine air wash through the car as she sang another line with Whitney, feeling lighter than she had in months. The closer she drew to downtown Harmony Grove Harbor, the more life stirred, the clinking of boat riggings at the marina, the chatter of shopkeepers setting out displays, and the cheerful ring of the bell above the Dockside Diner door every time a customer walked inside. She smiled. Harmony Grove Harbor had a heartbeat all its own, gentle, unwavering, full of grace.

Parking near the diner, she spotted Charlene through the window, already waving enthusiastically with a grin that could light up any room. Kendra shook her head, laughing openly as she stepped out of the car. "Some things never change."

Charlene met her halfway across the sidewalk, sunglasses perched on her head and mischief already in her eyes. "Oh, don't 'some things never change' me," she teased. "I want details…Sam Whitaker details. You two left church together last night, and don't think for a second I didn't hear about it. You know how news travels around here."

Kendra rolled her eyes but couldn't help smiling. "It was just a walk, Charlene."

"Mmm-hmm," Charlene drawled, looping her arm through Kendra's as they started toward the diner door. "A moonlit walk with Harmony Grove Harbor's most eligible bachelor in town? Sure sounds like just a walk."

Kendra and Charlene continued their casual chatter as they made their way through downtown Harmony Grove Harbor, which was quietly alive that morning. It was the kind of day where everything moved at an easy, unhurried pace. Sunlight pierced through shopfront windows, and flower boxes spilled over with late-blooming petunias. A pair of children walked along the brick-paved sidewalk with ice cream cones in hand while a delivery truck idled beside the local florist. People greeted one another as they passed; waves, smiles, and a few quick conversations between neighbors who'd known each other most of their lives.

Charlene gave a dramatic sigh, hands waving for emphasis. "You are *not* going to believe who my mom tried to set me up with last night after church."

Kendra grinned, already amused. "Oh, this ought to be good. Who's the lucky guy?"

"Gerald Boyce," Charlene said, drawing out his name like it had too many syllables. "You know… the sweet guy from the church tech team who quotes Scripture and science facts in the same breath? Apparently, he's been asking about me every time he sees my mom. Every. Single. Time."

Kendra burst out laughing. "Maybe God is trying to tell you something."

Charlene shot her a look of mock horror before joining in the laughter. "If that's true, I think God and I need to have a little talk."

Their laughter echoed lightly down the sidewalk as they wandered through the familiar stretches of downtown, sometimes stopping to browse a quaint new shop or try on a few trendy pieces from one of the newer boutiques. As morning eased into early afternoon, their stomachs began to remind them that lunch was overdue, and that the Dockside Diner was just around the corner, overlooking the marina.

Dockside Diner was just as they remembered it, its striped awnings fluttering gently in the breeze. The poet's blooming jasmines were tucked neatly beneath the wide picture windows, their fragrance drifting softly through the open air.

As they stepped inside, a small silver bell rang above the door, welcoming them in. The diner felt both familiar and renewed. A wave of savory warmth washed over them; the buttery scent of shrimp and grits mingling with notes of fried catfish, hushpuppies, and fresh-baked cornbread. Just past the entrance stood a chalkboard menu, its neat white lettering boasting the day's specials: crab cakes with lemon aioli, she-crab soup, and Low Country boil for two.

The aromas stirred something sweetly familiar…memories of Sunday lunches and summer evenings when the diner's windows fogged with kitchen steam, and laughter drifted out onto Oceanview Drive.

Jazz music played softly in the background as waiters weaved between tables with easy smiles…the clink of dishes and the low murmur of conversation creating a comforting rhythm. Sunlight streamed through the wide windows, framing the marina like a living painting; sleek yachts and modest leisure boats rocking gently in their slips, gulls circling lazily overhead, and people strolling along the boardwalk outside.

They made their way to a booth near the window, the polished tabletop gleaming beneath a vase of fresh daisies and a small container holding napkins, condiments; and menus tucked between them. Tables towards the center of the dining area were neatly covered in crisp white linen and topped with fresh flowers and a pair of votive white candles in glass holders added an elegant touch.

Sheryl Robbins approached their table just as bubbly and cheerful as she had been when welcoming them home at the airport. She pulled a notepad from her apron and greeted them with a wide grin.

"Well, if it isn't Harmony Grove Harbor's very own heroes! I didn't expect to see you again so soon. What can I get for you two today…sweet tea or lemonade to start?"

Kendra and Charlene greeted her just as warmly, the three exchanging a few quick laughs.

Charlene chuckled. "Okay, make that two sweet teas. Heavy on the lemon."

Kendra smiled, settling in as the light reflected off the harbor beyond the glass. "See, that's what's so good about being back home…always running into a familiar face. It almost feels like we never left, doesn't it?"

Charlene glanced toward the window, her eyes softening. "Almost. But I think it feels even better this time."

For a few quiet moments, they both watched the world outside; a few townspeople strolling along Oceanview Drive, pausing to wave when they recognized them through the glass. The easy warmth of home seemed to wrap around them like sunlight.

Charlene broke the silence with a grin, flipping open her menu. "You know what sounds good? The grilled seafood platter. I've missed real seafood; not whatever mystery meat of the day they tried to pass off in the mess hall."

Kendra laughed. "Agreed. Let's split it. It's way more than I can eat by myself."

Sheryl returned with the iced teas and a pleasant smile, pausing this time to take their food orders. Charlene ordered the grilled seafood platter for them to share, and Kendra added another iced tea. Sheryl jotted their choices quickly and promised, "Excellent choice. I'll have that right out for you," before gliding off toward the kitchen.

Charlene leaned back in her chair. "I had almost forgotten that this kind of peace still exists."

Kendra followed her gaze outside. "Yeah. It's strange hearing laughter without a sense of worry behind it…no alarms, no rush to a medevac helicopter or truck."

Charlene gave a low chuckle. "Just the sound of silverware and easy jazz music. I'll take it."

Kendra laughed too, but her expression softened. "I keep catching myself waiting for something to happen. It's like my mind hasn't quite learned how to be still."

“Give it time,” Charlene said gently. “We’ve been running on adrenaline for a while. Now we just have to learn how to exhale again…and maybe eat something that isn’t vacuum-sealed.”

That made them both laugh, the easy kind that felt like release. But inside both of them, an uneasiness churned; unwanted, but not yet ready to loosen its grip. Outside, the breeze shifted the reflections on the window, and the faint sound of harbor bells carried through the air…a needed reminder that they were home, safe, and beginning again.

When the food arrived, the sizzling aroma of garlic and lemon butter made both women sigh contentedly. Shrimp, scallops, crab legs, and clams were perfectly charred, served over a bed of wild rice and vegetables, alongside corn and potatoes. They shared bites between easy conversation; light, teasing remarks about the people they’d seen and talked with at the Welcome Home celebration the night before, memories from deployment that now felt oddly distant, and the comforting normalcy of a small-town afternoon.

Afterward, Charlene pushed her plate away with a satisfied sigh. “You go ahead and get dessert. I’m saving room for dinner at Mom’s.”

Kendra smiled. “You don’t have to tell me twice.”

She ordered a slice of lemon pie. The kind the diner was famous for, and it reminded her just how far she’d come from those long, hard months overseas. And yet, her shoulders stayed taut, waiting for a sound that would never come.

Sheryl reappeared with the pie, breaking the spell. “You ladies need anything else?”

“Maybe a time machine,” Charlene quipped, earning a puzzled laugh before Sheryl moved on.

Kendra smiled faintly as she took her first forkful, the tangy sweetness pulling her back to easier times, if only for a moment. Charlene must have noticed, because before Kendra could stop her, she dug in with her fork and stole a generous bite, a mischievous grin spreading across her face.

Hey!" Kendra laughed.

"Wha-at? I just wanted to make sure it was still as good as I remember," Charlene feigned innocence, then added with a satisfied swallow, "Still the best pie on the coast."

The mood lightened a little, helped by the sugar and sunlight. They were halfway through the pie when Kendra glanced up and saw Sam Whitaker walking along the sidewalk across the street. His head slightly bowed against the wind, a quiet confidence in his stride. Hands in his jacket pockets, his stride unhurried but thoughtful. The same easy stride that had first caught her attention was still there, though now it seemed something was different; something very different, something deeper… something heavier.

Charlene noticed her expression. "That's Sam, isn't it? He looks like he's carrying the weight of the world."

Kendra nodded softly. "Losing his brother has changed him. I know he's still wrestling with that loss…but he seems to be finding his way back again."

Charlene rested her chin on her hand. "He will and maybe we all are finding our way back again. In our own way, in our own time."

Their conversation turned to the hospital. The work ahead of them, and the kind of difference they hoped to make. "I'm looking forward to working in the new trauma unit. Looks like we made it here just at the right time. They're just days away from being fully operational."

"I just keep thinking," Kendra said, "after everything we saw, after everything we experienced…maybe being back here isn't just about starting over. Maybe it's about healing…for all of us."

Charlene smiled, her voice soft but sure. "I believe that. You know, sometimes God puts us right where we need to be. Even when we don't understand the timing."

They finished the pie and Charlene checked her watch. "We should get going, before the evening rush."

As soon as they were outside of the diner, Kendra looked out toward the harbor where fishing boats rocked gently against the docks. "Is it just me, or does it feel almost too good to be back?" she said quietly.

Charlene looped her arm through hers. "It does. And whatever waits for us at that hospital; I think we're ready. God didn't bring us this far just have us stand still and do nothing."

Kendra smiled, letting the breeze brush against her cheek. "No," she said, her voice soft but certain. "He brought us home to continue what we started over there."

Together, they started down the street, their laughter carried by the same gentle wind that swept through Harmony Grove Harbor…a breeze ripe for healing and believing.

A soft quiet spilled over Harmony Grove Harbor as the afternoon sun had already started its descent when Kendra pulled into her parents' driveway. The sunlight cast slender shadows across the driveway and porch, brushing over the immaculate flowerbeds and trimmed hedges that lined the front walk. Inside, the house was quiet except for the faint ticking of the old kitchen clock and the hum of the refrigerator. She had just set her purse on the counter when her phone began to buzz.

She glanced at the screen and smiled.

"Hey, stranger," she said, answering.

"Stranger? So you miss me, huh?" Sam's voice came through, warm and teasing. "Guess I made a halfway decent impression."

Kendra laughed. "You did all right for yourself."

"Well," he said, a playful note sneaking into his tone, "since I'm on a roll, how about I try again? There's a jazz concert down on the waterfront tonight; local band, food trucks, sunset over the bay. Thought you might want to come…with me."

She leaned against the counter, absently tracing a circle on the wood grain. "Jazz on the waterfront, huh? Sounds suspiciously like a date."

"Only if you want it to be," Sam replied. "Otherwise, we can call it... community support for the arts."

Kendra laughed again, shaking her head. "That's the worst cover story I've ever heard."

"Maybe," he said. "But it worked; you're laughing."

The pause that followed was comfortable, filled with the hush of the late afternoon and the distant sound of crickets tuning up for the evening.

"So," he asked softly, "what do you say?"

She hesitated just long enough to make him wonder. "Pick me up at seven?"

"Seven it is."

"Don't be late, Whitaker."

"Wouldn't dream of it, Williams."

When the call ended, Kendra lingered by the window, watching the sunlight glint off the neighbor's wind chime. She could still hear the smile in Sam's voice. The day suddenly felt brighter; full of something she couldn't quite name but didn't want to lose.

Outside, the breeze carried the faint scent of jasmine through the open window, whispering a promise that the evening ahead might hold more than just jazz.

Chapter 5

A Gentle Evening, A New Morning

A soft quiet lingered over Harmony Grove Harbor as the afternoon stretched lazily toward evening. Sunlight spilled through Kendra's bedroom window, laying warm streaks across the oak floorboards. She stood before her mirror, still uncertain what to wear, holding two hangers side by side.

The first was a casual blouse and jeans; safe, unremarkable. The second, a sleeveless summer dress in a soft coral tone she hadn't worn in years. With a faint, self-conscious smile, she chose the dress. The fabric slipped easily into place, fitting more gracefully than she remembered. Months of military routine had left her arms strong and her posture straighter, and for a brief moment she hardly recognized the woman looking back. She brushed a loose curl from her forehead and laughed softly.

"You're doing it again…overthinking, Kendra. It's just jazz."

She reached for a simple necklace and a light shawl; just in case the harbor breeze turned cool.

A few blocks away, Sam stood before his own mirror, tugging at the knot of a navy tie he hadn't worn since Easter service.

"Too much?" he muttered, loosening it slightly. He finally settled on a crisp white shirt, sleeves rolled once at the forearm, and khaki slacks tucked neatly at the waist. It wasn't fancy, but it felt right; comfortable, clean, and just enough to show he cared. He smoothed the front of his shirt, straightened his slacks, and gave his reflection a half-smile.

"Not bad, Whitaker. Just don't trip over yourself."

He checked his watch, then glanced toward the window where the harbor glimmered in the distance. A flicker of nerves passed through him; ridiculous, he told himself. It was just Kendra. Except it wasn't *just* Kendra anymore.

By the time Sam arrived at the Williamses' home, the soft gold of late afternoon had deepened, and a faint breeze stirred the palm trees lining the driveway. He parked neatly, close to the middle of it, took a quiet breath, and stepped out of his truck. The house stood in a comfortable hush, touched by the warm glow of the lowering sun.

Sam walked up the front path, nervously straightening his shirt again, and climbed the porch steps. He prepared to knock, but before his hand reached the door, it opened. Kendra stood there, framed in the doorway, the late-afternoon light spilling softly across her face and catching a gentle shimmer in her eyes. For a heartbeat, Sam forgot whatever polite greeting he'd meant to say.

"Hello again, Mr. Whitaker... You clean up nice," she said with a smile.

"You, uh…" He cleared his throat, trying again. "You look amazing. Not that you didn't before, but…wow."

Her laugh came light and genuine. "Thank you."

As she neared him, her eyes drifted briefly over him… the neatly pressed shirt, the sleeves rolled just enough to hint at the quiet discipline in his build. She didn't say a word, but the small, approving smile that touched her lips said plenty.

Sam offered his arm with a grin that mirrored hers. "Shall we, Miss Williams?"

Her smile softened as she looped her arm through his. "We shall."

He led her down the steps at an easy pace, mindful of her dress, the boards creaking softly beneath their feet. At the truck, he walked slightly ahead to open the passenger door and extended a sturdy hand.

"Careful now," he said gently.

Kendra placed her hand in his and let him guide her up into the seat, her laugh light as she settled in. "You really are determined to make a lady feel spoiled, aren't you?"

"Only when the lady deserves it," he replied, grinning as he closed the door with quiet care before circling to his side.

The harbor had come alive with music. The sun hung low over the bay, painting the water in rippled streaks of copper and rose as the first notes of saxophone drifted through the air. A soft breeze carried the mingled scents of salt, kettle corn, and sweet summer grass from the park that sloped down toward the boardwalk.

Sam reached for Kendra's hand as he guided her through the growing crowd, weaving between rows of picnic blankets and clusters of lawn chairs. Strings of Edison bulbs glowed overhead, their reflections trembling on the surface of the water. Near the edge of the dock, a small cluster of café-style tables had been set up with flickering votive candles and paper lanterns swaying gently in the breeze.

"Perfect," Sam said, pulling out a chair for her. "Front-row seat to the bay and the band."

Kendra smiled as she sat. "You know, this is a lot fancier than I expected for a hometown concert."

He grinned. "Harmony Grove Harbor's learned a few tricks since you left. Same spirit as ever; laughter, music, and a mix of old and new faces, generations blending together like they always do. Feels even better now that you're back in the middle of it again."

The band struck up a livelier tune, the trumpet blending with the rolling tide. Sam leaned closer with a grin. "Be right back, going to get us something refreshing to drink."

A few minutes later, he returned balancing two tall glasses filled with crushed ice and slices of lemon and mint. "Harbor Breezes," he said proudly. "A local favorite; lemonade, a splash of sweet tea, a hint of ginger, and just a splash of rum."

Kendra took a sip, smiling at the crisp, surprising mix as the rhythm of the music sank in. The late light danced across the water and through the strands of her hair, and when she glanced up, she caught Sam looking at her.

"What?" she asked, laughing.

He shrugged, a bit sheepish but smiling all the same. "Nothing. Just thinking how Harmony Grove feels much better with you here."

She tilted her head, still smiling. "That so?"

Sam hesitated, then added quietly, "It's just… you look different out of uniform. Not that you weren't beautiful before; but tonight…" He paused, the words catching slightly. "You're breathtaking."

Kendra felt warmth rise to her cheeks. "That's the smoothest thing you've ever said to me, Whitaker."

"Hey, I've had years to practice," he teased.

"Careful," she said lightly, her voice gentle but laced with warmth. "That Harbor Breeze might be stronger than you think."

Sam chuckled, raising his glass. "Maybe. Or maybe it's just the company."

They both laughed, and the easy sound of it mixed with the swing of the saxophone. The moment lingered, light and golden, before the singer's voice rose, something familiar and soulful, and couples began drifting toward the open space before the stage.

Sam tilted his head toward the music. "What do you say? Think you remember how to dance?"

Kendra raised an eyebrow. "If you're brave enough to risk those toes of yours, sure."

He stood and offered his hand. "I'll take my chances."

She slipped her hand into his, and together they joined the small crowd moving to the music. The dock lights shimmered around them; laughter and applause rippled through the night. Sam's hand rested gently at her waist, her other hand in his, the two of them swaying easily in time with the rhythm. For a while, the rest of the world fell away; no hospital, no memories of war, just the music, the harbor breeze, and the rhythmic pulse of the band.

When the song ended, they stayed close a moment longer than either meant to. Sam's smile was quiet, and Kendra's eyes shone with something soft and new. Around them, the band struck up another tune; faster, livelier, and the spell eased into laughter once more.

"See?" he said. "Didn't step on me once."

"Beginner's luck," she teased, still smiling.

They wandered back to their table, the sound of jazz and gentle waves mingling in the night. Kendra leaned back in her chair, content. It had been a long time since she'd felt this light, this present. And as the music played on, she realized that, maybe for the first time since coming home, she didn't want the evening to end.

When the final song ended, the band thanked everyone for coming and the crowd started to disperse, but Sam and Kendra lingered a moment longer, letting the night settle around them. The harbor lights shimmered across the bay, and the faint strains of a saxophone still drifted from the stage, mingling with the rush of the tide.

"That was… wonderful," Kendra said softly, gathering her shawl. "It's been so long since I've just had a chance to listen and enjoy a live jazz band."

Sam smiled, his eyes warm. "There's something about live music and sea air that makes everything feel a little clearer." He hesitated for a beat, then added, "It's still early. Would you like to see the view from my rooftop deck? It overlooks the harbor, it's nothing fancy, but the lights are something else this time of night."

Kendra's lips curved in a faint, curious smile. "Sure. I'd like that."

They walked back toward his truck, the boardwalk lamps guiding their steps. The crowd had thinned, leaving only the sound of gulls settling on the pilings and the gentle slap of waves against them. Sam opened the passenger door for her once again, and When their hands touched, an unspoken comfort and quiet understanding lingered..

The drive was short, only a few turns along the waterfront where the reflection of streetlights rippled across the glassy surface of the bay. The evening breeze drifted through the open windows. the silence between them was never awkward, just easy… like they'd both grown comfortable in it.

Moments later, Sam pulled into his parking space in front of his condo. "Home sweet home," he said lightly as he climbed out and circled around to her side. He offered his hand as she stepped down.

Kendra remembered this community from earlier that day. "This is a lovely community. I was thinking about moving here."

"Then you'll feel right at home. I can show you around."

Inside, the condo greeted them with soft lighting and from where she stood, Kendra could see the harbor through the wide balcony doors. Streetlamps cast wavering trails of gold across the dark water, and sailboats rocked quietly against its moorings. The view alone felt like a deep breath. Her eyes adjusted to the lighting and she took in the room itself. It was neatly kept but lived in from the framed photos on the mantel ,to a couple of old books placed near the sofa. Then, on the shelving unit, a particular photograph caught her attention. It showed a younger Sam standing beside his brother in uniform, both smiling beneath a bright summer sky.

Kendra took in a deep breath.

Sam followed her line of sight, his expression softening. "That was just before he deployed," he said quietly. "We'd gone to the lake the day before for one last day out. He made me promise to start the boat often while he was gone."

He gave a short, self-conscious laugh, but when he looked back at her, her expression had changed… eyes glistening.. shoulders drawn slightly inward.

"Kendra?" he asked gently. "Hey, did I say something wrong?"

She blinked, pulling herself back to the moment, and shook her head. "No," she whispered. "You didn't. It's just… seeing Joseph's picture; it brought something back. Something I have tried not to talk about."

He nodded slowly, not pressing, just waiting.

"Do you need to sit?" he asked after a moment.

She hesitated, then nodded, and they crossed to the small sofa near the window. The glow of the harbor lights spilled softly through the glass, reflecting off the photo frame. Sam sat beside her, just close enough for gentle support.

Kendra took a deep breath, and without realizing it, leaned against him. When she finally spoke, her voice was low, measured, but threaded with emotion.

"It was late into the night, later than it should've been. The med tent was already full that night..." Her mind slipped back to that night, when calm no longer existed.

— ✦ —

The sound came first.

The low chop of helicopter blades, the echo of artillery in the distance, and the harsh crackle of the radio.

The flaps of their medical tent ripped open, again and again, as trucks and helicopters rolled in wounded soldiers. As each soldier's injuries were assessed, fatigue pressed in, threatening to overwhelm the medical team. But it was the cries of the wounded that pierced the night's mercilessness, striking deeper than any shell.

Kendra and her medical team worked in tandem. The doctors, nurses, medics, each one running on instinct and prayer, sharing the unspoken understanding that every second could mean the difference between life and death. They didn't pause, didn't allow themselves to stagger. They lifted, bandaged, injected, sutured, all while the night dragged on, unending and relentless.

"Pressure here, keep it secure!"

"Vitals dropping, bring plasma!"

"Next wave incoming!"

Kendra could never forget a young private that night who had been severely injured. The doctors and nurses didn't hold much hope for him surviving, but Kendra whispered prayers between every instruction she was given by the medical team working with her. *Lord, steady my hands and guide me. Please, give this soldier strength and give me focus. Help us both to make it through this night.* Her voice was soft but sure, an assured faith that seemed to fill the tent with something stronger than fear.

By dawn, their tent was filled with the broken, the bleeding, the ones everyone whispered would not make it. Yet when the sun's pale light filtered through the torn canvas above them, a miracle revealed itself. Not one soldier in their care had perished. Not one. Some still clung to life by the thinnest of threads, but life remained. Against every expectation, every grim prognosis, the men under their watch still breathed. Kendra finally allowed herself to collapse to her knees, lifting trembling hands in praise.

It was then that Charlene had arrived back on base. That night she had been assigned as a flight nurse on the medevac helicopter. She found Kendra in the chapel and without saying a word, Charlene joined Kendra on her knees. The two nurses lifted up their eyes heavenward through sweat streaked and tear stained faces, offering whispered thanks, giving all glory to the One who had answered their desperate cries.

"Grace," Kendra had said through her tears. "Only His grace."

Charlene, weary but resolute, had nodded, her voice cracked and raspy. "And mercy."

"Because God was with us," Charlene whispered. "He was with us the whole time."

—✦—

The memory faded as Kendra opened her eyes to Sam's piercing eyes and the still waters of Harmony Grove Harbor. The same moon that had watched her through that terrible night and that place now hung over her in peace.

For a long moment, neither of them spoke. The room was still except for the faint rhythm of the waterfront below; waves brushing against the pilings, a soft, even hush that seemed to echo her heartbeat.

Sam rose quietly, moving just enough to sit on the edge of the coffee table directly in front of her. He needed her to see and feel the depth of his concern. He leaned in and reached out both hands to her, waiting. When she placed her hands in his, his touch was warm and comforting. His eyes softened as his gaze met hers… not fixed on her tears, but on the courage it took for her to speak them aloud.

Kendra drew in a slow breath, her gaze never leaving his. "I don't talk about that night," she said softly. "Not even with Charlene anymore. But seeing your brother's picture… it just came rushing back. We saw injuries that night worse than any I've ever seen. And even though we didn't lose anyone, and I'm grateful for that, I knew their lives were forever changed. I still wonder sometimes if we did enough. That feeling of being surrounded by helplessness, and yet somehow coming through it; knowing we weren't alone."

Sam's voice was low and intentional. "You weren't," he said. "And neither was he," his gaze shifting to Joseph's picture.

She met his eyes then, surprised by the quiet certainty in his tone.

He hesitated, glancing again toward the photo on the bookshelf before continuing. "There are days I still ask why it happened… why he didn't come home. But hearing you just now… maybe it's not about understanding why. Maybe it's about remembering that God was there even in the middle of it. I know I'm not quite where I should be right now, but I'm working on it."

Kendra nodded, her throat tightening. "Me too, Sam… me too," her voice barely above a whisper.

A long silence followed; the kind that didn't need to be filled. The harbor lights flickered gently across the room, glinting on the framed photo like a shared candle flame.

Finally, Sam rose and offered a faint, calming smile. "Come on," he said quietly. "You've got to see this view before the tide changes."

He led her out onto the small rooftop deck. The night air was cool, carrying the faint scent of salt and pine. Below them, the town stretched out in sleepy contentment, the church steeple, a dark silhouette against the moonlit bay.

Kendra rested her hands on the railing, the breeze tugging gently at her shawl. "It's beautiful," she murmured.

"Yeah," Sam said, his gaze fixed on the horizon.

"It really is."

For a while, they stood side by side beneath the silver wash of moonlight; two souls touched by memory, faith, and something unmistakably new.

The night deepened around them, the harbor hushed beneath a blanket of moonlight. The view said what words couldn't.

When the breeze turned cool, Sam glanced over, noticing Kendra pull her shawl a little tighter. "Come on," he said softly. "Let's head inside. This night air can get chilly suddenly"

She smiled faintly. "Alright, but only if you promise to keep showing me that harbor view."

"Deal."

Back inside felt even warmer after the night air. Sam crossed to a small cabinet near the kitchen counter and held up a bottle with a sheepish grin. "I've been saving this for company. Technically, it's local, one of those new vineyard blends up near Fairhope."

Kendra laughed softly. "Well, since you're offering, I suppose it would be rude to refuse."

He poured two glasses and handed one to her before sitting down next to her. They toasted quietly; just a soft clink of glass and the unspoken relief of shared understanding. For a while, they talked, reliving the concert and immersing themselves in the beauty of the moon-kissed oceanfront view.

After a while, Sam asked Kendra if she'd like to see some of the restorative projects he'd been working on recently. When she gave an inquisitive nod, he switched on the TV and queued up a set of short clips. He took a little more time with a documentary he'd been piecing together ever since the church bell had cracked and shifted off its yoke. The images moved from the damaged bell hanging crooked in the old steeple to volunteers bracing ladders, sanding beams, and securing new supports. Then came photos from bake sales, fish fries, and every fundraiser the congregation held to pay for the restoration.

Kendra leaned forward, her eyes following every frame. "Sam…this is incredible," she said softly. "I knew the bell was damaged, but I had no idea how much work is going into restoring it. You are a huge part of this. I'm really proud of you."

He didn't say much at first, just offered a small, thoughtful smile. Kendra could see something deeper working just beneath the surface. "Honestly…" Sam murmured, eyes still on the screen, "being part of restoring that bell… I'm honored. Humbled, really. And it's still a work in progress."

Kendra noticed the quiet confidence and a sense of pride behind his smile…a confidence that made sense now. Sam had spent the past few years training and working as a restoration project manager, totally committed to projects that protected the shoreline and the old structures rooted in it.

While Kendra watched him, she realized it wasn't just another project. The bell tower had become something more meaningful to him; a piece of Harmony Grove Harbor's heart, a symbol of endurance and hope. And Sam was pouring himself into bringing it back, the same way he poured himself into every project.

Kendra's expression softened. "Your dedication and pride in what you do, it truly shows," she said, her voice warm and reassuring. "What you're doing here…it's amazing, and it matters."

His quiet smile deepened, and their conversation continued, but gradually slowed, softened, and then drifted into a familiar comfortable silence.

Kendra leaned back, her eyes heavy but content. "It's peaceful here," she murmured. "Almost too peaceful."

Sam smiled, his voice low. "You can stay as long as you like."

She meant to answer, but her words melted into a sigh. Within moments, her breathing had evened out, in a soft and uniform rhythm. Sam sat there for a while, watching the faint rays of moonlight move across her face. The exhaustion of the evening, the long journey home the day before, the laughter, the memories, the ache of shared truths had caught up with them both.

He leaned his head against the back of the sofa, meaning only to rest for a minute.

Sleep found them both before they knew it.

The first light of morning crept across the harbor, slipping through the balcony doors and painting soft gold over the room. Sam stirred first. For a moment, disoriented, he blinked in the quiet space before realizing Kendra was still beside him; curled up, a blanket, gathered around her shoulders, a faint smile resting on her lips.

He sat up carefully, rubbing his eyes, and glanced at the clock. Nearly seven. The world outside was already awake; a fisherman's truck rattled past, gulls called somewhere over the pier.

Sam hesitated, debating whether to wake her. But she looked so peaceful, so far from the haunted weariness that had shadowed her eyes the night before, that he decided against it. Instead, he eased off the couch, draped a lighter throw blanket over her, and quietly slipped out to the kitchen to start the coffee.

The scent of it eventually stirred her.

Kendra blinked, realizing where she was, the couch, the sunlight, the blanket, and then her eyes went wide. "Oh no," she whispered, sitting up quickly and smoothing her hair. "Sam, what time is it?"

He turned from the counter, mug in hand, suppressing a small grin. "Just after seven. You were out cold."

Her eyes darted to the window, panic and embarrassment wrestling in her expression. "Sam, you know how people will talk if they see me leaving your apartment this time of the morning? This town doesn't need much to start a rumor."

He lifted a calming hand, his smile kind but teasing. "Relax. I think the harbor's too busy chasing seagulls to care." Then, softening, he added, "But you're right; small towns have long memories. Tell you what; finish your coffee, and I'll drive you home before the gossip brigade makes their morning rounds."

Kendra gave a half-laugh, half-groan, pressing a hand to her forehead. "Well, it's not like I'm eighteen. But I can hear them now. *Did you hear that Kendra Williams spent the night with Sam Whitaker*?"

He chuckled, sliding his empty mug into the sink. "Let 'em talk. We know what really happened; two tired people falling asleep after too much jazz and a little too much reminiscing."

That earned a small smile from her, soft but genuine. "You always know how to make things sound harmless."

"Maybe because they are," he said quietly.

She met his gaze then, something tender and uncertain flickering in her eyes before she looked away. "Alright," she murmured, pushing back the blanket and standing and gathering her shawl. "Let's get ahead of the rumor mill."

A few minutes later, they stepped out into the early morning light. The harbor was slowly waking; gulls circling above the docks, the scent of brine and freshly baked bread drifting from the café down the street. Dew clung to the hood of Sam's truck, glinting like tiny pearls in the rising sun.

The ride was quiet but comfortable. The windows were rolled down just enough to let the cool morning air in, carrying with it the familiar rhythm of waves against the pilings. Kendra cradled her coffee cup in both hands, gazing out at the pale shimmer of the water as the town came alive.

"I really didn't mean to fall asleep," she said after a while, her tone half-sheepish, half-sincere.

Sam smiled faintly, keeping his eyes on the road. "It happens. You looked like you needed the rest."

She glanced at him, a gentle gratitude in her eyes. "Thank you. For last night. For listening."

"Anytime," he said. Then, with a teasing note, "Besides, I couldn't let the night end without one more excuse to see you smile."

That earned a small laugh from her, quiet but real. The kind that eased whatever awkwardness had lingered.

By the time they turned onto her street, the sun was already climbing higher, spilling gold across the rooftops. Sam eased the truck to a stop in front of the Williamses' driveway, turned off the ignition, and stepped out. A moment later, Kendra watched as he rounded the front of the truck and opened her door with that quiet, gentlemanly ease that was becoming unmistakably him.

She smiled up at him. "You really don't have to do that every time, you know."

"Maybe not," he said with a small grin, offering his hand, "but I want to."

She hesitated, then returned the smile. "Fair enough. I guess we'll be giving the neighbors something to talk about."

He grinned. "Let 'em talk, let 'em wonder. they'll have moved on to the next headline by lunchtime."

She rolled her eyes, smiling despite herself. "You're terrible."

"Maybe," he said lightly. "But you're smiling again."

That made her pause, the humor softening into something tender. "Yeah," she said quietly. "I guess I am."

She stepped out, grabbing her shawl and catching Sam's hand as the cool morning air met her skin. The faint scent of her mother's roses drifted from the porch, wrapping the moment in quiet familiarity. Sam waited until she'd made it up the walk before giving a small wave.

Kendra lingered at the door a moment longer, watching as his truck pulled away toward the harbor road. For the first time in a long while, she didn't feel the familiar heaviness pressing in. Instead, something lighter, steadier... a promise of new beginnings.

The house was quiet when Kendra stepped inside, morning light spilling softly through the front windows. The faint aroma of coffee drifted from the kitchen. She set her shawl over the back of the sofa and let out a slow breath, grateful for the stillness.

No voices. No footsteps. No questions.

She slipped down the hallway to her room, easing the door closed behind her. A quick shower refreshed her from the peaceful night's rest, and by the time she'd changed and tidied up, the memories she'd shared with him felt a little lighter... no longer a weight, but a quiet reminder of grace.

When she finally joined her parents at the breakfast table, her mother was skimming the church bulletin while her father sat behind the morning paper.

"Morning, sweetheart," her mother said with a smile that was equal parts warmth and curiosity. "You're up a little late. Sleep well?"

Kendra returned the smile, careful to keep her tone easy. "Actually, I did. Better than I have in a while."

Her mother nodded toward the counter. "There's fresh coffee and some biscuits if you're hungry."

“Thanks,” Kendra said, moving to the counter and fixing herself a small plate before taking a seat. The biscuits were still warm, butter melting into golden pools.

Her father folded the paper slightly, one eyebrow lifting in that familiar, knowing way. “That’s good to hear,” he said. “Big day today; we still going to pick up that new car?”

She nodded, grateful for the shift in topic. “Yes, I thought we’d head over right after breakfast.”

Her mother exchanged a glance with her father, then said gently, “Your dad and I were just talking about Sam a little while ago.”

Kendra paused, her fork hovering above her plate. “Oh?”

Her father set the paper aside completely. “He’s a good man, Kendra. We know that. Dependable, respectful. We just want you to be careful, that’s all. You’ve both have a lot on your shoulders.”

Her mother reached over, resting her hand lightly on Kendra’s. “He’s been through loss and hard times too, sweetheart. Sometimes two people still healing can lean on each other so hard, they forget to stand on their own.”

Kendra looked down for a moment, then nodded. “I know. And I promise, I’m not rushing anything. Sam’s just been so kind… and understanding. That’s all.”

Her mother smiled softly. “Kindness has a way of taking more than we expect.”

Her father stood, sliding his paper onto the counter and giving her shoulder a gentle squeeze. “Just keep that level head of yours. Everything else will fall into place.”

Kendra smiled faintly. “I will, Dad.”

Her father nodded solemnly. “You know”, he paused, “That war has changed a lot of folks. It leaves more scars than the ones people can see.”

Kendra looked down at her hands, twisting her napkin slowly. "It's strange," she said softly. "Charlene and I made it home alive, but sometimes I wonder if a part of us is still over there. And Sam… he never even left, but I think part of him is even over there."

Her mother's expression softened. "Sometimes God moves and works in mysterious ways. We just have to be willing and open to where He's leading us."

Kendra met her mother's eyes and gave a faint, thoughtful smile.

The conversation drifted into gentler things after that; the new hospital, old friends, plans for Sunday service, and of course, picking up the new car. She couldn't wait to see Charlene's reaction to it tomorrow. But even as they talked, Kendra couldn't shake the image of Sam's eyes from the night before; calm, compassionate, yet shadowed by something he hadn't let surface. He'd listened to her, carried her pain as if it were his own, but she couldn't help wondering what he was still carrying inside and alone.

After breakfast, Kendra helped her mother clear the table before gathering her purse and keys. The morning sunlight slanted warmly through the kitchen window, glimmering off the polished countertops and her father's coffee mug.

"You about ready?" he asked, folding his paper and setting it aside.

Kendra nodded, smiling. "I think so. I'm kind of excited, actually."

Her mother grinned from her spot by the sink. "Well, I can't wait to see it when you get back. Drive carefully, sweetheart."

"I will," Kendra said, leaning over to kiss her cheek.

As she reached for her phone on the counter, a new message buzzed across the screen. It was from Charlene:

"Don't forget to send me a picture of that new ride! I want to see it before you get bug guts on the windshield!"

Kendra laughed softly to herself, shaking her head. She then reads Charlene's message to her parents, still smiling.

Her father chuckled. "That one hasn't changed a bit."

He grabbed his cap from the hook by the door. "Your mother told me the dealership said it'll be ready first thing this morning. Let's go make it official."

Before they headed toward the garage, Kendra paused by the table where she had taken out her old car keys. Her father followed her gaze, a small smile tugging at his mouth.

"You sure about giving it away?" he asked.

She nodded. "Yeah. That family over on Pine Street; the Johnsons? Their oldest just started a job out of town. It'll help him get back and forth until he can save up for something better."

He gave an approving nod. "That's a good thing you're doing, Kendra."

"It's just a car," she said softly, slipping the keys into his hand. "But maybe it can get him where he needs to go, like it did for me over the years, and like this new one's going to do for me now."

Her father smiled, pride and affection in his eyes. "You've got your mother's heart, you know that?"

Kendra followed her father through the kitchen as her mother wiped the counter, then turned toward them with a gentle smile. "Be safe, you two," she said. Her husband leaned in to kiss her cheek, murmuring something soft that made her smile even wider.

The garage door buzzed open, and the crisp morning air met them as they stepped inside. Her father's black Acura MDX gleamed beneath the light, the faint scent of leather and fresh citrus greeting them as they climbed in.

Kendra shared a laugh with her dad as they settled into the seats. The SUV eased out of the garage into the soft morning light, and their conversation flowed easily, the kind that needed no effort, just the comfort of years and understanding between them. It was that familiar rhythm of family... the grace, the laughter, and the simple blessings that kept them moving forward together.

Chapter 6

New Beginnings at Harmony Grove Harbor Hospital

Kendra Williams eased her brand-new midnight blue Honda Accord into the staff parking lot of Harmony Grove Harbor Regional Hospital. Sitting for a quiet moment, she drew a deep breath, controlling the mix of nerves and anticipation swirling inside her. Then, with quiet resolve, she opened the door and stepped out into the cool morning air. As she did, a lone seagull flew overhead, its long, outstretched wings gliding effortlessly across the pale sky. Kendra looked up, following its graceful path as it caught the wind, joined two more circling above, and lifted higher toward the dimly lit horizon… almost as if blessing the start of a new day. In the distance, the harbor was waking up; the low mournful call of a fishing boat horn, the clinking rigging against the metal masts, and the faint cries of herons and cormorants riding the morning air. The autumn sea air was fresh and crisp, and a tender breeze kissed her cheek as she opened the door.

Moments later, Charlene Matthews' fire-engine-red Jeep Wrangler wheeled by and slid into the parking space beside Kendra. The beat of an old R&B tune thumped lightly through her open window, the kind of song that always seemed to match her bright personality. Charlene leaned over the steering wheel with a wide grin the moment their eyes met.

"Well, now," she teased, eyeing the shiny blue car as she reached to turn the volume down. "Guess somebody decided to make an entrance."

She pushed her door open and stepped out, motioning dramatically toward the car. "New job, new hospital, new car... somebody's starting new and fresh in style!"

Kendra laughed, shaking her head as she adjusted the pants of her new scrubs. "My old one had served me well, and now hopefully it'll serve somebody else just as well. I gave it to the Johnson boy. He's been saving for his first new car, but hopefully, this will give him a head start."

Charlene's grin softened into something warmer. "There you go, always looking out for someone else."

Kendra shrugged with an easy smile. "It just felt right. That little car still has plenty of life left in it."

"Well, I'll give you this; you make kindness look effortless."

Charlene reached into her Jeep for her nurse's tote. "Well, it's a great little car…still looks like new."

Kendra nodded as she reached for her tattered old army tote that she had casually tossed to the back seat earlier, her nerves easing as Charlene's encouragement and light-heartedness filled the air with brightness. Charlene's sunny spirit was contagious, and Kendra felt some of the tension ease from her shoulders. "Guess it's a new chapter for both of us."

The two women fell into step together, their bags slung over their shoulders, side by side as they walked toward the main entrance of Harmony Grove Harbor Regional Hospital, Kendra paused, her gaze drifting past the hospital lot towards the harbor. The gulls wheeled in the rising sunlight of the morning sky, the echoes of waves against the shoreline, and the laughter of dockworkers carried faintly on the breeze. This time, she actually felt the lightness of peace embracing her.

Charlene noticed her pause and smiled knowingly. "I know. It's been a few days now, and it's still hard to take it all in. Every time I look over the harbor and enjoy a sunset or sunrise here, I marvel at not expecting to hear helicopter blades or the medical evacuation truck approaching in the distance. I don't think I really appreciated this peace until I *didn't* have it."

Kendra gave a soft knowing nod. "I know. …" She lifted her face to the breeze. "All I hear are gulls and ship horns. I didn't dare think *there* about how much I missed *here*."

Charlene bumped her gently with her shoulder, her sunny grin returning. "Yup, I'm with you. There's no place like home. And, now we get to continue what we started…over there."

Kendra nodded, her eyes softening. "And we get to do it in our hometown. Who would've thought?"

"Not me," Charlene chuckled. "But I'll take it. Harmony Grove Harbor may be small, but it's a great place to be. And with this new hospital and two of the best nurses this town could ever ask for…" She flashed Kendra a playful wink, then added with a touch more sincerity, "We've come a long way to get back, and I'm glad we are back."

And with that, they continued towards the gleaming glass doors of Harmony Grove Harbor Regional Hospital, carrying both the weight of their past and the bright hope of their new beginning.

The Army had taught them discipline, skill, and resilience, but Harmony Grove Harbor had always been the place that defined them. The place where their roots ran deep, where every street corner carried a memory. To Harmony Grove Harbor, they were daughters of the city; nurses who had left to serve and then came back to give their best to the people they loved. They had experienced many times over how to make life saving decisions in the span of a heartbeat when faced with injuries so severe that no one back home could truly imagine; the wounded soldiers whose cries haunted their sleep, friends carried back home in military coffins, the crushing weight of losing a soldier despite their best efforts. War had scarred them, yes, but hope and faith had sustained them. And in that crucible, their friendship had deepened into sisterhood. But even as Harmony Grove Harbor's sea air filled their lungs, memories of that place and that life followed them like a persistent unyielding shadow.

Charlene adjusted her stethoscope and gave the building a slow, approving look.

Kendra glanced at Charlene, her eyes bright with excitement. "This is way more than I imagined it would be. Can you believe this?" she said softly.

Charlene smiled, though her gaze stayed fixed on the hospital's entrance. "Yeah," she chuckled, "cause I'm looking at it! But it is amazing!"

They both burst out laughing as the sliding glass doors parted with a soft hiss, ushering them into the gleaming atrium of the hospital. Their brand-new clogs squeaked lightly against the spotless floors, echoing just enough to announce their arrival.

The atrium was bright and inviting, with sunlight spilling through the tall glass panels that framed the entryway. A soft murmur of voices drifted from the information desk ahead, where a friendly receptionist greeted visitors with practiced warmth. Off to one side, the aroma of fresh baked biscuits and fried chicken floated from a small café near the waiting area, its corner tables already occupied by a few early-rising staff and patients' families.

Charlene nudged Kendra lightly as they passed the café. "Now this is my kind of medicine," she whispered, grinning.

Kendra smiled, her earlier nerves easing more as they followed the signs toward Staff Orientation. The hum of monitors and the persistent shuffle of feet surrounded them, the hospital was alive with its familiar rhythm.

A few nurses glanced up from nearby stations, offering tired but welcoming smiles; an unspoken gesture that said, *You belong here.*

Inside the conference room, a small group of new hires gathered near a refreshment table, all wearing the same mix of first-day nerves and anticipation. Charlene's eyes lit up at the sight of coffee and snacks. "Now that's what I'm talking about," she said with a wink, drawing a quiet laugh from Kendra.

As they reached the table, a friendly-looking nurse smiled at them.

"Hey there, I'm Allison Parker. Nurse, medical-Surgical unit."

Charlene returned the smile. "Charlene Matthews, Emergency and Trauma."

Kendra followed with a polite nod. "Kendra Williams, also Trauma. Looks like we'll be seeing a lot of each other."

They exchanged quick laughs, the kind that broke the ice easily, before moving toward a table near the window. Around them, similar introductions rippled through the room; soft voices trading names, departments, and a few hopeful remarks about schedules and shifts to come.

Promptly at 8:30 a.m. Denise Parker left her post from the entrance doorway and made her way to the podium. She tapped the microphone gently. "Good morning, everyone. First, let me say how thrilled we are to have you here. You are the heart of this hospital. The hands, the compassion, and the skill that you bring will help us build something truly special for this community."

Her words struck something in Kendra. She looked out the tall windows where the morning light spilled through them and across the room, beaming rays like liquid gold. For the first time that morning, her excitement outshone her nerves. She suddenly realized that she wasn't just starting a job. She was returning to her purpose, her calling… right here in the place that she proudly called *Home*.

Denise began passing out the welcome packets around the room and allowed some time for the new hires to become acquainted with its contents. When Charlene received hers, she opened and flipped through the packet.

"Schedules, policies, emergency procedures, patient care philosophy…" She glanced up, eyes wide with mock exasperation. "Girl, they really expect us to read all this?"

Kendra laughed softly, the tension easing from her shoulders. "Yup. Guess it's official now. No turning back."

When they reconvened after lunch, Denise returned to the podium, her smile bright but relaxed. "Welcome back, everyone. I hope you enjoyed lunch and managed to recharge a bit. This morning, we covered the hospital's mission, vision, and values, as well as hospital-wide policies, compliance regulations, and procedural requirements."

The next hour, they spent meeting Nurse Daniels, whose calm presence and kind eyes instantly put everyone at ease, followed by two social workers who spoke warmly about patient advocacy and community outreach. Finally, a representative from Payroll and Benefits distributed folders, explaining the forms inside with practiced efficiency and a reassuring tone.

By late afternoon, Denise was wrapping up the first day of orientation. "You've all done great today. Tomorrow morning, please report back here, and then you'll be assigned directly to your departments. I hope your first day has been a good start. Remember… this hospital runs on teamwork, and every one of you matters here. I'll remain here for a few minutes in case you have any questions or concerns."

With that, the orientation group made its way back to the main lobby and entrance. Kendra, Charlene, and Allison lingered for a moment near the glass, exchanging contact information and making plans to get together after work.

"Great meeting you, Kendra and Charlene. See you tomorrow," chimed Allison.

"First day down," Kendra said softly.

Charlene grinned. "And only a lifetime to go."

They shared a quiet laugh before heading their separate ways; two friends, now three, walking into very different evenings.

The next morning, the soft hum of conversations again filled the orientation room as Kendra settled into a seat beside Allison, who had arrived just moments earlier, a steaming cup of coffee in hand. She glanced around, noticing that most of the new hires had already arrived, some chatting quietly, others reviewing their notes from the day before.

The clock on the wall ticked steadily toward the start time when the door swung open and Charlene slipped in, her tote slung over one shoulder, her hair gathered in a quick twist. She offered a breathless smile as she made her way to the empty chair beside Kendra.

"Morning," Kendra said softly.

Charlene smiled back, dropping into her seat. "Morning."

It wasn't unusual for Charlene to be lively or spontaneous but rushing in at the last minute just wasn't her style. Kendra didn't say anything, just offered a knowing look before turning her attention back to the front of the room where Denise Parker had started the day's agenda.

Orientation began promptly, and the room settled into focus. Discussions about unit-specific training filled the next hour; safety protocols, charting procedures, and introductions to the department preceptors who would be shadowing the new staff in the coming days. Kendra took careful notes, her pen gliding across the page with practiced neatness. Beside her, Charlene jotted quick bullet points, stifling an occasional yawn.

When Denise called for a short break, Kendra rose and stretched, then turned to her friend. "You okay? It's not like you to be sliding in at just the nick of time."

Charlene let out a quiet sigh, shrugging her shoulders. "Didn't sleep well last night. Running on fumes." She tried to smile, but it didn't quite make it. "It doesn't happen often, but when it does… it's like being run over by one of those military transporter trucks. I'll be okay, though."

Kendra studied her for a moment, sensing the forced humor in her tone. She thought about pressing further, but something in Charlene's expression said *not now.* So instead, she nodded and smiled gently. "Coffee refill?"

Charlene smiled only faintly. "Now that's a prescription I can follow."

The two walked toward the refreshment table, their quiet footsteps blending with the low chatter of other new hires. Whatever shadows lingered behind Charlene's smile, Kendra let them rest…for now.

A few minutes later, Denise's familiar voice carried across the room. "All right, everyone, we'll be moving on to the next portion of your orientation. You'll now head to your assigned departments for team introductions and area tours." She lifted a small stack of papers from the podium, passing them to the nearest table. "Please select the packet with *your* name on it, and pass the remaining packets on to your neighbor. Each packet includes a map with your department highlighted and directions to the nearest staff elevators. Your badges are now fully active, so you'll use them to access secured areas and staff lounges. Just tap them at any door marked with a blue light."

The room stirred with quiet energy as chairs were pushed back from the tables and voices mingled. Denise smiled. "Your department leads will be expecting you. Take your time getting there, but don't get lost; this place can feel like a maze your first week."

Kendra looked down at her map and noticed the bold print near the top: *Emergency and Trauma Services – Level One.* She glanced toward Charlene and Allison, who were standing nearby comparing their sheets.

"Well," Charlene said with a grin, "looks like the dream team's sticking together."

Allison laughed. "I was hoping we'd end up in the same unit. Guess somebody up there likes us."

Kendra smiled, tucking her map into her folder. "Come on then. let's not make Nurse Daniels wait on her new recruits."

Together, the three women followed the small stream of new hires into the hallway, their badges proudly dangling and softly catching the light as they passed through double width sliding glass doors. The corridor opened into one of the hospital's main arteries; a long, gleaming passage that connected the administrative wing to the patient care towers. The faint scent of fresh paint and new flooring still lingered in the air, a reminder that the building was barely broken in. Their footsteps echoed lightly against the polished tile as they passed empty waiting areas, unoccupied offices, and the occasional maintenance cart tucked neatly to the side. A few staff members in crisp uniforms moved with quiet purpose, testing equipment and checking monitors. Following the signs marked *Emergency and Trauma Services – Level One,* the trio descended a short corridor marked for *employees only* to a set of double doors illuminated by a blue security light. Kendra reached for her badge and, with a soft beep, tapped it against the reader. The lock clicked open, and the doors parted to reveal the entrance to the Emergency Department; the place where their new journey would truly begin.

The nurses' station was abuzz with the low hum of monitors, the shuffle of shoes on polished tiles, the quiet rhythm of conversation between staff, and the morning sun slanted its rays through the tall windows and brightly lit floors.

Kendra and Charlene didn't have a chance to say "hello", before, several nurses waved and turned to welcome the two new arrivals as they approached. Bright smiles broke across attentive faces as the nurses looked up from an EMR station, their focus shifting briefly from screens and setup tasks to the new arrivals.

"You must be the new trauma nurses," said a tall, sandy-haired RN, offering his hand first to Kendra, then Charlene, and finally Allison. "I'm David, night shift lead. Welcome aboard."

They introduced themselves in turn, returning his handshake with easy smiles as they met their new team.

Another nurse, a petite woman with a stethoscope draped loosely around her neck, leaned forward with a grin. "We've heard about you three; our new dream team," she said warmly. Her gaze lingered briefly on Kendra and Charlene. "You two are the Army nurses, right? Thank you for your service." Then, turning toward Allison, she added with a friendly smile, "And welcome aboard to you, too, Allison." The nurses nearby nodded and smiled in agreement.

Kendra felt her cheeks warm. "We were just doing our jobs," she said softly.

Charlene gave a modest "Thanks", though her eyes showed a flicker of embarrassment. "We're just happy to be here, working alongside all of you."

Allison smiled slightly and said graciously, "Thank you for such a warm welcome."

"Still," David said firmly, "what you've done matters. And we're honored to have you with us."

The sincerity in his voice disarmed them both. They weren't just newcomers; they were being welcomed into a family.

As the introductions circled, names, roles, quick handshakes, the conversation shifted naturally.

"You probably talked with nurse Daniels in your interview or met her during orientation. We are all under her," another nurse explained, lowering her voice slightly in the way staff always did when talking about leadership. "Tough as nails, but fair. She expects a lot. Organization, sharp thinking, and absolute commitment to patient care."

A younger nurse, clearly new herself, chimed in eagerly. "But she notices effort. She doesn't let good patient care and good record keeping go unrecognized."

"More than that," David added, resting a hand on the counter, "she's known for standing up for her staff. In hospital conferences, she won't hesitate to challenge policies if they put nurses at risk or pile on unreasonable workloads. She's makes sure our voices are heard, and genuinely cares for her staff."

Kendra felt a quiet sense of relief bloom in her chest. Authority could be daunting, but a leader who cared for her people, well, that was something she and Charlene respected deeply.

"She's popular," the petite nurse added with a grin. "But more important, she's well respected. Don't let the stern face fool you. Beneath it, she's probably one of the kindest people here."

Charlene smirked, a bit of her dry wit surfacing. "Tough but fair, respected by her staff, advocates in meetings… sounds like the kind of commander we used to wish we had."

That drew a ripple of laughter around the station, and the tension eased even further.

"Nurse Williams, Nurse Matthews, Nurse Parker?" a firm voice greeted them.

They turned to see Nurse Manager, Pauline Daniels, approaching; a tall, slender woman whose posture carried the quiet authority of someone who had led more than a few hospital departments in her time. Her dark brown hair was immaculately coiffed, with a graceful streak of silver framing her face; a touch that lent her both elegance and distinction. Though her presence at first glance seemed commanding, her eyes told another story; warm, assuring, touched with the kind of calm that instantly put others at ease. A pair of delicate teardrop earrings caught the light as she moved, a subtle accent to her tailored suit and soft, jewel-toned blouse beneath her crisp lab coat. Her high-heeled shoes clicked smartly against the polished floor; an unexpected touch of style in a world of rubber soles. Altogether, she looked every bit the poised, self-assured leader. Professional, capable, and undeniably confident.

"Welcome…it's good to see you again." Nurse Daniels extended her hand, her tone professional but genuine. "We've been expecting you. I just wanted to take a few minutes to formally welcome you. We're so glad to have you onboard."

Her grip was firm, her eyes thoughtful as they moved from Kendra to Charlene. "Your service records are impressive; Special Operations Battlefield RNs. This hospital needs nurses like you; calm under pressure, levelheaded when it counts." Then her gaze shifted to Allison, and her expression softened with appreciation. "And Allison Parker, our Medical-Surgical standout. Your clinical leadership during the hurricane relief effort last year caught our attention. That kind of experience says a lot about your dedication and heart. We're fortunate to have you with us."

Charlene chuckled softly. "We've had our share of pressure to be sure."

Daniels nodded, almost knowingly. "Good. Because you'll find that even in a place like Harmony Grove Harbor, crises don't wait. Patients come in broken, sometimes hopeless. And you'll be asked to do more than patch them up. You'll be asked to give them hope."

"And that's why we're here," Charlene had understood this when she agreed to come onboard at Harmony Grove Harbor

Regional Hospital. "We've been trained for this." She continued. "We're prepared for when the worst comes through those doors to stay focused, remain calm to provide the best possible care for folks when they need us the most."

"And we know that it will come," Kendra had replied, her eyes stern. "Accidents, storms, maybe even disasters. But God prepared us for this. For here."

Allison nodded thoughtfully, her expression calm but sincere. "I haven't seen the kind of things you both have," she said quietly, "but I've learned that compassion under pressure changes everything. I'm ready to do my part."

Standing here now, inside the bustling hospital, Kendra and Charlene felt the weight and truth of those words settle deep in their hearts. Kendra's chest tightened as memories flickered; of that night on the battlefield, when hope had faltered, yet God had sustained them and carried them through.

"Good." Nurse Daniels replied and nodded approvingly. "Let's get you familiar with your new surroundings and get you going, I know you're eager to get started. I've got to get to a meeting in a few minutes, but I'll have nurse Billingsley show you around. I have an open-door policy, so feel free to talk to me about any issues or concerns you may have or if you just need to talk. Enjoy the quiet for now, I'm sure it won't remain that way for long. I'll come by and check in on you later.".

Nurse Amanda Billingsley gathered her nurses' tablet and walked unassumingly from behind the nurses station Her movements were calm and deliberate, with an air of quiet confidence that immediately set Kendra and Charlene at ease.

"Hello again, Kendra, Charlene, Allison" she said, her voice soft but clear, each word carefully measured. "Welcome. I'm Amanda." She extended a hand, and all three women shook it, feeling the firm grip of someone used to command without raising her voice.

Amanda's presence was comforting in the understated way of someone who didn't need to assert themselves loudly to be respected. She smiled warmly. "I'll show you around the emergency department and the trauma center, just to make sure you're familiar with the latest equipment we have in the bays."

As they walked, Amanda pointed out the new monitors, ventilators, and trauma kits, pausing occasionally to let them get hands on with the devices. "Here, try the cardiac monitor," she suggested. "And these automated intelligent infusion pumps are intuitive; you'll get a feel for them quickly."

The hands-on practice and consistent encouragement reassured them. The equipment was familiar enough, intuitive enough, that the women felt a renewed confidence settle over them. Amanda observed silently, a faint smile tugging at her lips as she watched them move with precision and attentiveness.

"I have to say," she said quietly, "I'm genuinely impressed with you three. You adapt quickly, and your instincts are sharp. That will take you far here."

Kendra and Charlene exchanged a glance, a flicker of pride passing between them. The warm, measured words of acknowledgment reassured them, even as the calm of the morning began to press upon them. They knew the quiet could not last forever. The day could shift in an instant, and they were ready.

The call came through the intercom just as Amanda wrapped up the briefly interrupted orientation. "Code One, Emergency. Trauma incoming. ETA five minutes." The quiet had ended.

Amanda's serene demeanor didn't falter; she simply nodded toward the nearest bay. "Time to get back to serious business. Kendra and Charlene, stay with me," she said, her calm authority sharpening the focus in the room.

Kendra and Charlene responded without hesitation They fell into step behind her as she moved toward the trauma bays, her voice resolute and clear. “Bay Two and Bay Three are prepped. Oxygen ready, IV access set. Let’s move.”

Across the room, David motioned for Allison to join him. “Come on,” he said, his tone brisk but encouraging. “You’ll shadow me for now; see how we coordinate with Trauma when a call like this comes in.” Allison nodded, her pulse quickening as she followed his lead toward the monitoring station.

The atmosphere had shifted instantly. The low hum of conversation and the persistent beep of monitors gave way to focused movement. Nurses pushed stocked trauma carts toward the bays, physicians pulled on gowns and gloves, and the doors at the ambulance entrance swung wide open.

Paramedics and a stretcher rushed in, wheels clattering against the floor.

Kendra and Charlene fell into step behind Nurse Billingsley. Amanda’s calm voice guided them as the team assembled. “Bay Two and Bay Three are prepped. Oxygen ready, IV access set. Let’s move.”

“Car accident,” one of the paramedics announced, already rattling off vitals.

“Male, twenties,” the lead paramedic shouted, sweat beading down his temple. “Car accident, severe abdominal trauma. BP’s crashing, blood transfusion and fluid started en route.”

Amanda quickly assessed the patient and activated Trauma Bay One, directing Kendra to stay close with the assigned trauma team. Kendra had expected to simply observe her first critical case, but the gravity of the moment pulled her in. She stayed just behind the lead nurse, observing every move, ready to step in if called upon.

The patient, a young man, bloodied and pale was struggling to breathe, his chest rising shallowly beneath the mask. Monitors beeped in uneven rhythm, filling the room with urgency. Kendra’s instincts stirred, her hands tightening around her gloves as she anticipated the team's needs; oxygen ready, IV lines prepared, instruments within reach.

Then, amid the flurry of movement, the patient's eyes met hers, glazed with fear and pain, darting wildly until they locked on her face. His fingers twitched slightly, as if reaching for something unseen.

Kendra felt her heart tug. She started to reach for his hand, then hesitated, glancing toward the team for silent approval. The lead nurse caught her look and gave a quick nod.

With that unspoken permission, Kendra moved closer and gently took the patient's trembling hand in hers. "It's okay," she whispered, her voice calm and sure despite the chaos around them. "You're not alone. We're right here."

Even in the rush, she closed her eyes for the briefest moment and offered a silent prayer; words rising like instinct. *Lord, preserve his life. Guide every hand, every choice. By Your power and by Your Spirit, bring healing. Amen.*

Charlene had already been assigned to another incoming patient. Another set of sirens wailed closer, and within minutes a second ambulance delivered a middle-aged woman with burns and broken bones trying to escape through a second floor window from a house fire. Her face was ghostly pale beneath streaks of soot, her shallow breaths audible even over the clatter of equipment.

Charlene stood at Amanda's side, suited up and ready, her jaw tight with concentration as she observed and kept pace with the rapid demands. Amanda worked methodically, her calm presence anchoring the room. From just a step back, Charlene watched as Amanda moved with quiet assurance, pointing out equipment, steadying a shaking hand, confirming a quick decision with a firm nod. When the patient whimpered in pain, Amanda leaned close, her voice soft and unfaltering, offering words of comfort that seemed to soothe as much as the care itself.

Charlene felt a deep respect stir within her as she watched, understanding that healing wasn't always in the medicine alone. It was often paired with a calm, confident presence in chaos mingling with compassion.

Towards the end of their shift, the last patient had been wheeled off to recovery, leaving them with the subdued energy of exhaustion, relief, and quiet pride all wrapped into one. Kendra and Charlene peeled off their gloves and exchanged a glance that needed no words. Amanda walked them to the staff lounge as they prepared to clock out and gave them a satisfied nod.

"Good work today, ladies. Get some rest, you've earned it. We start fresh tomorrow."

They headed for the entrance doors and slowing their pace, waiting for a moment to see if Allison would join them. When several minutes passed with no sign of her, Kendra and Charlene exchanged a knowing smile and began walking toward their cars.

The evening sky had painted streaks of lavender and gold across the hospital' parking lot and in the soft glow of sunset filtered through the hospital's glass façade, casting warm shadows across its floors.

The cool evening air greeted them as the sliding doors parted. Just as they were outside, a familiar voice called out from behind them. "Hey, guys…wait up!"

They turned to see Allison hurrying out the exit, slightly out of breath, her ponytail bouncing as she jogged to catch up. "What a day, huh?" she said, laughing between breaths.

Kendra smiled, acknowledging the sentiment. Her shoulders finally released the last of the day's tension. "Grateful today," she said softly. "Days like this remind us why we do what we do."

Charlene nodded and chuckled. "Grateful, yeah, but still exhausted. I don't think my feet remember what it feels like not to ache."

Their laughter mingled with the evening breeze, softening tired eyes as they fell into step together toward their cars. Allison blinked, a faint smile curving her lips, grateful for the two new friends she'd found. Something about them had resonated with her over the last couple of days—Kendra's quiet reserve and strength, Charlene's search for humor even when all hell was breaking loose. There was a quiet peace she sensed, but couldn't yet name.

As they reached the parking lot, the trio slowed near their cars; Kendra and Charlene's parked side by side, Allison's a few spaces down beneath a glowing lamppost. Kendra paused, smiling at them both. "Enjoy your evening, ladies."

"Back at you!" Charlene and Allison replied in unison, sharing an easy laugh before heading to their cars.

The parking lot lights shimmered against the deepening sky, the first stars winking above Harmony Grove Harbor; a gentle close to a long, extraordinary day.

As they drove away in different directions, the hospital's glass façade reflected the soft shimmer of twilight, its lights glowing like faithful beacons against the deepening sky.

Kendra's car was the first to pull onto the main road. The quiet hum of the engine filled the space as she reflected on the day, on the faces, the patients, the unspoken prayers that had carried her through. Gratitude welled in her heart, not for her own strength, but for the grace that steadied her hands and heart. Yet as the road curved toward home, her thoughts drifted to Charlene. She hadn't had the chance to ask about her restless night, but something in her friend's eyes had lingered; something unspoken. Kendra whispered a soft prayer as she drove. "Lord, give her rest tonight… and whatever's heavy on her heart or her mind, comfort her, and give her the strength to bear it."

Charlene, a few miles away, sat behind the wheel with the radio low, the cool air brushing against her face. She, too, felt the day's weight lift into something quieter, almost holy. But beneath that calm, the unease still stirred. The dream had returned the night before; flashes of fire, rushing water, piercing wind, a storm with faces she couldn't quite see. She hadn't told a soul, not even Kendra. Deep down, she sensed it wasn't just a dream. *Lord, if You're trying to tell me something... help me understand.*

And a few parking spaces down, Allison rolled down her window, letting the evening breeze wash over her. She smiled faintly, still hearing Kendra's soft-spoken "Grateful today" echo in her mind. There was something different about the two of them; something deeply rooted. She didn't quite understand it yet, but she knew she wanted to. For now, she was simply thankful for the new friendships, and the quiet promise of a new beginning.

The night deepened over Harmony Grove Harbor, the stars bright against the quiet stretch of sky. Three women, three stories, each touched by a purpose they were only beginning to see.

And somewhere beyond the quiet hum of the harbor, grace was already preparing them for what was to come.

Chapter 7

The Weight of a Promise and the Grace That Follows

The sun was easing its way down when Charlene steered her Jeep away from Harmony Grove Harbor Hospital and towards home. The glass building gleamed in her rearview mirror, catching the evening light like a promise… beautiful in that promise, yet heavy with all it would require.

She rolled her shoulders as she drove, trying to shake off the long hours of shadowing in the emergency department—observing triage flow, meeting staff, and learning how ER and trauma units worked together as one. It felt good to be back with a medical team again… good to step into the rhythm of care instead of just talking about procedures on paper. And more than that, it felt good to be needed… to feel purpose again. Still, an unfamiliar sense of foreboding tugged at the edges of her thoughts… memories of visions in dreams she didn't yet know what to do with.

As the road curved toward her neighborhood, the scenery softened into neat lawns and broad driveways, framed by oaks dripping with moss and tall palms lining neatly trimmed walkways. The Matthews home came into view… gray stucco softened by bright white trim and warm sandstone accents. Large windows glowed with warm light, and the backyard pool gave off a faint shimmer through the side gate.

Charlene felt the cares of the day slip off her shoulders as soon as she pulled into the driveway. She eased into her family's generous three-car garage, guiding her Jeep into the same spot she'd claimed back in high school. She grabbed her nurse's tote and headed for the mudroom door… the one that opened into the center of the house, between the kitchen and family room.

Charlene was blessed to live in a community lined with gracious, spacious homes. She learned early on that those blessings came with responsibility. One of her dad's favorite sayings was, "To whom much is given, much is required." Because of that, her parents insisted she be approachable, gracious, and humble in all things and in all her ways. Gratitude was expected, as was a sunny spirit and an easy humor; no matter where she went or whom she met. It was never acceptable for her to cause anyone to feel overshadowed or small. Nursing had always tugged at her heart for that very reason, and enlisting later on felt like a natural extension of a deep desire to serve… to offer light wherever God called her.

Even before she reached the garage door, Charlene caught the rich, savory aroma slipping through the seam, hinting at whatever her mother had simmering on the stove… warm, familiar, unmistakably delicious.

She inhaled deeply. *"Cube steak, onions and gravy,"* she thought to herself. *"Mama's been busy"*.

Inside, the comforting aromas wrapped around her like a hug. Rice simmered on the stove, and buttered green beans waited in a serving bowl.

"Baby girl, that you?" her mother called.

"It's me, Mama," Charlene said, kicking off her shoes before tucking them into a mudroom cubby. "Smells incredible in here."

Margaret Matthews bustled at the stove in a soft floral blouse, her shoulders lifting with joy as she turned. "Well, I figured my girl would need something filling after the day she's had."

Her father, Harold, came in from the family room, folding his newspaper. He wasn't a particularly tall man, but his eyes spoke of gentle strength as he spread his arms wide.

"There she is," he said, pulling her into a hug. "How's Harmony Grove Harbor's newest trauma nurse?"

"One step at a time," Charlene laughed. "But it's going well."

They gathered around the dining table, filling their plates with generous helpings of the meal Margaret had so lovingly prepared. Before anyone so much as touched a fork, Harold bowed his head and reached out for his family to join him.

"Lord," he said gently, "bless this food to us, and us to Thy service. We thank You for the blessings of home. Amen."

"Amen," Charlene echoed softly.

They dug in, and her mother wasted no time.

"So, tell us everything. How's the new hospital? We've waited half our lives for this town to get its own trauma center."

"It's amazing," Charlene said. "State-of-the-art equipment, bright hallways, big windows overlooking the waterfront… and everyone really has been so nice. It feels hopeful and a little overwhelming at the same time."

Harold nodded knowingly. "New beginnings often are."

Margaret leaned closer, eyes twinkling. "And that new friend you mentioned? Allison?"

Charlene smiled. "She's great. Funny, quick on her feet. I think she'll fit right in with me and Kendra. We're already kind of adopting her. We invited her to come to church with us this Sunday."

Her mother beamed. "Oh, that's wonderful. Makes my heart happy. Good friends are hard to find, and a good one makes all the difference."

They talked about schedules, the upcoming hospital grand opening, and the excitement brimming about town. Between stories, Harold chimed in with warm jokes that made Margaret roll her eyes lovingly.

Charlene began to feel a little lighter by the time the dishes were cleared away, the edges of the day softened by the comfort of home.

"Well," Margaret announced, snapping her dish towel dry and then draping it over the sink, "your dad and I are going to watch a movie. Something light. I'm not in the mood for anything that requires thinking."

Harold chuckled. "Translation: your mother wants something where everyone ends up married."

Margaret raised an eyebrow. "And what's wrong with that? I like my movies with heartwarming endings."

Harold shot Charlene a look. "This is the woman who tried to set you up with that choir director from three towns over once."

"That was different," Margaret insisted. "He sang tenor."

Charlene nearly choked laughing. "Mama… please. Not the tenor again," she begged.

Margaret placed her hands on her hips. "Well, I still say there are some fine men around this town. And Raymond Carter, for example…"

Harold groaned. "Margaret, don't start."

"Mama!" Charlene cried, though her cheeks warmed.

"What?" Margaret said innocently. "The man is polite, handsome, owns his own business, and generously supports church fundraisers."

Harold folded his arms. "He's still not good enough for my girl."

Charlene shook her head, grinning. "Y'all are impossible."

Her parents settled into the family room, still bickering playfully as they chose a movie. Charlene joined them, allowing herself to sink into her favorite recliner, her eyelids growing heavy as the opening credits began to roll.

Her phone buzzed softly in her hand. She glanced down at the screen. Kendra.

"Be right back," she said softly. "Just need some fresh air."

"Don't stay too long," Margaret called. "Night air's cool."

Charlene answered her phone as she made her way to the screened-in lanai. The backyard spread out like a private oasis; shimmering blue pool, soft outdoor lighting, a tidy dining table beneath a ceiling fan, and the hum of crickets mixing with the distant hush of the marina.

"Hey, girl."

"Hey you," Kendra replied, her voice equally tired, but warm. "You home?"

"Yeah. Just had dinner with Mom and Dad. Mama's already matchmaking… Lord help me."

Kendra laughed softly. "I can only imagine." Her tone shifted; calmer now, more concerned. "How are *you*?"

Charlene leaned against the railing. After a slight pause, she continued, her voice soft… almost fragile.

"I just haven't been able to sleep well these last few nights. And when I do, I keep having the same dream again and again," she whispered. "And after that dream, I can't go back to sleep."

Kendra's voice tightened. "You want to tell me about it?"

"Well, it always starts with this medical helicopter, in the desert. It looks eerily like our medical camp where we were deployed." Charlene said quietly. "Rotors loud enough to feel in my bones… a bright sky, maybe too bright… we're loading wounded into the medevac helicopter. Then…"

She trailed off.

Kendra closed her eyes and took a slow, steady breath.

"Dark clouds start to roll in," Charlene continued. "A storm is coming, and it's moving fast… maybe too fast. The darkness settles in, and then the rain and the wind. The wind is so strong it's raining sideways. While I'm inside the helicopter, it begins to shake violently… but it doesn't tip over.

Storm clouds keep rolling overhead, thick and heavy, turning everything dark. When I look up, I see this light in the middle of the clouds. As the storm grows worse, the light grows larger. And then, just as suddenly as the storm came, it's gone.

The only thing left is that strange cloud with the light… and then it, too, is gone. I can't explain it, but I get chills even talking about it. And when I wake up, my mind just keeps replaying the dream over and over. I don't know what it means," she said softly. "But it really feels like God is trying to tell me something… I just don't know what it is."

Kendra swallowed hard. "Is there more?"

"That's the dream," she said quietly. "But there is more… the biggest part is the feeling it leaves behind. Every time, I hear the same whisper deep in my spirit… *I brought you back for a reason.*"

Kendra looked out past her bedroom window, moonlight casting shimmering shadows about the room. "Yeah, I understand. That *is* heavy, and God has brought us through heavy before."

She paused, then added gently, "That feeling that you mentioned, it reminds remind me of something. Do you still remember...in the chapel that day? Kendra asked gently. "You remember that?"

Charlene looked past the peace and calm of the backyard, her eyes drifting beyond what she could actually see. Twilight had surrendered to nightfall. Her voice softened to almost nothing, trembling at the edges. "Yeah… I remember."

She closed her eyes as the memory took over.

— ✦ —

Charlene sat in the small chapel of the medical base encampment, cap beside her, a single candle flickering before the wooden cross. Outside, the roar of the medevac helicopter engines rumbled back to life, preparing to send in a fresh team to pick up more evacuees.

She carefully unfolded a worn letter; her mother's handwriting faintly fading but still readable.

Remember, baby girl, we are all soldiers in the army of the Lord and God never leaves His soldiers... no matter where they stand.

"Even here, Lord?" she whispered. "Even when I'm this tired?"

A soft tap sounded at the canvas door.

"Char?" Kendra's weary voice drifted in.

Charlene turned. "You always know where to find me."

Kendra walked inside, scrubs stained, eyes shadowed. "Another convoy just came in. It's bad."

"They're all bad lately," Charlene said, swallowing.

They sat together, candlelight flickering. Helicopter blades thudded outside.

"I keep thinking about home," Charlene whispered. "Mama's Sunday dinners… Daddy's stories. I promised them I'd come back stronger. But some days… I'm not sure I can keep that promise.

Every time I go up in that medevac helicopter, I know there's a risk that I might not make it back. Right now, I don't feel strong at all."

"You're stronger than you think," Kendra said softly. "You're our anchor out here."

Charlene's tears brimmed. "You think God hears us?"

"Especially when it's hardest to believe," Kendra answered.

A quiet settled over them.

"Lord," Charlene whispered, "help us and keep us. And when this is over… if it is Your will that we make it home again, I promise to be a vessel of Your grace and mercy, no matter how heavy the shadows become. Amen."

It was a promise she wouldn't leave in the desert.

It would follow her *home...*

— ✦ —

Back on the lanai, the memory faded.

"And that promise is part of who I am now," Charlene said softly. "I made a promise to God… in front of you… and I plan to live by that promise, even when things get heavy, 'because I know He's got my back!."

Kendra exhaled shakily. "I needed to hear you say that. Char… would you pray with me?"

Charlene bowed her head, folding her hands gently.

"Father," Kendra whispered, *"You see every part of Charlene's heart. If these dreams are warnings... give her clarity. If they're wounds... give her peace. Surround her with wisdom, courage, and your divine presence. Guide her steps, and help us both walk in Your will. In Jesus' name... amen."*

"Amen," Charlene breathed. "And thank you for praying with me."

They talked a bit longer before saying goodnight.

Charlene stayed quiet on the lanai, the breeze brushing her face… peace threading through her. She remained there until she heard her mother calling out for her. Her spirit felt lighter now, and she chuckled softly to herself. "*Bless her heart"*, she thought. "*She still thinks I'm nine years old.*"

— ✦ —

A Couple of Days Later

Charlene was grateful for a day off… a much-needed break after two full days of shadowing in the emergency room. With no shift to rush to and nothing pressing on her schedule, she let herself slow down for the first time since coming home, settling comfortably into the family room as the quiet of the house wrapped around her.

She was half-watching a morning show and half-lost in her own thoughts when the soft chime from the home security panel lit up on the wall. She glanced over; someone was pulling into the driveway.

A sleek black limo appeared on the screen, the polished exterior gleaming beneath the late-morning sun. *Carter Coastal Transport*. She recognized the style before she even saw the logo.

But it wasn't the limo that made her sit up a little straighter.

A passenger door opened smoothly, and Raymond Carter stepped out.

Even through the camera feed, she could see the familiar way he carried himself; deliberate, confident, that quiet charm that had only grown stronger with age. And the same handsome face she remembered from her teenage years, now softened by maturity rather than time.

Charlene felt a small flutter she tried to ignore.

Lord have mercy... Mama's going to have a field day with this.

She slipped from the couch, smoothing her hair without thinking, and made her way toward the front door just as Raymond reached it and lifted his hand to knock.

Charlene pulled it open before he could.

"Morning, Raymond," she said, breathing calmly… mostly.

His smile warmed. "Well, good morning, Charlene."

He lifted a stack of sleek, glossy brochures.

"Your mom asked me to drop off the new marketing brochures for our luxury limo line. Figured I'd bring them by myself, since she's been telling half the town about us anyway."

Charlene laughed under her breath. "Oh, she's your biggest fan. She practically thinks she runs your PR department at this point."

Raymond chuckled, his eyes brightening. "I know. Believe me… I'm well aware. But truth be told, I had another reason for stopping by."

Charlene's heart fluttered. "Oh?"

He gestured toward the limo. "We just added a few new ones to the fleet. I couldn't help but notice how much you enjoyed the ride from the airport, so thought you might enjoy getting a little fresh air this morning… maybe a ride to the marina clubhouse. Fresh pastries, gourmet breakfast treats and coffees."

"You came just to offer me a ride?" she asked softly.

Raymond chuckled. "Well… I remembered a teenage girl who used to blush when I walked by. Thought I'd see if she still found my company worth blushing over."

Her cheeks flushed instantly. "Raymond!"

He raised his hands. "Hey now… I said maybe."

Charlene laughed despite herself. "Alright… it all sounds nice."

They settled into the spacious limo, and Charlene noticed a neatly dressed, uniformed chauffeur already behind the wheel. Raymond caught her glance and offered a small smile.

"I'm training one of our new drivers today," he said as he buckled in. "Upping the standard for the luxury fleet. Thought it'd be good for him to get a feel for the marina route… and figured I'd bring along the best company I could find."

Charlene felt a flutter she quickly pushed down.

"Well," she said lightly, "I guess I'm helping with employee development today."

Raymond chuckled softly. "You always did have that leadership quality."

And with that, the limo eased smoothly out of the driveway and toward the marina. Brunch at the clubhouse was simple but pleasant, and conversation came easily. Raymond listened more than he spoke, never pressing when her voice softened around certain memories.

By the time the limo returned her home, something within her felt lighter.

"Thank you," she said. "For today."

"You're very welcome," Raymond replied gently. "But I should be thanking you. The pleasure was all mine."

Charlene caught herself before raising an eyebrow, managing a smile instead. *That sounds familiar,* she thought, though she kept her smile wide and warm.

Raymond reached into his pocket and pulled out a sleek business card. "Feel free to stop by the office anytime. I'm usually there, and I'd love to show you around. Here's my card… call me anytime."

"Thank you," she said softly. "I'd love to… and I will."

And for a reason she couldn't quite explain, her gaze lifted to meet his.

Raymond held her gaze without flinching, something unspoken settling between them. They walked up the front porch steps together, the quiet between them not awkward at all… but full.

He paused, then leaned in and gave her a gentle, unrushed hug, finishing with a light peck on her cheek.

"I'll see you soon?" he asked quietly.

"I'd like that," Charlene replied.

And as he stepped back, that look lingered… the kind that said more than words ever could.

That night, long after her parents had gone to bed, Charlene stood at her bedroom window, overlooking the faint glow of the marina.

She folded her hands, bowed her head, and whispered:

"Lord… I don't understand what these dreams mean yet. But I trust You. Help me walk in Your grace. Prepare me for whatever comes. Amen."

The night was still… then softly alive with crickets and distant waves.

She didn't have full understanding yet.

But she had peace.
And for now…
that was enough.

Chapter 8

Because of Grace

Main Street Baptist Church had welcomed worshippers for more than a century, and this Sunday morning would be no different. It stood as a constant reminder that hope, help, and healing could always be found here. Sunlight streamed through its stained-glass windows in ribbons of color, settling over the pews like a promise. The steeple cast long, solemn shadows down Main Street, as though the church itself were extending a gentle hand to the town, calling its people home to worship in the serenity of God's presence.

In the quiet of his home study, Pastor Nathaniel Thompson knelt in prayer beside a window bench placed there for this purpose. The door was closed; a familiar signal that this was his sacred time with the Lord. Rays of morning light filtered through the window and rested on his head as he bowed and closed his eyes.

"Father, I ask You to give me the words to speak to Your children. Speak to my heart, Lord, that I may speak to them,

according to Your will. Prepare me, I pray, once again for Your service. In Jesus' name, Amen."

When he rose, he felt a calm settling over his spirit, knowing once again that a faithful God had answered his request. He now opened the door to find a patient and understanding Leah waiting; hands folded loosely, listening for the soft click that meant he was ready. When their eyes met, she reached for his hand with a knowing smile.

"Ready?" she asked.

He squeezed her hand gently, the peace of prayer still resting on him. "I am."

Pastor Thompson and Leah pulled into the church parking lot just as the early worshippers were beginning to arrive… those faithful few who always came early enough to secure *their* parking spots. As he took those familiar steps from the parking lot toward the church, he chuckled softly, shaking his head with affection as Mr. and Mrs. Carter, after settling into the same space they had claimed every Sunday for as long as he could remember, waved eagerly from across the lot.". Leah slipped her arm through his, and together they exchanged warm greetings as more families pulled in, some bustling with cheerful conversation, others approaching in quiet, reflective steps as the morning sun washed the church grounds in soft gold.

The Williams family arrived next. Thomas straightening his tie as Evelyn smoothed the front of her Sunday dress, both waving toward the pastor before joining the gentle flow heading toward the double doors. Moments later came the Matthews family. Charlene's parents chatted warmly with another couple, while Charlene, having parked a moment later, paused just long enough to wrap Kendra in a quick, bright hug.

Sam Whitaker crossed the lot shortly after, brushing a bit of imaginary dust from his sleeve out of habit. When he spotted

Kendra, he changed course and headed towards her. Their smiles were soft… a little careful, but full of warmth.

"Good morning," he said, gentle but sincere.

"Good morning," she returned, equally warm, equally guarded. She couldn't help noticing how handsome he looked in his suit, and that familiar flutter stirred before she could stop it.

Sam turned easily to her parents. "Good morning, Mrs. Williams… Mr. Williams. It's good to see you both."

Evelyn's face brightened. "Good morning, Sam. It's always good to see you too."

Thomas offered a warm, approving nod. "Morning, Sam."

The four of them entered through the sanctuary doors, the soft chatter of the gathering congregation drifting outward to greet them as they approached. And without overthinking it, Sam fell naturally into step beside Kendra. When they entered, he followed the Williamses down to their usual row, stepping aside to allow Kendra to be between her parents and him.

Kendra felt that small flutter again… stronger this time… and she couldn't help the soft smile that rose as he settled in right next to her.

As the sanctuary slowly filled, short conversations and soft laughter drifted between the pews. Raymond slipped into the sanctuary just as Charlene was making her way down the aisle, headed toward the pew where her parents were already seated. He stopped just in front of her and greeted her with a bright, shoulder-to-shoulder "gospel hug," warm and familiar. When they pulled back, their hands found each other for a light squeeze; two quick nods and a shared little giggle passing between them like an inside joke. From their seats, her parents raised matching eyebrows; her mom smiling with that unmistakable *I saw that look* as she nudged Harold with her elbow. He cleared his throat a little too loudly, pretending to study the bulletin as Charlene slid into the seat right next to them. Raymond continued down the aisle and found a seat a few rows back.

A few more minutes passed, and the organist settled onto the bench, followed by the pianist and drummer. The guitar player and saxophonist were the last to arrive and take their places among the other musicians. The first gentle chords of familiar melodies drifted through the sanctuary like a breath. Those lingering in the aisles made their way to their seats just as Allison slipped in through a side door, still a little breathless from hurrying. She chose a quiet place near the back, offering a gentle smile to anyone she passed.

The organist struck up a familiar chord and began playing the introduction to an old, familiar gospel tune. Double doors on each side of the sanctuary opened, and the choir members made their way down the aisle, wearing robes of cream and navy. They lifted their voices in the opening lines of "*Glad to Be in the Service (One More Time)*". Their harmonies rose strong and joyful, filling the sanctuary with a rhythm that made even the stained-glass windows seem to glow brighter. The congregation responded almost at once; hands clapping, voices rising, smiles warming the room as many rose to their feet in worship. The sound swelled into a unified, soul-stirring praise, the kind that wrapped itself around every heart and reminded them how blessed they were to once again gather in the house of the Lord.

The worship service continued with songs of praise and uplifting prayers that filled the sanctuary like a shared breath of hope. As the choir members took their seats in preparation for the sermon, Pastor Thompson rose and walked to the pulpit, his robe swaying softly with each measured stride. He rested his hands on the sacred desk… ready to deliver the message God had placed on his heart.

"Brothers and sisters," he said, letting his eyes sweep gently across the congregation. "The Lord has placed something on my heart that I want to share with you this morning. Our scripture this morning is coming from 2 Corinthians 12 verses 8-10.

For this thing I besought the Lord thrice, that it might depart from me. And he said unto me, My grace is sufficient for thee: for my strength is made perfect in weakness. Most gladly therefore will I rather glory in my infirmities, that the power of Christ may rest upon me.
Therefore I take pleasure in infirmities, in reproaches, in necessities, in persecutions, in distresses for Christ's sake: for when I am weak, then am I strong.

Our sermon title is: **Because of Grace** A reminder that even in tough times, God's grace is available

He paused, allowing the room to settle into a quiet stillness.

His voice carried a softness and strength that wrapped around the sanctuary like a sheltering hand. He spoke of physical and spiritual infirmities. He spoke about the blind man that Jesus healed and the power of praying in times of weakness, doubt and sorrow.

"God's peace can be found even in the darkest time of our lives," he said. He spoke with the gentle wisdom he was known for, smiling as he added, "Sometimes God doesn't fix our situation…He fixes us *in* our situation."

He closed by saying, "This is the same grace that holds you up in times of grief…the same grace that dries every tear…and the same grace that walks with you through every trial."

The congregation rose to its feet as Pastor Nathaniel Thompson closed the sermon. Waves of praise moved through the parishioners as they raised hands and voices in unified worship, hearts and spirits overflowing.

"Amen!"

"Thank You, Lord!"

"Thank You for the Word!"

"Praise Your name, Jesus!"

Some worshippers dabbed their eyes. Others lifted their faces heavenward; hands extended in humble surrender. A few moved gently in their pews as the Holy Spirit moved through the sanctuary. It was a heartfelt, Spirit-filled response that came when God's Word moved on the hearts of willing listeners.

Pastor Thompson stepped back from the pulpit, his head bowed, his hand pressed to his chest as he whispered his own prayer of thanksgiving. Every so often he lifted his eyes toward heaven, lips moving in quiet reverence. Leah watched him from the front pew, moved by the power and message from the man she knew God had made for such a moment as this.

Pastor Thompson moved away from the pulpit, walking towards his congregation. He drew in a strong breath and exhaled slowly, like a man listening for something beyond the room… something only his spirit could hear. And when he lifted his eyes again, they shimmered with a deep, stirring conviction. Heaven was moving.

And then… he began.

At first his voice was low, almost conversational:

"A-maz-ing Grace…How sweet the sound"

The musicians, recognizing the lyrics, joined him. The congregation and choir moved together in rhythm as the music swelled and filled the sanctuary. Kendra was swept by a sudden chill that settled deep within her spirit.

Pastor Thompson nodded once, moving closer to his congregation.

"that saved a wretch like me!

"I once was lost, but now I'm found,"

Pastor Thompson continued with conviction:

"Was blind…but now I see."

Tears streamed down Charlene's face as she closed her eyes. Memories of her recurring dream, the strange fog and that unexplainable light flickered through her mind. For a moment, the song felt like a message meant for her alone… a reminder that even what was unknown to her was known by an omniscient God.

Pastor Thompson's voice deepened, strengthened, placing one hand over his heart.

"Through many dangers, toils and snares"

"I have already come."

"Twas grace that brought me safe thus far…

Sam Whitaker let out a slow breath he didn't know he'd been holding. He leaned forward, resting his hands on the back of the pew in front of him, his gaze fixed. Something about *this* song; something rich, powerful, and raw tugged at that place within him that still wrestled with grief; layers of grief he'd been carrying too long

"And grace will lead me home."

"Twas grace that taught my heart to fear,"

"And grace my fears relieved:"

Sam's breath shuddered.

"How precious did that grace appear"

"the hour I first believed!"

Kendra pressed her palm lightly to her heart, tears ready to fall but not released. The words and the melody wrapped around her like a warm protective embrace… a balm to the places inside still wrestling with their deployment memories, her readjustment to civilian life, and the quiet questions she didn't dare speak aloud.

Pastor Thompson continued, humming the familiar melody for the last verse.

Hands still raised, many pointed towards heaven, voices joining, tears released. It was worship. It was communion, recognition, and gratefulness outpouring from within the hearts of God's people.

Sam swallowed hard, rose from his seat with his arms raised toward heaven, fighting the tremor rising in his throat. The words struck deep, like they were calling him to release something he'd been holding onto for too long.

The musicians took over playing the familiar melody so fervent that it spilled outside the walls of Main Street Baptist Church.

Pastor Thompson worshipped with his congregation allowing the lyrics and melody to sink deep within him.

It was clear… this was worship. A testimony of a God whose grace was overflowing. It was Nathaniel Thompson pouring every ounce of faith he had back into his flock.

When the last note faded, the sanctuary was filled with the praises and prayers of the people within it.

Reverent. Full. Reassuring.

Leah bowed her head, raising one hand, the other wiping a tear from the corner of her eye.

Kendra exhaled shakily. "My Lord…" The tears flowed freely now, and she didn't care who saw.

Charlene's voice trembled, then failed. No audible words came from her mouth as her lips moved and uttered a praise and prayer that only God Himself would hear. She then bowed slightly with outstretched arms, saying, "Yes God, yes God," and nodding her head as if hearing directly from Him. Her dream felt clearer now… less confusing… but more urgent.

Sam could not stop the tears that flowed. A slow release followed; something that had held him prisoner for far too long. When he came to himself, he wiped at his eyes quickly, wondering if anyone had noticed. But Kendra turned just enough to see his face and reached for his hand. Their eyes met and held. And in that shared moment, they both felt it and knew it. The message, the song. It was as if God had sent it especially for them, because it had reached and touched something deep within. A place in need of healing. A place ready for healing.

Pastor Thompson smiled gently at his congregation, his voice warm again, though tired around the edges.

"Church… it is because of grace that we are still here, and because of God's grace, He will carry us through."

The benediction was short, simple, and gentle.

Pastor Thompson lifted both hands over his congregation, his voice reassuring and deep.

"May the Lord bless you and keep you… May the Lord make His face to shine upon you and be gracious unto you… May the Lord lift up His countenance upon you and give you peace."

"Amen," the people replied, almost as one.

The sanctuary, moments ago filled with thunderous praise, eased into a calmer rhythm. People began waving goodbyes to one another, shaking hands, embracing, exchanging soft laughter and words of encouragement. Mothers grabbed their children's hands. Deacons straightened hymnals. Ushers opened the double doors to the now approaching noonday outside.

Charlene found Kendra and Sam and the three of them moved slowly toward the exit with the flow of people.

"Yes sir, that was a Word this morning," one man said, clasping another's hand.

"You feel that? My Lord…" a woman whispered to her friend with tears still shimmering.

Near the front, Pastor Thompson stood greeting members as they approached; shaking hands, hugging a few, listening closely as they spoke to him. His smile remained warm, but there was a tiredness in his eyes, and a slight raspiness in his voice; nevertheless, he insisted on knowing his flock and shook every hand who waited patiently to do so.

The three made their way down the aisle and out into the parking lot before Kendra spotted Allison.

"Hey Allison!" she called gently.

Allison turned, brightening instantly when she saw them. She hurried over to them, an excited smile lighting her face.

"There y'all are! The church was full today. I was looking for you; hoping you were in the service today!" Allison wrapped Charlene in a tight hug, then turned to Kendra with equal warmth. "Wasn't that service something? Lord have mercy… I felt that one."

"You and me both," Charlene breathed, still feeling the lingering spiritual high.

Kendra smiled and leaned in a little closer to Sam as he reached for her hand. "And this is Sam."

"Pleased to meet you, Sam," Allison said. The sidestep by Kendra did not go unnoticed by Allison. She extended her hand with cordial and respectful flair.

Sam smiled and accepted the handshake. "Pleased to meet you too, Allison."

As the four of them continued with casual conversation, a warm coastal breeze swept across the parking lot, carrying the soft sounds of car doors opening and closing, friends calling out goodbyes.

"Y'all be blessed now!" a church mother called, waving her handkerchief with a bright smile.

"You too, Mother Jenkins!" another member chimed back, her spirit still lifted from the service.

Sam, still joined hands with Kendra, said, "Well… nice talking with you all. I guess we should get going soon."

Kendra nodded, looking at Sam. "Yeah, Mom and Dad took off without me. I guess they just assumed you would take me home. Is that okay?"

Sam smiled easily, almost snickering. "Um… I'm a little ahead of you. I told your folks I'd take you home after church… maybe grab a quick bite to eat and then a stroll, maybe?"

Kendra nodded, looking straight into his eyes. "Well, yes, I would love that!"

Charlene and Allison exchanged an all-knowing glance, eyebrows raising in perfect unison.

"Hey, it was good seeing you guys today," Allison said warmly. "I really did enjoy the service. I'll see you at work tomorrow." And with that, she offered a little wave and headed toward her car.

Sam glanced at Kendra. "Ready?"

They started walking toward his truck, but as they got close, Kendra stopped and turned to him.

"Just a sec, Sam… be right back," she whispered.

He nodded, leaning against the truck with an easy smile.

Kendra hurried back toward Charlene, who was just reaching her own car. The parking lot was thinning out now; a few families chatting, a few cars pulling away, their passengers ready to claim the peaceful bliss of a Sunday afternoon.

Kendra lowered her voice. "I didn't want to bring it up in front of the others, but… about your recurring dream. If you really feel that God is trying to tell you something, I think that maybe you should meet with Pastor Thompson and see what he thinks… soon."

Charlene's face grew thoughtful. "Yeah… I've been thinking about that too."

Kendra squeezed her arm gently. "We'll talk more later. Just… don't put it off."

Charlene nodded slowly. "I won't."

Just then, from the church's side entrance, a familiar voice called out:

"Charlene! Charlene!"

Both women turned as Raymond Carter jogged across the parking lot; not panicked, just eager, moving with that polite urgency only Raymond could pull off while still looking composed. His Sunday suit jacket was unbuttoned now, his tie slightly loosened, but his gentlemanly charm very much intact.

He reached them just as Charlene opened her car door.

"Whew…" he laughed lightly, catching his breath. "I was hoping to catch you before you left."

Charlene straightened with a surprised smile. "Well, you got me, Raymond. What's going on?"

He cleared his throat, suddenly a little shy, but still smooth. "I just… ah… wanted to ask if you had any plans for this fine Sunday afternoon?"

Charlene blinked, caught off guard in the best way. "Um… no, not really. Why?"

Raymond gave a modest, gentleman's nod. "Well… if you're free, I wondered if you might like some company. Maybe a little drive… a stop for lunch… or just conversation. Only if you're willing, of course."

Kendra unintentionally let out a soft chuckle, delighted.

Charlene's eyebrows lifted just slightly as a slow smile curled onto her lips. "Well… Raymond Carter… It just so happens that I am free."

His whole face brightened. "Wonderful. Take your time, no rush."

Kendra cast Charlene a questioning stare. "We'll talk later."

With a knowing smile, she headed back toward Sam, who was already opening the truck door for her, a habit forming faster than she had expected.

He helped her up into the seat, just as naturally as always.

The church parking lot had quieted down to only a few cars, the earlier bustle fading into the soft quietness of a peaceful Sunday afternoon. The sanctuary doors swung open one more time; Pastor Nathaniel Thompson and Leah exited, side by side… the final two to usually leave.

Nathaniel's shoulders relaxed slightly now that the responsibilities of the morning had settled. His steps were stable but noticeably slower, the fullness of the sermon and the song finally catching up to him. Leah slipped her arm through his, supporting him without him really being aware.

She glanced up at him with a glow of pride. "Nathaniel… I don't believe you've ever preached a more powerful sermon. And then that song… Lord have mercy. I don't think there was a dry eye in the house."

Pastor Thompson chuckled softly, shaking his head with humility. "It was all God, Leah. Every word."

She nodded, giving his arm a gentle squeeze. "Surely God has blessed us with His presence today."

They walked together across the quiet lot, the afternoon breeze lifting her hat slightly and carrying away the last echoes of the worship service. When they reached their car, Leah walked to the driver's side. Sundays always took the most out of him, and she knew better than to let him drive when he had poured out so much. But he still insisted on opening the door for her, and she slipped in behind the wheel. He circled around, opened the passenger door slowly and eased into the seat, letting out a soft breath as he settled in.

For a quiet moment, they sat there, the distant sound of a child laughing somewhere across the lot, a breeze rustling the magnolia leaves nearby. The kind of Sunday stillness that wrapped itself around the heart.

Nathaniel turned his head slightly and looked at his wife. Really looked at her.

Her hands rested lightly on the steering wheel. Her face still carried the afterglow of worship. And the love in her eyes that he never took for granted.

"Leah," he said gently.

She turned toward him, her expression softening even more. “Yes, baby?”

He reached for the steering wheel and took her hand in his; gentle, warm, and familiar.

“Did I ever tell you how much I thank God for blessing me with you?”

A tender smile curved across her lips, one she’d worn for him countless times over the years. “All the time, baby… all the time,” she whispered. “And all the time, I love to hear you say it.” He met her halfway across the console, and they shared a slow, lingering kiss; gentle, heartfelt, full of the history and devotion between them.

When they parted, Leah kept his hand in hers for another quiet moment before turning the key. The engine hummed to life, soft and smooth.

She eased them out of the parking lot, the afternoon sun warming their faces as they pulled onto the quiet road, content, peaceful, enjoying the beauty of the day.

Unaware of the storm that waited somewhere in their future.

For now, it was just the two of them; blessed and grateful for the gift of each other.

Chapter 9

Echoes of a Brother's Love

Sam eased the truck out of the church parking lot, the whole worship experience still resonating in his spirit even after the last Amen. Without realizing it, he began humming the last few bars of "Amazing Grace", the soft notes carrying a weight Kendra could feel.

She glanced at him, pleasantly surprised. "You know… you have a really nice voice," she said, gently stroking his arm in quiet reassurance.

Sam offered a small, almost shy smile, but his gaze stayed fixed on the road ahead. He swallowed hard, his jaw tightening, just a little. Something about him felt different. Kendra studied him, her concern rising.

"You OK?" she asked, her voice warm and low.

Sam exhaled through his mouth, a shaky breath he didn't fully hide. "Yeah… I guess I'm still trying to get myself together after that sermon and that song, "Amazing Grace", this morning. It got into me deeper than I was expecting. I don't think I was quite ready for that."

Kendra nodded slowly. "I know… I felt it too. It hit deep."

"It did." He paused, fingers tightening slightly on the steering wheel as he bit his lip. "I think this message is going to stay with me for a while."

A few more seconds passed; only the hum of the engine broke the silence. Then Sam spoke again, even softer:

"Kendra… there's something I need to ask you. But it's not something I want to just… blurt out."

She turned toward him. "Okay. Whenever you're ready."

He nodded once, eyes still on the road ahead; the winding stretch of road that would take them to the neighborhoods just outside of town. "I was thinking… maybe we could have lunch with my parents. They have been asking about you since you got back, and I know they would love to see you again."

"I'd love that," she said with a small smile, wondering why he had changed the subject so quickly.

"Great," he said, trying to force a smile, "because I already told them you'd be coming."

His tone was calm, but she heard the undercurrent. Something deep was wrestling inside of him; something she had sensed since she first saw him again... a quiet burden he carried, heavy enough that she could almost feel it sitting between them. He started glancing toward her as though the words were right there, pressing against him, but every time he opened his mouth, they stalled on the edge of his breath.

They continued the ride in silence for a while, through tree-lined streets where sunlight barely flickered through the trees. Then Sam's voice returned, low and controlled.

"Kendra… there's something I haven't been able to do since Joseph died."

The admission came out haunting and somber. She felt the sorrow within him, and her heart filled with compassion, ready to give whatever strength and support he needed.

"You don't have to tell me right now," she said gently. "Just tell me how I can be there for you."

His hands grasped the steering wheel a little tighter, his voice strained, barely above a whisper. "There's something I know that I need to do… but I really need you there with me."

Kendra lowered her head just a moment, then quickly lifted her gaze to look straight ahead with him, fighting back tears she knew she could not release. Not now. This time, he needed strength, and she intended to be just that… for him. She reached across the console, resting her hand lightly on his arm.

"Then that's where I'll be. Whatever you need… I'm there."

A slow breath slipped from him; not shaky, but a quiet release, as though her words had given him something to hold onto. Still focused on the road, he slid his hand toward hers, their fingers weaving together in a gentle, unspoken promise. He lifted their joined hands and pressed a soft kiss to the back of her hand before settling them back on the console.

His eyes stayed forward and some of the tension in his shoulders eased… somewhat.

The Whitaker home stood warm and inviting under the Sunday afternoon sun as Sam pulled into the driveway; its white siding catching the light in a soft, welcoming way. The truck hadn't even come to a full stop before Mrs. Whitaker opened the front door, waving to them in with a bright smile, full of excitement and joy.

"Kendra Williams!" she said, pulling her into a hug that nearly lifted her off her feet. "Look at you, sweetheart. Oh, I'm so glad you are joining us for lunch and it's so good to have you back home. Great seeing you at the celebration."

Mr. Whitaker joined them on the porch, grinning broadly. "Well now, Kendra, you just come on in and make yourself at home. Just like you used to!"

Sam rubbed the back of his neck, offering a faint smile. "Hey, Mom… Dad… thanks for having us."

"Having you?" Mrs. Whitaker scoffed. "I've been praying the Lord would put some sense into you and bring this girl back into our lives."

Sam groaned softly, but Kendra laughed, the sound of her laughter easing some of the tension that still rested in his shoulders.

Inside, the house smelled of fried chicken fresh from the skillet, mashed potatoes whipped to creamy perfection, a crisp garden salad, and warm homemade rolls cooling on the counter. The dining table was already set, the room softly lit by the afternoon.

Sam reached for a drumstick as they passed through the kitchen, but Mrs. Whitaker swatted his hand away with a dish towel. "Samuel Whitaker, you know better than to sneak that chicken before the blessing."

He chuckled; a soft, genuine sound that hadn't come that easy in a long time. Mrs. Whitaker paused; a smile crossed her lips as she watched him. His shoulders seemed more relaxed, and there was a lightness even in his walk that she hadn't seen in months. Mr. Whitaker noticed it too; their eyes met in a knowing exchange. Their boy was different today; not the carefree Sam of old, at least not yet, but something about him just seemed a little lighter.

Lunch unfolded in easy conversation; stories, memories, laughter, and Kendra found herself slipping right back into the simple comfort of the Whitaker home.

Mrs. Whitaker observed the gentleness and effortless ease between them; the way Sam leaned just slightly toward Kendra… and how Kendra's presence seemed to comfort him.

Kendra helped Mrs. Whitaker wash the dishes and put them away, Conversation tapered into a quiet lull and then Sam took a deep breath.

"Kendra," he whispered, barely audible, his voice tight again. "Can I borrow you for a sec?"

She turned toward him, her eyes finding his; letting him know that she understood more than he'd been able to say.

"Of course."

Across the kitchen, Mr. and Mrs. Whitaker met each other's eyes; sharing a quiet, knowing glance. They sensed something moving in their son's heart, something they hoped he was finally ready to face.

Sam reached for Kendra's hand. His grip was gentle, but there was a tension in it, like he was holding on to someone he couldn't let go of.

He led her down the hall. Paused at the door. A door he hadn't opened… a room he hadn't entered in over two and a half years... Joseph's room.

He reached for the doorknob and turned it slowly. At the soft click, he closed his eyes for just a second; not in hesitation, but in acknowledgment of what he was about to do. Kendra moved a little closer, her presence quiet but unmistakable, a nearness he could feel without even looking at her. Then he drew in a deep breath, as if pulling strength inward. When he exhaled, it wasn't surrender, it was release.

Inside the room, it felt like stepping into a memory. A guarded memory frozen in time waiting to be set free.

Afternoon light slipped through the blinds in narrow bands, casting gentle stripes across the neatly made bed and the shelves lined with model airplanes Joseph had collected over the years. Sam could feel his shoulders tighten as he took in the once-familiar space. The air felt heavy with memories that seemed to rise from the quiet corners of the room.

He guided Kendra toward the bed and motioned for her to sit, his hand slipping from hers as gently as he had held it earlier. Then he sat next to her, his eyes skimming the room as if he was missing something, and then it caught his eye. Not on the desk but placed carefully on a shelf high above it. Half-shadowed and inconspicuous, unless you knew exactly where to look.

He spoke at last, his eyes widening. "I don't remember that being up *there* before."

Rising slowly, he moved closer and reached up to take down a photo album; its spine worn, its edges frayed from younger, heavier hands. He held it as though it was something fragile and precious.

"This…" he said softly, glancing toward Kendra. "We started this when we were kids. And the day before he left, we sat right here putting in the last pictures we had taken together." His voice wavered. "I haven't touched it since the day the commander came to the house and told us he'd been killed."

His eyes softened as he brushed a corner of the album, the weight of old memories pressing against him. "He said, just in case you can't reach me over there, or you start to miss me too much." A small, broken chuckle escaped him. "As if a scrapbook could ever make up for not having him here."

Sam's hand hovered over the album, before he lowered it to his lap, placed it across them, and opened it.

The first page held a photo of two little boys sitting on a swing set; Sam missing his front tooth, Joseph's arms thrown around him in a proud, big brother grip. Sam lovingly circled his fingertips over the image, his eyes filling with tears that were not yet ready to fall.

Kendra reached out, her voice barely above a whisper. "You can take your time, Sam… take all the time you need. I'm here for as long as you need me."

He faced her, lifted his eyes to hers, and for a moment the room grew still. They leaned closer, drawn by something quiet and unspoken, their foreheads touching in a gentle, familiar closeness. His breath mingling with hers when he spoke.

"Thank you," he murmured. "But it's time… and I'm ready. I need to do this… and I need to do it now."

Page after page, the story of their childhood unfolded: fishing trips, scraped knees, football games, goofy grins, sitting with Santa at Christmas time, birthdays marked by crooked cakes and handmade cards, high school graduations. The last few pages shifted to adulthood. The two of them standing tall beside their parents at a Fourth of July parade, Joseph in uniform, Sam helping him pack.

Sam's voice fractured. "We made this, together… all of it… just the two of us." His voice trembled, the realization of the significance of a simple photo album of shared memories.

"It's almost like he knew what it would mean to me or us… later."

Kendra shifted on the bed, turning toward him. She tucked her feet under her to move closer to him, her knee brushing his as she wrapped both arms around him, her head resting gently on him. She was there to comfort him… ready to walk with him through the grief he could no longer bear alone.

"He knew that he might not be coming back." Sam whispered. His voice splintered. "But he went anyway."

It happened before Sam even realized it. Something deep inside him; the dam he'd built over years of silence began to crack. But before the dam, there had always been Kendra. She had encouraged him through his awkward teenage years, comforted him long before the uniform, long before the loss. She had always met him with grace and understanding instead of judgment. And she was here now. She wasn't just a friend; she had become the one person who held a place for him at his best and at his worst.

The one he trusted to carry what he had never said out loud. The one he trusted without even having to think about why.

He turned to her, his head sinking against her as the album remained clutched in one hand, the other arm reaching for her and holding her as if his very life depended on it. Grief unattended was finally given notice, the weight of it loosening its grip. The release built slowly at first… then broke into deep, shuddering sobs rising from a place so deep inside him that they shook him to his core.

Kendra didn't speak; she only held him tighter, drawing him closer to her; until the raw anguish in his sobs reached a place inside her that she could no longer hold. She felt his pain as if it were her own heart breaking, stirring emotions she dare not embrace. Her tears fell freely, joining with his. She let them fall…for him, for his brother, for every unspoken ache he had borne. She drew him closer still, letting their grief meet in the quiet space between them, a wordless promise that he wasn't alone.

When his grief began to ease, even slightly, a memory flashed; vivid and uninvited:

They were all together that morning in the staging area behind the battalion building, where families gathered in clusters beneath a few canvas tents. Soldiers stood with their duffels at their feet, last-minute checks happening all around them. The buses were parked in the departure lot, forming an angled row where soldiers would soon board.

Joseph stood in uniform, straight-backed and fighting misty eyes, but Sam thought he could see a flicker of nerves beneath the determination. Mom clung to Joseph's arm, tears slipping silently despite her efforts to stay strong. Mr. Whitaker kept a hand on her shoulder, his own eyes misty despite the brave smile he wore.

"Y'all don't start crying now," Joseph said with that familiar half-grin. "I'll be back before you know it."

Then he turned to Sam, pulling him into a hug so fierce it knocked the breath from him. "Keep the faith for me, Sam," he'd said, voice low but calm.

Sam laughed through the sudden sting in his eyes. "I'll do my best. You know I will."

Joseph's grin widened. "Then we're covered."

Sam blinked hard, the memory fading as the room came back into focus. Their tears had mingled on the album's cover, dampening its worn edges.

Slowly, he lifted his head from her shoulder, and Kendra drew back just enough for their eyes to meet. For a moment, neither of them spoke. They simply breathed the same breath, foreheads touching gently… two hearts finding a calm in the quiet.

Sam exhaled and eased the photo album onto the far side of the bed, his hand lingering on it briefly before he let it go. Then he turned back to Kendra, and the two of them folded into each other's arms; no words, no explanations, just the quiet refuge of shared grief and presence.

They stayed like that for a long while, long enough for the storm inside him to soften, long enough for his breathing to return to normal… long enough that, from the doorway, Mr. and Mrs. Whitaker peeked in, witnessing their son held in the kind of comfort and reassurance they had prayed he would find. They slipped away quietly so as not to disturb the tender moment unfolding between their son and thc woman he had chosen to share it with.

Sam stood, taking the album with him and gently set it back on the shelf.

"Kendra…" he said hoarsely. His head was bowed, still full of emotion. "I know that I would not have been able to do this without you. I know this is just a start, but I'm grateful that you were willing to take that first step with me. Thank you."

She stood with him and closed the distance between them. Then cupping his face into her hands, she brushed away a lone tear. "I will always be here for you, Sam, for as long as you need me, and as long as you let me."

Something had changed in *him*. Something had changed in *her*. Something had changed between *them*. An unbreakable bond, and unspoken love, a release and an awakening: as if a door in front of them, once held only slightly ajar, had finally opened wide, waiting for them to walk through it.

— ✦ —

They walked back to the kitchen together, Sam's steps a little lighter now, though still measured. The change in him was obvious. It showed on his face, in his eyes, even in the way he carried himself. The undeniable presence of peace. Even if it was only the beginning.

Mother, father, and son stood facing one another. Kendra recognized the significance of it and eased back just slightly, giving them the space they needed… together. But not so far that Sam couldn't reach for her if he needed to.

They embraced; not in sorrow this time, but in relief, in healing, in a shared release they had waited for, far too long. Mrs. Whitaker peered over her son's shoulder, her eyes finding Kendra's. She mouthed a grateful, silent "*thank you*". Kendra answered with a soft acknowledging nod, one filled with humility and understanding.

Mr. Whitaker kept his arms around Sam as he whispered into his ear, "You alright, son?"

Sam's response came quiet but sure, his voice no longer breaking. "Yeah, Dad… I'm good. I'm getting there."

Mr. Whitaker lowered his head, his voice quivering as he spoke into his son's shoulder. "That's all I needed to hear."

The Whitakers slowly released one another, and Sam reached out for Kendra. She took his hand into hers, the other hand wrapping around him in gentle support. Sam turned and looked into her eyes, deeply, finding again that place of comfort and consolation, and a quiet, growing emotional intimacy between them that ran deeper than either of them had spoken out loud.

They drifted into the living room together, the weight of the afternoon giving way to the softer edges of familiar comfort. Conversation found them naturally; little stories, small memories, a few light jokes that brought a warm chuckle from Mr. Whitaker and even coaxed a smile from Sam. As Sam and Kendra readied to leave, Mrs. Whitaker hovered near the arm of the couch, her eyes resting on her son too long for it to go unnoticed.

Sam caught it. He moved toward her, his expression gentle. "Don't be sad, Mom," he said softly. "You know I'll be by tomorrow after work."

She managed a smile as he leaned in and kissed her cheek, his hand brushing her shoulder with quiet affection.

"Well… alright then," she murmured, trying to make the smile stick. "I'll hold you to that."

They gathered themselves and headed toward the front door. Sam reached for Kendra's hand again, not out of need this time, but out of newfound closeness, and together they walked out into the late afternoon light, walking toward his truck as the Whitakers watched them go with a gratitude and emotion too deep for words.

They reached the truck together, a quiet calm wrapping around them like the full afternoon sun. Sam paused by the passenger door, turning toward her with a vulnerability he didn't try to hide. He reached for both her hands and held them.

"Kendra," he said, his voice low, shaped by truth instead of fear. "I need you. I've needed you for a long time. And… I think I've loved you for longer than I should probably admit."

Kendra drew in a soft breath; not from surprise, but because that flutter that she always felt near him had blossomed to a full blown leap. She moved closer to him, her eyes locked on his, her heart open, full, unguarded.

He held her gaze, searching for something; assurance, permission, hope.

Kendra paused, not out of uncertainty, but searching for the right words. She cupped his face in her hands, her touch gentle and loving.

"I've cared about you for so long," she said softly. "Longer than I would ever admit even to myself. I just… I didn't think you saw me that way back then. I was young, we were young and unsure, and too scared to risk losing each other completely."

"But when I saw you at the welcome celebration… the way we looked at each other, I allowed myself to feel something that I had pushed back for years. And when I saw Joseph's picture at your apartment… I understood your pain. I felt your pain join with my pain…Sam, I knew right then that whatever we had in the past was not what we have now. And now, after everything you shared today, everything you let me walk through with you… and what we are sharing right now, I realize that I don't have to hold back anymore. I love you more than the air I breathe."

Sam caught his breath, before smiling, really smiling. "Yeah?... Really?", almost boyish in his uncertainty of what he had just heard. His gaze held hers, almost searching.

"Yeah!... Really!" She was smiling now too, and couldn't stop the little laugh of relief as she nodded several times continuing to look into his eyes.

Sam let out a breath that trembled with relief and joy, his forehead gently leaning on hers. For a long time, they simply stood there, breathing in the same warm afternoon air… two people finally speaking a truth they had hidden for years.

His voice dropped to a whisper. "Kendra… I've wanted to hear you say that for so long."

She wrapped her arms around his neck and looked deeply into his eyes. "Then hear it again," she whispered. "I love you."

Something within him softened, his heart opening to a love and joy that felt almost unreal. His hands found her waist, drawing her in with a tenderness that spoke of every unspoken moment between them.

Their lips met softly at first, gently, almost reverently; a kiss that felt like a promise, a beginning, a release of years of held-back hope. Then, as they both exhaled, the depth of the bond between them finally revealed itself; not hurried, not desperate, but warm and certain, like two hearts finally choosing to move in the same direction.

When they finally pulled back, their foreheads rested together, breaths mingling, smiles trembling between laughter and tears.

"I've got you," Sam murmured.

"I know," Kendra whispered, gently allowing their lips to touch again. "And I've got you right back."

The afternoon sun wrapped around them, the world quiet and full, as if all of Harmony Grove Harbor paused long enough to let this time belong only to them.

Still wrapped in each other's arms, Sam let out a soft laugh. "Kendra… you know they're watching us, right?"

She chuckled, her forehead still resting lightly against his. "Yeah… I know."

Sam pulled back just enough to glance toward the house, and sure enough, he caught a quick flash of movement. Mrs. Whitaker ducked behind the curtains with all the subtlety of a church usher trying to sneak a peppermint to a child. Mr. Whitaker wasn't any better; he was pretending to adjust something on the coffee table, though his eyes were still angled toward the window.

Sam shook his head, amused. "Gotta love those guys."

Kendra laughed, brushing her fingers down his arm. "It's alright… I love them too."

He smiled; a warm, unguarded smile that made his heart full. "I know," he said gently. "And they love you."

Reluctantly but still smiling, they eased out of each other's embrace. Sam moved around her and opened the passenger door with easy, natural grace; not because he felt he had to, but because it was *who he had always been with her.*

"My lady," he said softly, bending in mock chivalry.

Kendra climbed in; and she gently placed her hand over his and their eyes met once more. Sam closed the door gently, still grinning as he rounded the truck.

He circled around to the driver's side, and once they were both in, neither spoke immediately. They didn't need to. The oneness between them spoke *for* them.

As Sam backed out of the Whitaker driveway, Kendra cast one last glance toward the house. Mr. and Mrs. Whitaker had walked onto the porch, standing side by side, waving at them with gentle smiles. Sunlight spilled across the yard in soft afternoon gold, framing them in a warmth that felt every bit like a blessing.

Kendra couldn't hear what they said, but she felt it; the quiet gratitude in their faces, the unspoken prayer in the way they lifted their hands toward their son… and toward her.

Sam shifted the truck into drive, the engine rolling to life as they eased down the street. Harmony Grove Harbor stretched before them, wrapped in the gentle glow of the late afternoon sun; warm, hopeful, and full of promise.

"You up for a late afternoon stroll by the waterfront?" he asked, eyes brightening. "Just you and me… taking a little walk?"

Kendra laughed, warm and light. "With you? Anytime." Then she looked down at her shoes and groaned playfully. "But you gotta take me home first so I can get out of these shoes. My feet are killing me."

Sam chuckled. "Fair enough."

A few minutes later, he pulled into the Williamses driveway. Before he could even reach for the door handle to get out, Kendra touched his arm, her eyes shining.

"Don't move," she said softly. "I'll be right back."

She slipped out of the truck and hurried up the front steps. The front door swung open and she practically floated inside, joy trailing behind her like a ribbon. Evelyn and Thomas Williams looked up from the living room, instantly catching the glow that lit their daughter's face.

"What's the rush?" her father asked, brows raised, amused.

Kendra darted toward her bedroom as she called back, "Sam's waiting…Just changing shoes!"

In what felt like seconds later, she came running back through the hallway again. "Love you, see you later!" she called over her shoulder, taking a second to adjust a strap on her sandals and then flying back out the door.

Evelyn watched the front door swing open and then swing shut in one movement, one hand slowly lifting to her heart. A knowing smile spread across her face.

"Lord, have mercy," she murmured, shaking her head with a joy that couldn't hide the hint of concern only mothers carry. "My child has come home and fallen in love."

Thomas chuckled softly beside her. "About time," he said with quiet approval.

Outside, Kendra hurried back to Sam's truck, her smile echoing his. Sam watched her with a warmth that spread across his entire expression as she climbed back in.

He backed out of the driveway, the two of them headed toward the Harmony Grove Harbor waterfront… but more than that, toward a destiny that had patiently waited for them to claim it.

Chapter 10

The Light Over the Harbor

Kendra stirred at the sound of her alarm buzzing on the nightstand. She reached out a sleepy hand to silence it, then rolled onto her other side with a soft groan… not quite ready to surrender to the morning. She lay there with her eyes drifting toward the ceiling, quietly reflecting on the fullness of emotions from the previous day. Sam's breakthrough… Pastor Thompson's soul-reaching message… the shared confessions of love between her and Sam…and her promise to stand by him. It all felt as though blessings from above had rained down and settled gently over her. She exhaled, letting the stillness of a new day wash over her.

Her phone buzzed again, this time an incoming call…Sam.

A smile tugged at her lips before she even picked it up.

"Good morning, beautiful."

"Good morning, handsome," she replied, her voice still hushed with sleep.

Sam chuckled, that warm, gravelly sound she was beginning to crave. "I was hoping you'd sound like that."

"Like what?"

"Like you just woke up… and like you're still smiling."

Kendra rolled onto her back, lowering the comforter to just beneath her arms. "Well, someone on the other end of this phone gave me a reason to smile."

"Well," he said, "now you've given me a reason to smile."

She heard the gentle rustle of covers on his end and pictured him lying in bed, his head resting on a pillow, a soft ray of sunlight brushing softly across his face.

"You woke up early?" she asked.

"Couldn't help it," he said. "Been thinking about you. About yesterday. About… everything."

She caught her breath gently. "Sam…"

He cleared his throat lightly. "Nothing heavy. Honestly… I just wanted to hear your voice and say good morning before you started your day. After everything yesterday, it reminded me that you've got my back… so I wanted you to know I've got yours too, Kendra."

The lightness and tenderness in his voice made her smile.

"Thank you," she whispered. "I know you do… but it means a lot to actually hear you say it."

An easy pause unfolded between them… gentle, unhurried.

"And Kendra?" he added.

"Yes?"

"You're going to look great in those scrubs… but I'm still thinking about that dress you wore to church."

She let out a surprised laugh. "Sam Whitaker…"

"What?" he teased. "Just being honest."

She shook her head, laughing softly. "You are too much… but you know I love it."

"Good. I'll let you get ready. But I'll see you later tonight. I don't care what we do…I just want time with you. I've got to be at the church today for the final phase of the bell's restoration, but I'll call you when we're done… if that's alright?"

Her heart warmed. "More than alright."

"Good," he said, his voice softening. "Have a beautiful morning, Kendra. Love you."

"Love you too, Sam."

They lingered on the line a second longer before she finally ended the call, still smiling. For a few quiet moments she lay there… letting the warmth of his voice rest within her, letting her heart calm itself before the day pulled her forward.

At last, she pushed the comforter back and swung her legs over the side of the bed. Discipline and military training had prompted her to lay out her scrubs neatly on the chair beside the dresser, with her Crocs lined up just beneath them the night before. She headed straight for the shower, lathering in the gentle scent of fresh linen.

The warm water rushed over her shoulders, easing the faint tension that had long followed the memories of wartime deployment. But today felt different. It felt as though a heaviness she hadn't even realized she'd been carrying had suddenly been lifted. Hopefully Sam felt it too.

She closed her eyes beneath the spray, letting the water cascade over her with an enveloping warmth. She pressed her palms against the shower wall and bowed her head.

"*Thank You, Lord, for this day*."

When she stepped out of the shower and slipped into her scrubs and Crocs, she felt renewed from the inside out. She tugged her hair into a loose pouf, looped her lanyard and ID badge over her head, and finally lifted her old army tote over her shoulder. It was worn around the edges, but she kept it as a reminder of where she'd been… and how far she'd come.

Kendra looked forward to her shift at the hospital today, but she couldn't deny she was looking forward to seeing Sam even more. The thought of just being with him again drew a quiet smile to her lips… one she couldn't quite make go away.

Kendra pushed through the double doors leading into the ER, the familiar burst of antiseptic and disinfectant greeting her as soon as she was inside. The unit wasn't busy; only four people sat scattered throughout the waiting area, quietly scrolling through their phones or talking in low tones. A tech rolled a vitals cart toward triage, and a couple of monitors beeped softly from behind closed curtains.

Charlene had arrived only moments earlier when she spotted Kendra coming in. "Good morning, sunshine. Somebody's glowing this morning, and it's not from the overhead lights," she said, narrowing her eyes with a knowing grin.

Kendra paused mid-step, feeling the warmth rise in her cheeks. "Good morning to you too, Charlene. And don't start."

"Oh, I'm starting," Charlene said, lifting her coffee cup like she was making a toast. "So let me guess *who* you were talking to this morning?"

Kendra tried, unsuccessfully, to hide the small smile tugging at her lips. "We just talked, that's all."

"Mm hmm… talked," Charlene echoed, drawing out the word as she picked up her tablet from the counter. "Oh, so you're admitting that you talked this morning? Anything else you want to tell me? That little glow of yours practically followed you through the door. Even Ray Charles could see that."

Before Kendra could respond, Allison walked over from an ER bay, snapping off a pair of exam gloves. "Hey guys, and good morning. We only have two patients holding right now, so this might actually be a peaceful shift. I hope it lasts."

She glanced at Kendra and smiled. "Geez, Kendra… something about you looks different today. You've got to tell me your secret."

Charlene leaned closer. "It's called Sam Whitaker… trust me."

Kendra shook her head, laughing softly, though she couldn't deny it. Something about this morning… this peace, this ease, this joy and new closeness with Sam was resting easy within her.

Charlene glanced up to the patient status board above the nurses' station to confirm what Allison had just said, then leaned in just a little, lowering her voice as if saying it out loud would jinx it. "We might actually get to drink our coffee while it's still hot."

Allison stood beside her, finishing the log record from the last patient. "Those two cases holding," she said. "One mild asthma flare in Bay 3, waiting on respiratory to reassess, and a sprained wrist in Bay 1 waiting for imaging transport. That's literally it."

Kendra laughed softly. "Well, that *is* a rare Monday morning blessing."

They walked together toward the nurses' station inside the ER's main horseshoe. The scene was calm in the best way… no sirens pulling into the bay, no overhead calls for rapid response. Just the gentle rhythm of a department exhaling.

Kendra logged into her tablet and pulled up her patient assignments, glancing toward Bay 3. She heard a soft wheeze drifting faintly through the curtain, followed by a gentle cough.

"I'll go check on Mr. Harris," she said. "If respiratory hasn't been in yet, I don't want his anxiety to spike."

"Good call," Allison replied. "He asked for you by name earlier. Said he remembered you from the last time he was in the ER."

"That's because she's the nice one," Charlene added with a dramatic sigh. "I, apparently, intimidate people."

Allison raised an eyebrow. "*You*? No."

Charlene placed a hand over her heart. "See? This is the kind of disrespect I get when the ER has no real emergencies."

Kendra shook her head, smiling as she left the nurses' station and walked toward Bay 3. She drew the curtain back to check on the older gentleman inside, greeting him warmly. The ER may have been quiet, but its quiet had a rhythm she appreciated… quick conversations, small reassurances, gentle hands guiding patients through discomfort. Nothing like the battlefield tents she had once worked in. And every calm moment still felt like a gift.

Behind her, she could hear Charlene and Allison slipping back into their light banter again… the kind that helped the hours pass easily when the unit wasn't demanding their full attention.

Kendra glanced back briefly, grateful for the ease of it… grateful for the peace in her spirit today… then turned her focus fully toward her patient.

By early afternoon, the ER had settled into an easy rhythm. Imaging had picked up the sprained-wrist patient, respiratory had checked in with Mr. Harris, and the waiting room hadn't grown beyond a handful of quiet visitors. When their lunch break finally rolled around, Kendra and Charlene slipped into the break room, grateful for the breather.

Charlene set her container on the table and exhaled. "Well… if this shift keeps going like this, I might actually survive till dinner."

Kendra smiled as she unwrapped her sandwich. "You needed an easy day."

"No kidding." Charlene sat down, stirring the ice in her cup before taking a sip. "Between the dream and that nagging feeling I woke up with this morning… I'll take all the peace I can get."

Kendra looked at her, gentle concern softening her expression. "Speaking of that… have you had a chance to talk to Pastor Thompson yet?"

Charlene shook her head. "Not yet. I called the church office during my morning break and asked if I could meet with him sometime this week. They said I could stop by on Tuesday…

anytime." She hesitated, the joking edge in her voice fading. "Kendra, to be honest with you, there's still something else I need to tell you about that dream… just not yet."

"What part?" Kendra asked quietly.

Charlene traced the rim of her cup with her fingertip, her gaze drifting toward the window. "The fog… the light… this town… the feeling that something was coming. I don't want to sound dramatic. Not until I talk it through with Pastor face-to-face."

Kendra nodded slowly, her eyes widening just a bit. "*This town*? Yeah, you definitely didn't tell me that part. But I won't pry now. You'll feel better, and maybe you'll get some answers once you talk to Pastor. And he'll listen… you know he will."

"Oh, I know," Charlene said, blowing out a small breath through her mouth. "That's why I need to talk to him… face to face. I just really have this feeling that this isn't just one of my random dreams. It feels heavier. And it's the *same* dream over and over again."

They both paused, looking beyond one another, the silence between them thoughtful. Only the hum of the refrigerator filled the quiet, along with the faint sound of distant footsteps outside the room.

Kendra reached over and nudged Charlene's arm with a soft smile. "Hey… whatever this is, we'll walk through it together. You're not alone in it."

Charlene looked up, a faint smile appeared, but what lingered in her eyes told a different story. "I know. That's why I told you about it. You've always been there for me."

Their lunch break continued in easy conversation, and Kendra, sensing the need to lighten the mood, perked up.

"So," she said lightly, "do you have something to tell me about this Raymond fellow?" She smiled sweetly, though it was almost a smirk.

"We just talked… that's all." Charlene raised an eyebrow, giving her that *you know* look.

And with that, they both shared a hearty laugh. But underneath the laughter and light teasing, something else lingered... a shared awareness that whatever Charlene's dream meant, it mattered… and both of them sensed it.

And in the quiet recesses of Kendra's and Charlene's hearts, Pastor Thompson's sermon echoed again… the power of grace, even through mysteries they didn't yet understand.

— ✦ —

Charlene's shift ended quietly, and by early evening she found herself pulling into her driveway with a long exhale. The sky above Harmony Grove Harbor was a dusky lavender… the kind that always made her think of God's hand of protection over the town. Normally, that alone would calm her. But tonight, she just wanted answers… clarity on something that was persisting longer than she thought it should.

The foyer was warmly lit, and she could feel a calmness beginning to embrace her. She dropped her keys into the bowl on the console table by the door and peeped around the corner.

"Mama?" she called, softly.

Margaret Matthews finished a sip from a cold glass of lemonade before looking up. Her face brightened when she saw Charlene. "Hey baby… you're home earlier than I thought. Everything alright?"

"Mm-hmm," Charlene said with a small smile as she walked toward her mom, then leaned in for a quick hug. "A pretty quiet shift today. Where's Daddy?"

"Still at the office," her mother sighed good-naturedly. "You know your father. If he's not home by seven, he's going to be there until ten."

Charlene chuckled softly. "Yeah… that sounds about right."

"Did you eat? I put some baked chicken in the fridge."

"I grabbed something at work. I'm just… a little tired." Something in her tone made her mother study her face, but Charlene offered a reassuring smile before Margaret could ask more.

"Well, go on and get some rest," her mother said gently. "You look worn out."

"I think I will," Charlene replied, giving her mom a grateful hug around her neck and a kiss on the cheek.

She headed down the long hallway toward her private wing, a quiet corner of the house her parents had renovated just after she left for active duty overseas so she would have a place of her own to come back to… a place to recuperate, to heal, to relax, and to renew. It had its own sitting room and bathroom, and a large balcony overlooking the backyard, the magnolias, and the swimming pool. A small sanctuary she was grateful for…especially tonight.

Charlene usually couldn't resist spending a few hours on her phone, listening to music, or letting the television play softly in the background after work…but not tonight. As soon as she stepped into her suite, she closed the door behind her, letting the calm and quiet settle in and around her.

She found herself absorbed in her own thoughts, drawn inward in a way she hadn't experienced before… as if something deep within her spirit was being gently tugged. Closing her eyes, the words surfaced again in her mind.

The fog... the light... this town...

When she came back to herself, Charlene knelt beside her bed. She bowed her head, turning her palms upward as they rested on the mattress. Closing her eyes once more, she began to talk to God.

"*Father,*" she began. Her prayer rose in silence and humility. "*You have safely brought me home. You have kept me safe in times when I didn't think I would make it. You have been my constant friend. So please… increase my faith and my trust in You, even when I don't understand what You are doing. And if this thing I am wrestling with is not of You, I pray that You rebuke it. In Jesus' name, Amen.*"

She stayed on her knees a little while longer, meditating on Him… recalling moments from His holy Word that had encouraged her, lifted her, and reassured her.

"*He that dwelleth in the secret place of the most High shall abide under the shadow of the Almighty. I will say of the Lord, He is my refuge and my fortress: my God: in him will I trust."*

"Wait on the Lord; be of good courage, and He shall strengthen thine heart: wait, I say on the Lord"

When she stood up, Charlene realized she was simply Charlene Matthews… laughing loudly, loving deeply, and doing her best to walk faithfully every day. She didn't have to understand what God was doing. She didn't even need to know what He was doing. All she needed to do was trust Him.

Comforted and reassured, Charlene decided that a long hot bath would further relieve any remaining tension, and definitely soothe tired feet from another long day at the hospital. She let the tub fill with the water temperature set to the highest she thought she could stand and threw in an abundance of lavender bath salts for good measure. She sank deep into the warmth of the water and rested her head back on the pillow rest. For a third time she closed her eyes. When her fingers and toes began to prune, Charlene rose and stepped out of the tub, wrapping herself in a towel as she moved toward the mirror. Its surface was completely fogged over, not surprisingly. She reached out to wipe away the condensation, but then she hesitated. She thought she saw something… something different.

Then she froze.

At the very edges of the mirror, where the steam was still thickest, a rolling cloud began to form…the same pattern she had seen in her dreams. And then it was there. A pale, gentle light began to glow… slowly growing. As it expanded, its intensity strengthened. When the light had consumed the cloud, Charlene turned around, needing to see it with her own eyes.

She saw it for only a heartbeat.

Then it was gone.

She felt no fear. She neither trembled nor shook. Her eyes remained fixed on the place where she had last seen it, and she reached toward that space as if she might feel its essence still lingering there.

And then the voice:

"Peace I leave with you, My peace I give unto you… not as the world giveth, give I unto you. Let not your heart be troubled, neither let it be afraid."

Charlene dropped to the floor, covering her head as her knees struck the cool tile. It wasn't fear; it was reverence.

"Lord…" she whispered.

"Why me?" she breathed.

When she was able, she gasped… not from fear, but because she felt as if something holy had passed through her, leaving a whisper she was longing to hear. And then came the peace.

Charlene swallowed as she stood, with her head still bowed, not sure she should raise it. She simply thought to herself; *Pastor Thompson and I have much to discuss tomorrow.*

Chapter 11

A Meeting with the Shepherd

Morning daylight had yet to touch Harmony Grove Harbor when Charlene pulled into the small parking area beside the administrative offices of Main Street Baptist Church. She had slept peacefully for the first time in days, wrapped in the quiet certainty that the vision she'd seen in the mirror the night before had come from God. She felt ready… willing… settled in a peace she couldn't explain. But she just didn't feel worthy. And she couldn't help feeling a little guilty for having Pastor Thompson awake at such an early hour.

The church felt different on a weekday. In the dim, pre-dawn stillness, it was solemnly quiet. A faint glow of lingering moonlight refracted through the stained-glass windows, scattering soft colors onto the carpeted floor. Charlene stepped out of her car quickly and hurried up the steps leading into the office entrance. She had forgotten her jacket and wanted to shorten her time in the crisp autumn air.

At this hour, the staff wing would normally be empty, but Pastor Thompson and Leah were already waiting, watching for her. She opened the entrance door to the offices gently.

"Good morning, Charlene. He's waiting for you; just down the hallway to the left. The door should be open."

"Thanks, Sister Thompson, and good morning to you too. I'm really sorry for getting you all up this early."

Leah waved it off. "Think nothing of it. You didn't wake us. Nathaniel's always up before the crack of dawn; says he can hear better from the Lord then."

Charlene smiled, relieved, as she walked with Leah down the hallway that led to Pastor Thompson's office, their quiet footsteps echoing as they talked softly. The corridor itself felt like a walk through history; framed photographs of former pastors, black-and-white images of the sanctuary before renovations, and an old picture of the steeple being raised.

The closer they got to Pastor Thompson's office, Charlene became aware of her own footsteps, sounding too loud even on the carpet. Out of nervousness, she smoothed her scrubs top, hoping whatever she gained in this meeting would strengthen her for whatever the day held.

Leah tapped lightly on the door before easing it open. Pastor Thompson looked up from notes sprawled across an open Bible, a soft lamp casting a warm glow over the room. Books lined every shelf, their spines worn from years of use, and a faint scent of old paper and polished wood wrapped around the space like something familiar and safe.

"Charlene," he said, rising slowly from his chair and moving around the desk to greet her. He motioned gently toward a comfortable-looking chair across from him. His eyes held both concern and gentleness.

"Come in, daughter."

"Thank you, Pastor." Charlene stepped further into the room and allowed herself to sink into the chair. Something about the way he said *daughter* spoke straight to her heart, and she had to stop herself from nearly breaking. She had known this man for more than half her life. He had prayed with her and for her, guiding her to grow stronger and deeper in her faith…always gentle, always kind, never judgmental. It wasn't until this moment that she realized how much she had taken his presence for granted, and how deeply she had depended on the quiet strength he offered without ever expecting anything in return.

Leah slipped quietly away and closed the door behind her.

Pastor Thompson began, "So, tell me what's on your heart."

Charlene swallowed, lacing her fingers together for a moment before the words finally came.

"I've been having this dream, Pastor…every night for almost two weeks. And last night, it wasn't a dream. I was fully awake."

There was no skepticism or uncertainty in her voice. Pastor Thompson's eyes softened, inviting her to continue.

She explained how the dream always began the same way…a storm rising over the desert, the darkness, the glowing light within the rolling cloud. Then the scene shifted to Harmony Grove Harbor in a storm…the same darkness, the same radiant light appearing once again.

She paused, just long enough to choose her words carefully.

"And Pastor," she said quietly, "last night wasn't a dream. I was standing in front of my mirror…the same cloud appeared there, along with the same light. But this time, it grew bigger and brighter. I turned to look, and it was only there for a moment…but I know what I saw."

Her expression didn't waver as she told him about the voice…clear and unmistakable, the scripture it spoke, and how her knees gave way beneath her, not from fear, but from the overwhelming presence of God.

She paused before continuing. "Pastor, I don't want to sound crazy or overly dramatic. I just…I just don't know what God wants me to do with this, and why me?"

Pastor Thompson didn't speak right away.

He sat back slightly, his eyes never leaving hers…not in shock, not in doubt, not in judgment, but in recognition, as though something in her words confirmed what his spirit had already begun to sense.

At last, he nodded, slow and thoughtful.

"Charlene," he said softly, "the Lord does not reveal Himself without purpose. He speaks to His children to lead and guide them."

A soft smile touched the corners of his mouth. "And why you? Because God does not choose the perfect. He chooses the willing. And you, daughter, have a willing heart…a heart attuned to compassion, to intercession, to listening. That is far more rare than you think."

Charlene blinked hard, feeling a lump rise in her throat.

He leaned forward, his elbows resting lightly on his knees, his voice lowering into a tone she had heard countless times in sermons, prayer meetings and prayer vigils.

"What you saw… what you heard… I believe it was from God. I believe that fully."

Charlene felt her breath catch, not in fear but in relief… the confirmation she had prayed for.

Pastor Thompson continued, "Dreams, visions, whispers of Scripture in the stillness…these are not foreign to the God we serve. And when the same message comes again and again, whether in sleep or waking, I believe it means the Lord is preparing your heart…and you…for something."

He paused, letting the weight of that truth settle between them.

"I don't know yet what He's asking of you," he said gently, "but I do believe this: you were chosen to receive it. And God does not choose lightly."

His expression warmed with that familiar mixture of fatherly affection and spiritual certainty.

"Just trust in God for now; understanding will come later. We won't always understand God's will, but we can always trust His will."

"Come," Pastor Thompson said gently, rising from his chair and moving toward Charlene.
"Let's pray."

Charlene stood as he reached out his hand. She placed her hand in his, and together they bowed their heads.

"Father," he began, his voice low and reverent, "we thank You for who You are...for Your presence that guides, Your mercy that covers, and Your wisdom that never fails."

"We lift up Charlene to You right now, Lord. You know her heart. You know what You've shown her, and You know why. Give her peace as she walks in the light You've given...and patience where the path is not yet clear."

His tone softened even further.

"Let no fear touch her, Father. Let no confusion take root. Let her spirit remain anchored in You. And when the time comes for understanding, open the doors...and speak to her in a way that only You can."

He paused, letting the quiet of the moment settle like a blanket of calm over the room.

"We trust Your will, Lord. We trust Your timing. And we trust that whatever You are preparing...You are already in it."

He lifted his head slightly.

"In Jesus' name...Amen."

Charlene whispered, “Amen,” an inner peace coming over her that hadn’t been there when she walked in. Tears slipped quietly down her cheeks, but these were tears of gratitude.

Pastor Thompson understood. He gave her a reassuring nod and then pulled her into a gentle hug.

“God is with you, daughter,” he said softly. “And so are we.”

She managed a smile. “Thank you, Pastor.”

Charlene’s footsteps felt lighter now as she left Pastor Thompson’s study. The hallway glowed with a new morning’s light, one that had risen while they talked and prayed.

Stepping outside, she felt the sunlight greet her like a gentle embrace.

Charlene walked toward her car, then paused for a moment. She lifted her face toward the sky, a quiet reminder of the One who had walked with her through good times and bad times, through every trial, every heartache, every storm—and the One who would continue to walk with her long after this day.

She let the warmth of the morning sun chase away the chill of the early breeze before sliding into the driver’s seat. She took a quick glance into her rearview mirror, not to look back in expectation, but simply to exhale.

And in that stillness, she knew one thing for certain: whatever God was preparing her for… she would not have to walk into it alone.

Chapter 12

The Bell, The Tower and Main Street

Sam Whitaker stood beside the temporary rigging frame the crew had set up at the base of the tower, his tablet in hand as he reviewed the checklist for what felt like the tenth time. The restoration team had been moving since sunrise… checking the pulleys in the block-and-tackle system, testing each rope line for load tolerance, and inspecting the reinforced beams inside the tower where the hoisting point had been anchored. Every detail mattered, and Sam wasn't about to risk a single oversight. Not today.

"Still planning to raise her by noon?" Sam asked as the crew chief cinched the last of the heavy-duty rope through the pulley wheel overhead.

"Right on schedule," the man replied with a confident nod. "Once we adjust tension on the main line, she'll lift smooth. We'll have her back in the tower before lunch."

Good. Exactly where they needed to be. Sam checked a few boxes on his tablet, marking off the completed inspections and progress milestones. Weeks of planning… precise measurements… and careful structural work had brought them to this moment. The tower's aging support frame had been strengthened with new steel brackets; the old mounting bolts replaced with corrosion-resistant hardware; and the headstock refitted to ensure the bell would hang level and secure. Even the interior platform had been reinforced, its joists tightened to safely bear the bell's weight during the installation.

The bell had been polished, rebalanced, fitted with a new clapper assembly, and tested for tone and stability. All repairs had now been finalized. All adjustments had been fine-tuned and all safety precautions had been followed.

Now… it was ready to return to its place.

He breathed a slow sigh of relief as a quiet wave of pride washed over him, everything moving so smoothly. He could finally take a short break and call the one person he knew would be just as excited as he was to see the bell going back up in the tower. *Kendra*. Besides, any excuse was a good excuse just to hear her voice.

He slipped his phone from his back pocket, the motion almost automatic. These days, being apart from her for even a few hours felt painfully long. He craved that warmth she carried… the way she had of calming him with just a few simple words.

He checked the time. Right about now, Kendra should be almost ready for her morning break. As he thumbed the screen awake, another thought rose up and deepened his smile. Maybe she was thinking about him too.

Sam tapped her name and lifted the phone to his ear… already grinning at the thought of hearing her voice. The line rang once… twice… then clicked softly.

"Hey you," Kendra answered, her voice warm in that way that always found him, no matter where he was.

His smile was instant. "Hey. You on break yet?"

"Just now stepping off the floor," she said. He could hear the familiar sounds of the hospital on her end, the faint voices over the public address system. The hurried squeaks of Crocs and sneakers against the floors, the diminishing soft beep of a monitor. "Everything OK over there?"

"Oh yeah," he said, glancing back at the tower with quiet pride. "More than OK, actually. We're right on schedule. The team's got the block-and-tackle rig tested, and we should be lifting the bell back into place around noon."

Sam heard a small gasp on the other end of the line… softly delighted, absolutely genuine

"Oh Sam… that's amazing. I wish I could see it."

That was exactly what he'd been hoping to hear.

"Well…" he drawled lightly, trying (and failing) to sound casual, "if you happen to get a little time around lunch… you could swing by. Just for a few minutes. If *you* want to see it."

Kendra laughed, and the sound of her voice reminded him just how much he wanted to be near her.

"Uh-huh. You mean if *I* want to… or if *you* want me to?"

He chuckled under his breath. "Maybe both."

She sighed warmly. "Send me a text when you're close to lifting. If I can slip away, I'll be there."

And just like that, the whole morning got brighter.

Sam ended the call with a lingering smile and slipped his phone back into his pocket as he walked toward the base of the bell tower. The restoration team was already adjusting the guide ropes and checking the tension on the main hoist line, their movements precise and well practiced. He walked over to the team lead for a quick update, asked a few clarifying questions, and gave a nod of approval as they confirmed each step of the lift sequence. Satisfied, he drew his tablet up again and resumed his checklist.

Sam nodded, scanning his tablet and marking off another line. "We'll run any remaining diagnostics once the final safety checks are done… then we can test the striker assembly."

Sam stepped back to exit the tower, giving the team room to make their final preparations for the lift. Ropes were being checked again, knots inspected, pulleys tested under light tension; small but critical steps before committing to the full hoist. The morning breeze met him as he moved onto the pathway leading to the parking lot, cool and refreshing, carrying faint scents of pine and sea salt drifting in from the harbor.

As he glanced across the grounds, he spotted Pastor Thompson walking toward him from the side entrance of the church, his pace unhurried but purposeful.

"Sam," Pastor Thompson called warmly.

Sam turned, straightening instinctively. "Morning, Pastor."

Pastor Thompson's gaze lifted to the bell, his expression softening. "I've been praying for this day. To see it back where it belongs…" He exhaled, almost reverently. "It's more than I can put into words. It's a real blessing, Sam… and your role in making this happen cannot be denied. You have truly been a blessing."

Sam followed his gaze for a moment. "Thank you, Pastor. She's in really good shape," he said quietly, touched by the pastor's words. "Better than she's been in decades. We repaired and saved everything we could, and everything else we replaced. What was failing has been reinforced and renewed, including the support beams. She's ready."

Pastor Thompson nodded, emotion flickering behind his eyes. "I can't thank you enough for your hard work… for your dedication. You've treated this as if it were your own calling."

Sam swallowed, unsure how to respond to something that sincere. "It means a lot to me, sir. This whole project… it's been my privilege."

"I'm grateful you're the one overseeing it," the pastor said gently. "You've honored its history… and its purpose."

For a moment they stood together, watching the bell where it rested on the platform—silent for now, but almost longing for Harmony Grove Harbor to hear its voice again.

Pastor Thompson offered a small smile. "When the time comes for its first ring… I hope you'll be the one to pull the rope."

Sam blinked, surprised. "Me?"

"After everything you've poured into this," Pastor Thompson said softly, "I can't think of anyone more fitting."

Sam lowered his gaze, humbled. "Thank you, Pastor. Truly."

Pastor Thompson lingered, his gaze still lifted toward the tower. "When are you all planning to raise her today?"

Sam glanced down at his tablet, then checked for the time. "In less than an hour. I asked the team lead to give me a signal when they're ready."

"Excellent," the pastor said, the excitement in his voice gentle but unmistakable.

Sam nodded, but his eyes drifted past the tower, toward the church parking lot almost without thinking. *He hoped she'd make it in time.* She'd sounded excited on the phone. And he wanted her here. Wanted her to share this moment with him.

Then he saw her.

Kendra was already walking the main pathway from the parking lot with a purposeful stride, her lightweight jacket catching the light breeze as she headed straight toward them. Even from a distance, Sam felt that familiar tug in his heart; the same one he felt every time she walked into a room.

"Speak of an angel," Pastor Thompson said softly with a warm smile of his own. When she was close enough, he stepped forward to greet her warmly.

Her face softened with familiar affection. "Pastor," she said, walking into a gentle embrace. He wrapped his arms around her with the ease of someone who had held her in prayer since she was a child. Then her eyes brightened as she took in the sight of the rigging and the tower. She slipped an arm around Sam, her hand resting for a heartbeat against his back.

"Hey," she said softly, her smile carrying everything they didn't have time to say.

"Hey," Sam replied, unable to hide how happy he was to see her.

Pastor Thompson noticed the ease and gentleness between them and smiled. "It's good to see you, dear," he said. "I'm glad you made it."

"I wouldn't miss this," she replied, glancing again at the resting bell.

Just then, the team lead walked out of the tower door and called over to Sam, "We're ready!"

Sam breathed in deeply… not from what was about to happen, but because the two people he cared deeply for were standing right there beside him as it happened.

"That's our signal," Sam said, glancing between Pastor Thompson and Kendra. "Let's go."

Together, they walked toward the tower entrance. The restoration crew moved with coordinated rhythm; hands on ropes, eyes on pulleys, each man taking his place. The block-and-tackle system creaked softly as tension settled into the main line.

"All right," the team lead called. "On my count… three… two… one… lift!"

The ropes tightened. The bell rose smoothly from the ground, guided by practiced hands on tag lines, its bronze surface catching the shifting light as it climbed. Higher… higher… until it cleared the tower opening. The workers eased the ropes, steadied by practiced hands on the tag lines

"Set it there… hold… hold… good." Bolts slid into place. Wrenches tightened. A final check. The team lead stepped back, satisfied.

"She's mounted."

Kendra exhaled softly, awe widening her eyes.

Pastor Thompson pressed his hands together as if in prayer and breathed softly, "Beautiful." The emotion in his eyes said the rest.

The team lead turned to them. "Well… someone's gotta ring this restored beauty for the first time. Who's it gonna be?"

Pastor smiled and immediately motioned toward Sam. "There's only one choice."

Sam's eyes widened. "Pastor… I…"

"Go on," Pastor said gently.

Kendra softly rubbed his back, her hand resting near the center in quiet, reassuring support, and followed it with an encouraging smile. "Go ahead. You deserve this."

Sam lowered his head in humility for a moment, then looked to Pastor Thompson for confirmation. When he smiled back, Sam lifted his gaze toward the bell and the sky. He wrapped his hand around the rope, took a deep breath, and pulled.

The bell rang out in a bright, resonant peal; clear, strong, and full of life. The sound filled the churchyard, bounced along Main Street, and carried straight toward the harbor. Kendra instinctively lifted her phone and snapped a photo, capturing a moment he'd never forget.

Pastor Thompson laughed softly, his eyes glistening. "Wonderful… absolutely wonderful."

Sam turned to the restoration crew, shaking each man's hand with genuine gratitude and thanking them for their hard work and committed dedication. The team accepted his appreciation with tired but satisfied smiles before gathering their tools and heading out of the tower.

Pastor Thompson reached the tower exit first, stepping out into the open air while Sam and Kendra followed just a few steps behind. As they crossed the threshold, Kendra reached for Sam with one hand, drawing a little closer as she leaned in and whispered warmly, "Congratulations, baby… I am so proud of you."

Sam stopped just long enough to look at her softly, dip, and give her a quick, full kiss on the lips before they fell back into step together behind Pastor Thompson.

As they followed the pathway leading toward the parking lot, daylight suddenly dimmed. Pastor Thompson slowed a little, feeling something rumbling before glancing toward the darkening sky.

A thick bank of clouds had begun rolling in from the west—dark, heavy, moving faster than seemed natural. But what caught his breath wasn't the oncoming stormfront itself… it was the light. Just above the church steeple, the last bit of sunlight broke through the advancing clouds in a soft, concentrated glow shining from behind the darkness, the exact way Charlene had described in her dream. A halo of brightness, brief and trembling, as though trying to hold its place in the sky.

Pastor Thompson's eyes widened.

"Dear God…" he whispered, voice barely audible. "Whatever Charlene saw… or thought she saw… it's here."

Kendra heard him and lifted her gaze. For a heartbeat, she saw it too… the light glaring through a narrowing gap in the clouds, glowing with a strange, haunting familiarity. As the clouds threatened to overtake it, the light shone all the brighter, leaving only its rim of brightness where the sun had shone moments before.

The wind sharpened, whipping across the parking lot.

Almost on cue, all three of their phones buzzed at once.

Severe Weather Alert: Strong storm approaching Harmony Grove Harbor. Take shelter.

Sam saw the expression on both their faces… not fear, but something deeper. Recognition. Awe. As if the two of them were seeing the same truth unfold right in front of them… something they had already known long before the clouds rolled in.

He didn't know the details yet, but he didn't need to.

"Come on," he said gently but firmly, placing a guiding hand at Kendra's back. "Let's get to the cars. Storm's closing in fast."

"I better get back home," Pastor said. "We may be in for a rough one."

Sam glanced back at the tower one more time… the echo of the bell still ringing. A flicker of worry stirred in him. After everything they'd done, he prayed the restored bell would stand strong, whatever was coming. The bell had endured more than weather. It had known a season of silence, years when its voice was not heard but not forgotten, when storms came and went without its sound to mark them. And yet it had been restored…lifted back into place not because the storms would stop coming, but because life endures through them. Sam wondered if that was what the bell was really meant for; not a promise of calm skies, but to keep ringing in spite of them.

The thought passed quickly before the first cold drop of rain touched his cheek.

Chapter 13

The Storm

The first cold drop of rain slid down Sam's cheek… colder than it should've been for even a late-season coastal storm. He stopped for half a second, looking up at the sky as the three of them approached the open stretch of the parking lot. The clouds had seemed to darken too fast… too soon… swirling and rolling in such a way that carried a strange, unearthly heaviness beneath them. And what unsettled him even more was the look he'd seen on Pastor Thompson's face, and on Kendra's. Those two were imperturbable in almost anything. If *they* sensed something coming and it unnerved them… it had to be serious.

Pastor Thompson reached his sedan first, opening the door just as the first wind gust swept across the church grounds, swaying and bending the trees with the intensity of it. Still no rain beyond the first intermittent drops … but it was coming.

He pulled his phone from his back pocket, and tapped Leah's number as he started the engine.

She answered on the second ring.

"Nathaniel?"

"I'm leaving now," he said softly. "Headed home."

She exhaled in relief, her voice warm and full of love. "Be safe… there's a storm brewing. I love you."

He smiled, even as a softer gust of wind brushed against the side of the car. "I love you too. See you shortly."

He ended the call and eased out of the parking space, turning toward Main Street. He noticed that a slight misty fog was drifting downward, threatening to swallow the visibility of the road ahead with each passing second.

The first bolt of lightning cracked overhead, turning Main Street Baptist Church into a flash of white and momentarily startling Sam and Kendra as they quickened their pace toward their vehicles.

The two of them had been walking hand in hand, but when Kendra subtly attempted to pull away to head toward her car, Sam held on, just firm enough to cause her to turn and face him. Neither of them seemed to care that the rain was now upon them.

"Hey… wait," he said, voice low, tense. "If this storm turns into what I think it will… based on what I just saw in your face and his back there…" He shifted his gaze to where Kendra's car was parked. She followed his eyes. "You are not getting in that car alone."

"Sam, I have to get back to the hospital," she argued, eyes sharp with concern and purpose. "You know that. They're probably already calling in extra staff."

Sam did not blink. "And I've got you covered."

He closed the small distance between them, his hand settling gently on her arm.

"You're staying with me. I'll get you there… wherever you need to go. But you're not leaving my sight. Not in this."

A stronger gust whipped around them, carrying the first hard spray of rain.

Kendra hesitated… then finally nodded. This was a side of Sam that she had not seen. Non-negotiable protection coupled with determination. But now wasn't the time to try to analyze it.

"Okay…" she said quietly and almost immediately. "Hey, Sam?"

"Yeah, baby," he replied, guiding her toward his truck.

"Thank you."

His smile returned. "Anytime."

He hurried around the truck and slid into the driver's side. "We'd better get moving. This storm is moving in fast."

Sam turned the key, and the engine faithfully purred to life. The windshield wipers started and almost immediately they struggled to keep up with the first descent of the storm and its deluge upon Harmony Grove Harbor.

Pastor Thompson eased onto Main Street, the storm gaining strength by the second. What had begun as scattered droplets was now falling sideways into thick, blinding sheets. It was the kind of rain that turned headlights into pale smudges and taillights into red glowing globes, erasing everything beyond them in a few feet. As intense as the storm was now, it had yet to pour out its full vengeance on Harmony Grove Harbor. It was almost as if the full power of an omnipotent God was being unleashed on the small town, His mercy on it, yet to be revealed.

He tightened his grip on the steering wheel, leaning forward slightly as the windshield wipers worked furiously, struggling to carve even a fleeting glimpse of the road in front of him. They failed. Miserably.

He turned up the radio, checking for any updates on the weather and road conditions, but all he could hear was the pounding rain and the blistering gusts of winds that howled all around him.

"*Lord, have mercy*!" he whispered, the prayer rising naturally, "*Wrap your hand of protection around us, dear Father.*"

He rounded a gentle bend; one that usually offered a clear stretch of road and distant marshland beyond. But today, nothing was clear. The rain thickened into a fog-like mist, a water curtain that swallowed every shape ahead in white-gray shimmer. The familiar road felt unreal, distorted, dissolved beneath the storm's fury.

Pastor Nathaniel Thompson took a right turn onto Coastal Highway 17, a scenic stretch of road that divided traffic moving in opposite directions. Unbeknownst to him, further up ahead, what would eventually become a forty-five-vehicle pileup was already setting itself into motion. An SUV, unfamiliar with the winding nature of the road, misjudged the sharp curve, swerved, and came around facing oncoming traffic. A heavily loaded trailer traveling too closely behind it had no chance of slowing in the deteriorating conditions. It slammed into the SUV and jack-knifed, the trailer violently folding across both lanes and blocking the entire flow of traffic on that side of the highway. By the time Pastor Thompson approached, fifteen other cars had already been pulled into the growing entangled mess.

Pastor Thompson did not realize he was seeing less than half mile ahead. By the time he saw the faint glow of motionless headlights and taillights, it was already too late. He braked hard, swerving to a jarring stop with only inches to spare from the wrecked vehicle in front of him. He had barely taken a breath before a small pickup truck plowed into him, jolting his car sideways and dislodging the dashboard enough to expose a jagged metal shard that tore deeply into the calf of his right leg. The airbag exploded against his chest in a violent burst, forcing the air from his lungs. He tried to cry out, but the pain stole his voice, leaving only a strained whimper.

Hard pellets of rain and hail beat against Sam's windshield like handfuls of thrown gravel. The wipers could barely keep up, allowing only a brief sliver of visibility between sweeps

Kendra reached for the dashboard with one hand, catching her breath as a wild gust of wind shoved the truck slightly sideways.

"This is getting worse," she managed, her voice tight.

Sam leaned forward, jaw set, both hands tightly gripping the wheel. "Yeah… way worse than it looked a few minutes ago."

They rode in tense silence for a few seconds, the storm swallowing the sound of the engine, the tires, even their own breathing. Lightning flashed again, followed by a deep thud of thunder so forceful that it seemed to rattle inside them.

Kendra jumped lightly. Sam reached across the console without taking his eyes off the road and placed his hand over her hand with such gentleness and assurance in his touch that she felt the release of the tension that was building in her.

"You okay?" he asked.

"Yeah, I'm good." She nodded, though her eyes stayed fixed on the rain-sheeted windshield. "Just… thinking about what's coming. The hospital will probably be assembling the response team for emergency preparedness by now."

"I know they'll be glad to see you walking through that door," Sam said quietly.

They turned onto Harbor Loop Road; the final stretch leading up to Harmony Grove Harbor Regional Hospital. The building came into view only as a muted silhouette through the wall of rain.

"Just drop me off at the ambulance bay. That will keep me out of the rain and hopefully the wind too."

"Kendra…" He eased the truck beneath the covered entrance and finally stopped. Once the wind and rain weakened under the shelter, he slipped the truck out of gear but left the engine running.

"Once you're inside… don't worry about me, okay? Just do what you do."

She looked at him… really looked. Then she wrapped her arms around his neck, pulling him close. Her cheek brushed lightly against his, a warmth passing between them, rebuking the chill of the angry storm, and she placed a soft kiss near his ear. Another flash of lightning burst across the sky, sending exaggerated shadows through the cab.

"Sam… please be careful. This storm isn't like anything I've ever seen here."

He held her tighter… just for a few seconds more. His throat tightened as he swallowed. "I will. I promise."

“Hey, don’t try to pick me up after my shift is over, okay? I don’t want you back out in this. I’ll see if I can get one of those new sleep cocoons. I hear they’re pretty comfortable.”

“Well… okay. I guess it’s going to be a long night for you anyway,” he whispered.

Slowly, reluctantly, they eased out of their embrace, holding each other’s hands for a moment before finally letting go.

“I’ll walk you to the door,” he said softly.

“Sam…” she began, but he was already opening his door and running around to the passenger side of the truck before she could finish.

He rounded the front of the truck, rain slanting sideways across his jacket, and opened the passenger door for her. The wind pushed against them, but his grip was strong and firm; guiding her down from the seat. She landed close enough that he could draw her into one last brief embrace, landing a tender kiss to her forehead.

They were close enough to the entrance doors that they opened automatically for her. She touched his arm once more, and slipped between them, looking back once more to wave and blow a gentle kiss to him.

Sam stood there long enough to see her disappear beyond the reception desk, but not before he noticed the receptionist tilt her head with a twinkly-eyed nostalgic smile.

Sam shook his head, chuckled and thought to himself, “*Everybody loves a good love story, I guess*”.

He went back out into the storm, the wind immediately grabbing at his jacket as he climbed into the truck. He tugged the door shut hard against the gusts, shifted into gear, and eased toward the road again… the storm waiting for him like a hungry lioness poised to pounce on her prey.

Once back inside the ER, Kendra was immediately met by the bustle of nurses and staff. The emergency preparedness team was already assembled and in place, ready for incoming casualties. The storm howled outside, and unknown to her, a night much like one from her past…one that still haunted her…was already unfolding.

Charlene pushed the privacy curtain aside and eased out from the small exam bay, jotting a quick note on her tablet. Behind her, the older gentleman she'd just treated, the one who insisted he was "*fine enough to walk it off*" despite a clearly fractured ankle, was finally settled and resting while awaiting imaging.

The wind rattled against the ER windows again, a low groan of protest that seemed to echo through every hallway.

For the moment, though, the unit was strangely quiet.

Kendra sat perched on the edge of the nurses' station, elbows resting on the counter as she scrolled through patient charts. Allison wheeled over in her chair, sipping from a cup of lukewarm coffee and eyeing the weather on the small television mounted in the corner.

Charlene joined them, letting out a soft breath. "Alright… one slip-and-fall ankle fracture down. Hopefully that's the last storm-related mishap tonight."

Kendra glanced up with a faint smile. "Wishful thinking."

Charlene leaned closer, her voice dropping into a casual tone, though her eyes held a hint of something more serious. "Hey, Kendra… you heard about that multi-vehicle accident out on Highway 17?"

Kendra's eyes widened, a sudden awareness sparking in them.

"That's the road Pastor Thompson takes home," she said quietly. "I… I hope he made it home okay."

Allison swiveled her chair toward them, clearly unable to resist sharing the latest. "They're routing the most critical trauma cases here because of our trauma center," she announced, lowering her voice as though passing secret intel. "The others are being diverted to St. Mary's Regional over on the east side."

Kendra nodded slowly, her gaze drifting.

Allison continued, "But EMS is having a hard time getting to the injured. The whole scene's a mess; tangled vehicles, trapped folks, rain blowing sideways, debris everywhere. They're fighting the storm just to reach people."

The three nurses exchanged a look; a familiar one they'd shared too many times; one that spoke without saying a word.

Quiet now. But the storm was about to deliver its first victims.

Allison stood, setting her coffee aside. "I'm gonna get on the list for one of those sleep cocoons before the wave hits. I'll get you all setup too. We're all going to be here for a while." She hurried off toward the nurses' recharge area.

That left Kendra and Charlene alone at the nurses' station.

Charlene rested her elbows beside Kendra, speaking gently. "You've got that look."

Kendra hesitated. "Char… does this storm feel anything like your dream?"

Charlene's eyes softened; a calm, knowing look. "Yeah. It does. Actually… I've been sensing something all day. What had me panicked and frightened before doesn't feel that way now. I do believe that God is about to show me something. I can't say that I understand it all, but I trust Him, and I trust His will. And that gives me an enormous sense of peace. The same God that brought us back safely from over there, is more than able to take care of us over here. So I'm good."

Kendra studied her friend for a minute; unable to ignore how unusually calm Charlene seemed. Charlene was never one that would be called out for lack of confidence, or self-assurance, but this was different. This calm came from a much deeper place. A place Kendra knew too well. A place that only God alone could reach.

"You seem so peaceful in all this. It's… kind of remarkable."

That familiar twinkle in Charlene's eyes returned. "When God tells you something's coming, He also gives you the peace to face it and the strength to go through it."

Kendra nodded in agreement, and then asked Charlene something that she hadn't planned to ask.

"When I was leaving the church today, I noticed Pastor Thompson looking up at the sky when the storm was just starting to roll in. He had a really strange look on his face, so I looked up too. There was this light… right in the center of the rolling clouds. And even when the clouds tried to overtake it, you could still see the light glowing through. Does that mean anything to you?"

Charlene tilted her head slightly. "Yes, it does."

"And the way it stayed there; it reminded me of what you described from your dream."

Charlene spoke softly, "Honestly, Kendra, I don't know or fully understand what the light means. At least not yet, but…"

A sharp gust of wind slammed against the ER windows, followed by a blinding fork of lightning that flashed the entire hallway in stark white. An instant later, thunder cracked so hard it vibrated through the floor tiles.

Charlene and Kendra were still seated at the nurses' station when they noticed the dispatcher suddenly lean forward, her eyes locking onto her monitor.

On the large screen above her console, a bold red banner flashed across the EMS intake dashboard:

Multi-Casualty Alert – Highway 17

The red indicator pulsed sharply, catching Kendra's and Charlene's attention.

Before the first casualty arrived, they slipped into a quiet alcove and made quick calls home, letting their families know the ER was bracing for an influx of patients and that they would be staying overnight. It was a small courtesy… one meant to spare unnecessary worry, especially with the storm raging and reports already spreading across town.

When they arrived back at the nurses' station, Allison returned, brushing crumbs off the front of her scrubs from whatever snack she'd inhaled on the way.

"Hey, so I got us the sleep cocoons, but they were out of those vanilla protein bars, and so…"

Her words stopped mid-sentence.

All three of their digital alert pagers buzzed simultaneously. Charlene grabbed her pager first and read through the scrolling message.

Trauma alert – multiple incoming

Est. Arrival: Immediate

Severe trauma injuries reported

"Party's over ladies, time to get to work."

Allison's face sobered instantly. "Well… there it is."

Before anyone could respond, the ER doors burst open.

Paramedics rushed in with the first stretcher; soaked, breathless, shouting vitals as they pushed forward, the storm snarling behind them like it was trying to shove its way inside.

Kendra and Charlene exchanged a look; that silent, determined, resilient, battle-forged look.

We're ready.

And just like that—the storm outside had found its way in.

The automatic doors burst open again as paramedics rushed in with another stretcher. A man in his mid-forties lay pale and trembling, his shirt soaked through with dark, spreading blood. His breaths were shallow… ragged.

"He was pinned under the wreckage of an SUV," one of the paramedics shouted as they pushed forward. "Crushed pelvis—possible internal bleed. Vitals unstable!"

Nurse Amanda Billingsley was already there, jogging alongside the gurney as it barreled through the corridor. Her eyes swept over him in a single practiced motion—skin ashen, pulse thready beneath her fingertips, abdomen distended, blood pressure tanking.

Her voice sharpened instantly.

"Let's go! He bypasses imaging; straight to OR!" she commanded, raising her arm to motion the trauma doors open. "Call Trauma Red! Now!"

A resident darted toward the phone. Another nurse grabbed the IV bag and jogged to keep pace.

The paramedics hurried after Amanda as she steered the gurney toward the surgical wing.

"Keep pressure on that pelvic binder!" she barked. "If he crashes, I want blood ready before we hit the doors!"

The stretcher disappeared with her down the hallway, the storm's rage echoing faintly behind them as the ER swallowed its next crisis.

The next hours were relentless.

The trauma bay flooded with movement; stretchers rolling in rapid succession, doctors calling for scans, nurses spiking IV bags, a surgeon snapping for vitals over the roar of the storm outside.

A woman in her thirties arrived pale and barely conscious, having lost a dangerous amount of blood in what felt like mere seconds. Her vitals plummeted twice. The surgeon bent over her, whispering more than once that she might not survive long enough to reach the OR.

Kendra hurried from one patient to the next, her pulse racing with the pace of the chaos. But even in the blur, she paused for the briefest breath.. one heartbeat of stillness amid the storm, and prayed under it, the words rising like instinct.

Lord, preserve the lives of these people. Please guide my hands, the doctors' hands, and every decision made in this place. I pray for Your healing over every person we touch tonight.

Then she moved again, the storm finally at its peak and pressing in from all sides.

Chapter 14

In the Shelter of His Arms

The automatic doors slid open again, this time slower… almost forced by the wind. Allison glanced up from the medication cart she was restocking. After hours of battling grueling, life-threatening trauma injuries amid the brutal storm, she was hoping for a minor injury… or someone stable enough for fast-track. But the stretcher pushed through the entrance was anything but routine.

Two paramedics fought the gale behind them, rain dripping from their faces and caps as they maneuvered the gurney inside. The man lying on it was drenched, his clothes soaked with rain and streaked with blood. His skin was ashen… too ashcn. An oxygen mask covered his face, fogging faintly with each strained breath.

"Male, sixties," one paramedic called out, voice tight. "Severe lower-extremity trauma, suspected internal bleeding. He coded once en route, but we got him back. BP's crashing… again."

"All available hands, Trauma Red!" an ER nurse called out over the din.

Allison hurried over, reaching for gloves. She didn't see a face… only injuries. Training narrowed her focus long before recognition could catch up.

"Let's get him to Bay Three. What's his name?"

The paramedic scrolled through the tablet and hesitated for half a heartbeat… just long enough for Allison's stomach to drop.

"It's… Nathaniel Thompson."

The world seemed to tilt sideways for a moment, but training had prepared her. She moved decisively, assessing his injuries as they walked.

"Notify OR…we're incoming!" she shouted toward the nearest nurse. "The trauma surgeon should already be prepped. Clear the hallway…we need a path now!"

A second nurse sprinted ahead to alert the surgical team.

The ER doctor appeared from around the corner, snapping on gloves as he moved. "What've we got?"

"Severe trauma, unstable vitals," the paramedic replied. "He's crashing."

The doctor nodded once and came alongside the gurney. "Let's move. Keep that airway sealed. Allison, tighten that dressing."

She pressed down firmly, feeling the warm surge of blood fighting the bandage. Too much… far too much.

"He's losing pressure again."

"Then we keep him alive until OR takes over," the doctor said, already adjusting the oxygen mask and checking the pulse.

They pushed the gurney forward, wheels splashing through streaks of rainwater on the tile. Nurses hurried ahead, pulling carts aside, holding doors open, clearing the path with practiced urgency.

"Hang another unit of O-negative!" the doctor called out.

"I'm on it," Allison said, spiking the bag and connecting the tubing as they walked.

A faint groan escaped Pastor Thompson's mask.

Allison leaned close. "We're right here with you… just hold on."

The monitors beeped in erratic, unstable bursts. Thunder boomed overhead, rattling the corridor lights.

"Let's go," the doctor urged. "OR's ready for him."

They rounded the final corner. The double doors to surgery were propped open, sterile light spilling into the hallway. Two surgical nurses stood waiting.

"This way!" one of them called out.

They accelerated toward the doors.

"He's critical," the doctor said as they rolled him through. "They need to take him now."

They burst through the double doors into the bright, sterile light of the operating suite. The OR team was already waiting…masked, gowned, gloved…the room alive with controlled, deliberate urgency.

"Bring him straight to the table," one of the surgical nurses instructed.

The ER doctor moved alongside the gurney, giving the rapid handoff as they pushed him in.

"Male, early sixties. Severe lower-extremity trauma with suspected internal bleeding. Coded once in the field. BP unstable in the sixties. Two units O-neg infused. Dressing applied, but bleeding's still heavy. Airway supported."

"Copy," the trauma surgeon said, already assessing the leg. "Let's move him over."

Hands lifted, guided, slid him from the ER gurney to the OR table in one practiced motion.

"Anesthesia, take airway," the surgeon said.

"Got it," came the response.

The monitors beeped sharply as new leads were connected.

Allison stepped back, chest tightening, watching as the OR team formed a circle around him… calm, focused, intentional.

"Alright," the surgeon said quietly, almost to himself. "Let's save this man's life."

The OR nurse saw Allison's expression, then touched her arm lightly. "We've got it from here. We'll take good care of him."

Allison nodded, swallowed hard, and backed out through the doors as they swung shut behind her.

Allison took the stairs down from the surgical wing. She had no time for elevators right now. She tried to focus on calming her breathing and exhaled heavily and took in one shaky breath.

Please... God... let him live.

She rounded the final corner toward the ER waiting area, rehearsing in her mind how she would break the news to Kendra and Charlene. How could she prepare them for this, and how would she comfort and reassure them; all while keeping herself and her voice calm?

She looked straight ahead and stopped dead in her tracks.

They were all already there; Charlene, Kendra, Leah Thompson, and even Raymond Carter.

Allison cautiously approached the group, fearing that words would fail her.

Kendra and Charlene looked physically drained, still dressed in their scrubs, their badges hanging loosely from their necks. They had just finished a grueling twelve-hour shift, yet neither had been willing to leave Leah alone tonight.

Charlene stood behind Leah; sometimes pacing, then stopping, then pacing again… her breaths shallow, her fingers flicking in erratic motions, almost as if typing on an invisible keyboard.

Kendra sat beside Leah; arms folded, rocking back and forth, shoulders tight, as if holding herself together by sheer force. Her face was stoic, her shoulders tight and her gaze fixed. There were no tears… only the heaviness of trying to hold herself together.

Standing next to Charlene was Raymond Carter. His presence was quiet and calming tonight. He had stood in the gap for Leah Thompson, knowing that Leah needed to be at the hospital *no matter what*, and he was one of the few people with a vehicle capable of getting her there safely. He still appeared damp from the storm, his raincoat carelessly draped over an unoccupied chair, dripping onto the tile.

Leah Thompson sat rigidly at the center of them in one of the high-back padded chairs. She appeared calm, her hands gently folded in her lap, but her eyes gave her away. They shimmered with the mist of many tears… and yet, even now, she greeted Allison the moment she recognized her.

"Hello, Allison," Leah said softly. "They told me you went up with Nathaniel to surgery. Do you have any news on how he's doing?"

Allison swallowed hard. She had dreaded giving them the news… but their presence told her they already understood the seriousness of his injuries.

Kendra looked up first. Their eyes met.

"Allison…" Kendra whispered. "Is he…?"

Allison began, drawing closer to the group. "He's in surgery. That's all I know right now."

Leah caught her breath, then whispered, *"Please, Lord... don't take him right now... not yet."*

Allison continued softly. "He has one of the best surgical teams working on him. It's very serious… but with God's help—" She paused.

Charlene closed her eyes, tears falling freely.

Leah bowed her head into her hands.

Kendra's breath left her in a broken exhale.

Raymond placed a gentle hand on Leah's shoulder, offering quiet strength, and reassurance.

Allison nodded, reassuring but honest. "They're doing everything they can. He's strong, and he's fighting."

Kendra drew in a slow breath and glanced toward Charlene, her voice just above a whisper. "Maybe… maybe we should all go to the chapel for a moment. It's quieter there, and we need to pray. He needs our prayers, and Sister Thompson does too. And to be honest… I need prayer too."

Charlene's eyes softened at the sound of Kendra's voice. It was faint, almost fragile; a tone she had rarely heard from her friend. Kendra wasn't known for falling apart, but something in her eyes looked different: strained, weary; bearing the weight of too many emotional layers over too many hours. Charlene shifted her gaze quickly, not wanting to be too obvious in her concern for Kendra. She bowed her head just long enough to whisper a quick prayer.

"*Lord, I really need You now. Bless us with Your divine strength to help us all make it through this. Amen.*"

Lifting her head again, Charlene mock-ironed her scrub top with one hand, swallowed, and stood a little straighter.

"Yeah," she said gently. "That's exactly where we need to be in a time like this."

Leah looked up at them through tired eyes, grateful for their care and support.

Charlene reached for Leah's hand, offering gentle support as she and Kendra helped her to her feet. Together, the small group began making their way down the quiet hallway toward the chapel.

Allison stayed behind. She watched them go, wishing she could be with them but knowing she still had responsibilities in the ER. She drew in a measured breath, composed herself, and turned back toward the nurses' station.

Outside, the storm pressed against the windows… but something in its rhythm had begun to weaken. The violent gusts softened, as though the wind was finally tiring. The pounding rain eased from sheets to steady drops. A distant rumble of thunder rolled away instead of toward them. The storm was passing. Finally.

A few minutes away, Sam paced nervously in front of his parents' living-room window, watching as the storm slowly lost its fury. Thunder no longer shook the house, and the rain had thinned into a restless drizzle sliding down the glass.

The phone call from Raymond had come over an hour ago and it was still replaying in the back of his mind. "*Hey man, there's been a serious accident on Highway 17. Pastor has been injured and it's bad, but he's en route to Harmony Grove Harbor Regional ER now. I'm on my way to pick up Sister Thompson now to take her to the hospital. I'll be spending the night at the hospital with her tonight. You know she's always been like a second mom to me. Later, I'll hit you back when I know more.*"

A short message had followed not long after. *Allison took Pastor Thompson straight into surgery.*

The urgency in Raymond's voice had left Sam on edge. His concern for Leah and Pastor Thompson pressed heavily on him… but his thoughts kept circling back to Kendra. She had been at that hospital since the crack of dawn. He knew she was strong; stronger than most, but he also knew there were places inside her still raw, still healing. Ever since she'd shared that painful memory from overseas; that night of overwhelming casualties, he understood her limits in a way he would never have before. And tonight… this storm, this tragedy… it was far too close to that.

If she needed him, and he felt in his gut that she would, he intended to be there for her. No excuses. No hesitation. Just present.

His mother, watching him from the kitchen with a mother's eye, dried her hands with a kitchen towel, walked closer to her son, and gently placed a hand on his shoulders to reassure him.

"Honey… is there any update on Pastor Thompson?"

Sam shook his head. "Not yet. Raymond said Allison took him straight up to surgery. I don't know any more than that."

He exhaled slowly, watching the last streaks of rain slide down the windowpane, his jaw tightening. "I'm really worried about him… about Sister Thompson too."

He hesitated, then added quietly, "But.. I just have this feeling that Kendra is going to need me, and I know I need to be there."

His father rose from his recliner, rubbing a hand over his jaw as he studied him. "Son… are you sure the roads are safe enough?"

"Well the storm is easing up, and as long as the roads are passable, should be good to go." Sam replied quietly. "It's been over an hour, and I haven't heard back from Raymond. Nothing from her in a while either. That ER and trauma center must be overwhelmed."

Both parents exchanged a look; not quite approval, not quite resistance; more an understanding born from years of watching Sam protect his heart, fiercely. But now, he was finally opening it again, and for that, they were grateful.

"Be careful," his father said. "That's all we ask."

"I will," Sam promised.

He kissed his mom goodbye and hugged his dad. Then he grabbed his jacket and keys and headed for the door… pausing for one last glance at the weakening storm. It only confirmed what he already knew deep inside himself. He was going… to Kendra.

A soft knock sounded at the chapel door before it opened quietly. Deacon Eric Bennett walked inside, his damp coat draped over his shoulder. Behind him came Deacon Morris and Deacon Ellis, followed by two longtime church members who lived only a few streets from the hospital. The storm had eased just enough for them to make their way here, and none of them had wanted Leah to be alone on this night.

They slipped into the back row without a word, bowing their heads as the small chapel filled with the gentle murmur of whispered prayer.

Leah looked over her shoulder and managed a grateful smile.

"Thank you for coming," she whispered.

"We wouldn't be anywhere else," Deacon Bennett replied quietly. "We're here for you and Pastor, Sister Thompson."

The chapel was dimly lit and quiet, lit only by a single lamp near the small wooden podium. A row of flameless candles glowed along the platform, their warm halos settling over the room like a whisper of peace. Leah, Charlene, and Kendra sat close together in the front row; Leah in the center, Kendra and Charlene on either side, and Raymond just behind them, standing watch like a silent guard.

Leah held her small, worn Bible open in her hands. Her voice trembled, but the words carried borrowed strength.

> "*I will lift up mine eyes unto the hills, from whence cometh my help.*" she read softly.
>
> *"My help cometh from the Lord, which made heaven and earth."*

A fragile peace began to settle over them, but only for a heartbeat.

Before Leah could continue, Kendra abruptly rose from her seat, pressing a hand over her mouth as she rushed out of the chapel.

Charlene was immediately on her feet, hurrying after her.

She found her just outside the door, bracing herself against the wall, breathing hard… eyes closed and face pointed slightly upward, but not crying, not speaking… Her expression was tight and her lips were trembling.

"Kendra… hey," Charlene said gently, touching her arm. "Talk to me. Girl, you scared me."

Kendra shook her head. "I'm okay… I just… I just needed air. I'm fine." Her voice wavered too much for the words to land.

Charlene studied her friend, seeing everything Kendra was fighting so hard to hide: exhaustion, fear, haunting memories… the strain of being strong for everyone but herself.

"Girl," Charlene said softly, leaning in with a faint smile, "uh, you mean fine as in on a billboard selling perfume?"

Kendra let out a tiny, helpless genuine laugh… and that alone told Charlene how close the edge really was.

"Seriously, are you *sure* you're alright?" Charlene asked quietly.

Kendra shook her head and her eyes shimmered but no tears fell. "I just… I need a moment. You go ahead. Check for an update on Pastor Thompson. Please. I'll go back in a minute"

Charlene hesitated, but Kendra gave her a small, brave nod.

"Okay," Charlene whispered. "But I'll be right back."

As she headed toward the ER, her already had her phone in her hand. Sam answered before she even heard the first ring after tapping on his name.

"Charlene?"

"Sam—"

"I'm already on my way," he said immediately. "I know why you're calling. It's Kendra, isn't it?"

Charlene exhaled shakily. "Yeah… she's trying to hang in there, Sam. She's trying really hard. But I think… this is just too much… this whole night is just too much."

"I hear you," Sam said quietly. "Hold down the fort till I get there. You know that's my girl."

Charlene's lips curved with a tired smile. "Yeah… I know."

She ended the call just as she reached the ER waiting area. The overhead lights were dimmer now, the storm's fading rumble only a distant echo against the windows.

Charlene approached the desk just as a nurse glanced up. "Nathaniel Thompson. I'm checking for his wife, Leah Thompson. Is there any update?" Charlene asked softly.

The nurse shook her head. "Oh yes, I remember seeing ya'll with Mrs. Thompson earlier this evening. Pastor Thompson is still in surgery. It's been about two hours. He's still listed as critical."

Charlene closed her eyes for a moment, whispering under her breath, "Lord… have mercy, please."

The ER doors slid open with a tired, mechanical groan as Sam burst through them, rain still clinging to his jacket and jeans. He wasn't just damp… he was drenched, breathless, chest rising and falling in sharp, uneven pulls from sprinting across the parking lot.

He scanned the waiting area quickly—almost wildly—until his eyes landed on Charlene at the nurses' station. She had just started to walk away, headed toward the chapel to give the update on Pastor Thompson.

"Charlene!" he called as softly as he could, his voice edged with urgency.

She turned, startled, but then her expression softened as soon as she recognized the familiar voice and face.

"Sam… geez, you got here so quickly. I'm sure it's a mess out there. But thank God you are here."

He reached her in three long strides, bracing a hand on the counter as he tried to catch his breath. "I… was already on my way when you called. Coming from my folks' house. They're literally five minutes away." He swallowed hard. "Pastor Thompson… is there any update?"

Charlene shook her head, her voice gentle. "Still in surgery. Still critical. It's been over two hours now."

Sam exhaled slowly, rubbing the back of his neck, eyes lowering for just a moment as he absorbed the weight of that answer.

"Okay… okay." He nodded once, trying to control himself. "And Kendra? How's she doing, and where can I find her?"

Charlene glanced toward the atrium and main hallway she had come from earlier, her expression shifting into something out of concern.

"She's just not herself right now, Sam, but she's trying to be, she said quietly. "I think between the long shift today, the back-to-back trauma cases, and Pastor Thompson's injuries, I'm afraid she may be on overload. I was just headed back to the chapel. She had just stepped outside of it when I last saw her. I'll walk with you over there."

Understanding Sam's urgency, Charlene quickened her pace through the ER and past its entry door, then headed in the direction of the atrium and the main hallway that led to the chapel. When they got to the chapel, they both peeked in, opening the doors as quietly as possible.

No Kendra.

They closed the chapel doors carefully. "She stepped out of the chapel for air," Charlene said. "She won't go far because she's waiting on an update for Pastor. She probably found somewhere quieter."

Sam nodded quickly. "I'll find her." Then he paused, touching Charlene's shoulder lightly. "Can you update Leah? Let her know I'm here?"

"Of course," she said with a tired smile. "Go. Kendra needs you."

Sam turned almost immediately and jogged the short sprint back toward the central corridor and atrium, his shoes squeaking against the polished tile. His heart beat hard against his ribs, not having had a chance to fully rest from his sprint to the ER. When he rounded the corner into the hospital atrium, he spun around looking for any sign of her.

And he found her… in the quietest, dimmest-lit corner of the atrium, facing the floor-to-ceiling window with one hand pressed against it.

Sam slowed his pace, approaching as quietly as he could, trying his best to neither startle or frighten her. When he thought he was close enough for her to hear his voice, he wrapped both arms around her and pressed his face into her hair for a moment… then turned just enough for his lips to reach her ear.

"I'm here, Kendra."

She heard him.

But before she could speak, lightning flashed for the last time, casting a muted grayish-blue hue over them both in the window. A steady, almost solemn soft patter of rain followed, and the thunder's reply was so distant that their breaths could be heard above it.

She did not turn to face him, but she leaned on him. Really leaned on him. Still facing the glass, staring at their reflections, she whispered, "Sam…"

And just like that, the last thread holding her together broke.

She turned to face him, but her knees buckled, and he felt her full weight collapse against him. Instinctively, he lifted her and carried her to a nearby bench beside the window. He positioned himself across the bench to set her down, and she wrapped her arms around him and let her head rest against him. She did not sob. She did not speak, and for what seemed like an eternity, she did not look at him.

Only when he saw Charlene approaching did he release his hold on her just long enough to raise a hand towards her in gentle, protective authority… asking for a moment alone… in stillness and quiet. He drew closer to her and thought to himself, but did not speak... "*I will hold you all night if that is what it takes.*"

And then, quietly… desperately… he prayed.

Lord... I don't know what to do. I can't fix this. But You can. Please... hold her where I can't.

Give her your peace

Lord... please have mercy on us.

And Sam continued to hold her as though the world itself depended on it. Kendra stayed close against him, her breath trembling with each exhale. He didn't rush her… didn't ask her to move or speak. He offered himself as a quiet shelter. And then he began to take longer, deeper breaths to guide her breathing back to normal, all the while shielding her from everything the night had demanded.

Slowly her breathing began to calm. He felt the tension in her shoulders ease just as the tremors settled into stillness. He wasn't sure how long they held on to each other, but finally, she drew in a longer calmer breath and lifted her head slightly… just enough to meet his eyes.

"I… I didn't know you were coming," she whispered, her voice thin but not faltering.

"I know," Sam smiled softly, brushing what he thought was a tear from her face. "But I just couldn't stay away. I felt like I needed to be here… for you… so I came back as soon as I could."

She closed her eyes again… not in weakness, but in relief.

"I just needed a minute," she said softly. "I was trying to hold it together, but I felt myself losing that battle… and I didn't want to do that… not in front of everyone. It just felt like everything came crashing down on me all at once."

Sam shook his head slightly as he gently lifted her chin, guiding her face up to meet his for the briefest moment. "Kendra… you don't have to be strong every second. Not with me."

Just then, Sam felt his phone buzz in his back pocket. He saw that he had a new text and tapped the phone to read it. "It's from Charlene," he said.

Sam read the text to Kendra. *"Didn't want to disturb you. Pastor is out of surgery. He will spend the night in ICU. Still critical."*

Sam slipped the phone away. "Come on," Sam said quietly, easing out of the position he'd been holding on the bench and releasing her just long enough to stand. He helped her to her feet, keeping an arm around her as they began to walk. "Let's go check on everyone… and wait together."

She nodded, leaning into him just enough to feel steadied but not enough to seem fragile. That balance came naturally for them; a quiet strength shared without needing words.

Sam and Kendra approached the chapel slowly, their steps hushed in the dim hallway. Just ahead, and moving toward them, a surgeon in blue scrubs with his mask hanging loose walked beside Nurse Daniels, her clipboard held close, her expression serious but softened by compassion..

"They must be headed to the chapel," Kendra whispered.

Sam nodded. "Looks like it."

When he reached the chapel, Sam opened the door and held it as the surgeon and Nurse Daniels passed ahead of them. With his other hand, he kept his hold on Kendra. He paused just long enough to give her space to gather herself and draw in a slow breath. Then, together, they walked inside.

The chapel was still dimly lit with an atmosphere of peacefulness; the flameless candles still casting warm halos across the room. Sam noticed as he entered the room that several deacons and church members appeared to have dozed off in their seats: Some were visibly nodding and one man's Bible still propped open on his lap, another leaning slightly to the side with a soft snore escaping. The soft rustle of Nurse Daniels' and the surgeon's scrubs broke the silence and stillness just enough to stir the room into a disjointed ripple of startled awareness.

Sam leaned toward Kendra with a whisper that wasn't nearly as quiet as he thought he was. "These jokers are worse than Jesus' disciples in the Garden of Gethsemane."

Kendra gave him a small, tired elbow to the ribs, her lips tipping into the faintest almost-smile. Together, they continued making their way toward Leah, Charlene, and Raymond at the front of the chapel.

Up front, Leah had already started to rise to her feet, feeling the need to stretch her legs after sitting so long. She held onto her small, worn Bible to the center of her with both hands.

The surgeon moved toward her with a gentle nod. "Mrs. Thompson?"

"Yes," Leah replied softly.

"I'm Dr. Michael Greene, the trauma surgeon who operated on your husband," he said. "I wanted to come down personally and give you an update."

"Thank you," Leah whispered. "How is he doing?"

Dr. Greene exhaled with the kind of compassion that came from hours of fighting for someone's life.

"He has done better than we initially expected," he said. "Your husband is a strong man. He survived the surgery, and he is breathing on his own."

A noticeable wave of relief spread through the room; quiet amens, a soft exhale, a hand pressed to a chest.

"We did find internal injuries," Dr. Greene continued calmly. "There was bleeding in the abdominal cavity. We cleared the blood and repaired the sources of bleeding. The damage was significant, and his condition is still critical, but the surgery addressed the immediate threats. The next several hours will be very important. We'll be monitoring him closely for any complications, and we'll reassess him in the morning."

He paused, letting that sink in before continuing with the harder part.

"The most severe injury was to his lower left leg," he said. "There was significant trauma and a substantial loss of blood to the limb. We repaired the damaged vessels and soft tissue, and right now the leg is perfusing. That's a positive sign. But we'll be monitoring circulation closely over the next several hours. We've done everything we could to save the leg."

Leah's breath shuddered, "Oh my Lord", but she remained calm, her focus fixed on every word the surgeon was saying.

"I wish I could tell you he's out of the woods," Dr. Greene said gently, "but I will not give you false hope. He is still critical. The fact that he made it through surgery is very encouraging. It tells me he's fighting."

The quiet in the room deepened. Some of the parishioners exchanged quick glances; not fearful, but reverent.

Dr. Greene looked around the chapel, taking in the faces of the small gathering; family and close friends who had come together in prayer and support for the beloved man of God… and for Leah.

"And I think," he said softly, "I feel safe in saying to you folks here tonight…well, this morning, now, I suppose… that we, as doctors, have gone as far as we can for him now."

He bowed his head slightly.

"The rest," he said, "is in God's hands."

The response generated a gentle wave of whispered *amens;* some heads nodding in acknowledgement, some lips whispering more prayers, others from focused eyes misty with tears.

Leah pressed a hand to her heart. "Thank You, Lord," she breathed.

Dr. Greene gave a respectful nod. "He's being transferred to ICU now. Mrs. Thompson, you'll allowed to be with him tonight. If you need anything, please let our nursing staff know. They will be happy to accommodate you."

Leah's eyes filled. "Thank you… thank you so much."

"We'll be monitoring him closely through the night." Dr. Greene turned his gaze to Raymond, who had maintained his vigil for the entire evening. "If there are any changes, you'll be notified immediately."

With that, he offered the room a final nod and slipped out as quietly as he'd entered.

Nurse Daniels spoke to Kendra and Charlene next, her sharp professionalism softened by something unusually tender.

"Kendra. Charlene," she said, addressing them directly.

Both women instinctively straightened.

"Yes ma'am," Kendra said.

"I'm glad you're both here," Nurse Daniels continued. "I wanted to tell you this face to face. You've been here all day,… and most of the night… and now into the morning. You've both done outstanding work. But I need you at your best."

She studied them with a look that was firm, yet caring.

"You will *not* be at your best in a few hours if you try to push through without rest," she said. "So I'm ordering both of you to take the next couple of days off… Longer if needed."

Charlene blinked. "A couple of days?"

"Yes," Nurse Daniels repeated. "At least. The unit is covered. The ER and ICU are staffed. You've done more than enough for one day."

Kendra let out a slow breath, humbled and relieved all at once. "Thank you, Nurse Daniels."

A small nod. "Good."

Then Nurse Daniels turned to Leah.

"Mrs. Thompson," she said, her tone gentling even more, "your husband has made quite an impression upstairs. The staff can't stop talking about him since they learned who he is.

Leah smiled faintly. "That sounds like Nathaniel."

Nurse Daniels hesitated, glancing around at the chapel… at the candles, the praying hands, the open bible, the quiet reverence.

"You know," she said slowly, "I don't have a church home here. Haven't in a long time. I guess it just hasn't been my thing"

The deacons looked up, listening.

"But if this Nathaniel Thompson is half the man my post-op staff says he is…" she continued, her voice nearly warm, "then I'm going to have to give church another serious look."

A ripple of soft laughter and gentle amens passed through the chapel.

Leah reached for her hand. "You will always be welcome," she said. "Anytime."

Nurse Daniels gave a small nod, tucked her clipboard against her chest, and stepped back.

"Get some rest," she said to Kendra and Charlene. "That's an order."

"Yes ma'am," they answered together.

Sam's fingers threaded naturally through Kendra's, their clasped hands a silent testimony of the connection between them; a quiet anchor in a night that was not quite yet over.

Nurse Daniels lifted her clipboard from the pew, then paused long enough to glance at her watch. Her shift had officially ended nearly twenty minutes ago. She exhaled softly; not out of fatigue, but from the quiet tug of something she wasn't used to feeling. Pastor Thompson, his wife, the young nurses who had worked beside her all day, the church members who had filled this tiny chapel with prayer… they had become more than names on a chart or faces passing through a corridor. She tucked the clipboard beneath her arm and gave a small nod, her tone gentler than before.

"Mrs. Thompson, I can escort you to ICU, if you like. It's the least I can do."

Nurse Daniels' gaze shifted to Kendra, Charlene, and Raymond. "You can walk up with us too and say your goodbyes just outside ICU."

There was no protocol in her voice now. No duty-bound firmness. Just compassion; simple, willing, and sincere.

Leah placed her bible back in her purse and when she stood, the entire group rose with her. Sam, Kendra, Charlene, Raymond, and the deacons. They moved together through the quiet corridors, their footsteps soft against the tile as the hospital settled into the last hours before dawn. When they reached the ICU double doors, Nurse Daniels turned around to face them and said softly.

"This is as far as everyone can go, except for Mrs. Thompson."

Leah turned to the small circle around her, her eyes shimmering with exhaustion and gratitude. One by one, they embraced her, whispering words of encouragement.

Kendra hugged her first, holding tightly.

"We're praying, Sister Thompson. For both of you."

Charlene wrapped her arms around her next. "Anything you need…anything…you call me, okay?"

Sam was next, and he gave her a gentle hug. "We love you and we're here for you… every step of the way."

The deacons offered gentle words and promises of prayers through the night.

Raymond was last. He pulled her into a quiet, heartfelt embrace. "You're not alone," he whispered. "Call me if you need anything. Just try to get some rest tonight, if you can, OK?"

He stepped back and Nurse Daniels opened the ICU doors. Leah looked at all of them once more, breathed in their strength, then followed Nurse Daniels inside.

The hallway to the ICU rooms was brightly lit, but the room itself was dim, almost peaceful… illuminated by the soft glow of monitors. Nurse Daniels parted the curtains and motioned for Leah to enter.

"Reverend Thompson is in here, Mrs. Thompson, room 605."

Just as Leah entered the room, an ICU nurse parted the curtain on the other side of the room and quickly recorded Pastor Thompson's vitals and checked his bandages. She was a little taken aback in seeing Nurse Daniels on the other side of the room, and gave a quick nod of acknowledgement before quietly slipping away to check in on the next patient. Leah watched the steady rise and fall of her husband's chest and placed her hand over his heart for just a few beats before taking the chair next to his bedside. Leah's gaze turned to Nurse Daniels and she whispered a quiet "Thank you."

"They'll take good care of him, Mrs. Thompson. I will check in on you later." Nurse Daniels returned a slight smile, visibly moved and then quietly slipped away.

"Nathaniel," Leah whispered, her voice low but filled with love and faith, "I'm right here. The Lord has kept you this far. And I know that He has the power to heal you."

She opened her bible and began to read from his favorite translation, starting with Psalms, and continuing with all the scriptures that they had read and meditated together over the years. Though her voice was low, the heart of the scriptures filled the quiet room, each word settling over them like a blessing of peace.

Chapter 15

The Long Night that Wakes a Gentle Tomorrow

Outside the ICU doors, Sam, Kendra, Charlene, Raymond, and the deacons stood in solemn quietness. The storm had weakened considerably outside, but inside these walls, the air carried the weight of everything they'd still have to face.

The deacons carried the weight of supportive care for a severely injured pastor, his beloved wife, and the congregation of Main Street Baptist Church.

Sam and Kendra carried the weight of supporting each other.

Charlene carried the weight of a vision she still didn't fully understand and the fragile friend she was determined to stand beside.

And Raymond carried the weight of just being present; whenever he was needed and however he was needed.

No one spoke at first. It felt as though the hallway itself was holding its breath.

Deacon Eric Bennett finally cleared his throat, his voice low and thoughtful.

"Before we go our separate ways," he said, "we ought to pray together. Pastor would want that… and truth be told, we all need it."

Everyone nodded; tired, but grateful and willing.

They formed a loose circle, holding hands gently. Sam took Kendra's hand; Raymond reached for Charlene's. The other deacons closed the circle and bowed their heads.

"Father, we come to You in the wee hours of this morning, proclaiming that You are still God... in spite of the situation. So we come to You as humbly as we know how, and we ask for divine healing grace, and mercy for our shepherd, Pastor Nathaniel Thompson. We ask for strength, and the peace that passeth all understanding, for Sister Thompson. And for all gathered here in this small circle, I pray that You bless them with the comfort and peace that only You can provide. We thank You in advance for the blessing. In Jesus' name... Amen."

The group responded in unison, "Amen."

Deacon Bennett shook everyone's hand graciously, then placed his other hand over Kendra's for a brief, gentle moment before letting go.

"Y'all get some rest," he said softly. "Tomorrow will be another day that tests our faith."

"Yes," Deacon Morris added quietly. "And God's already ahead of us… ready, willing, and able to be a shelter in a time such as this."

One by one, the deacons began to gather their coats, their Bibles, their hats. Deacon Bennett paused again before leaving, his gaze full of the calm steadfastness he was known for.

"We'll be back later today," he said. "Pastor Thompson's in God's hands now… and that's the safest place he could ever be."

With that, they made their way down the quiet hallway, footsteps soft against the polished floor, their presence slowly fading until only the four of them remained.

Charlene rubbed at her eyes, suddenly aware of how heavy her limbs felt. The hallway seemed longer now that the deacons had gone, the silence stretching out around them.

Before she turned to leave, Charlene moved toward Kendra and wrapped her in a warm embrace. Kendra hugged her back, letting out a soft breath of quiet relief at being understood without judgment. For just a moment, she let herself recognize and appreciate the blessing of having a true friend who was simply available.

Charlene whispered near her ear, "You call me if you need me, you hear?"

Kendra nodded gently, her voice calm and soft. "I will."

Charlene then turned to Sam and gave him a brief, sincere hug. "Take care… and I'm trusting you to take care of her too," she said quietly.

"You too," Sam replied, accepting the weight of that responsibility.

With that, she stepped back, and Raymond glanced over at her.

"You ready to head out, Charlene? I'd be happy to walk you to your car." His voice was low, kind… the sort of tone someone used when they understood the night had already taken more than it should.

She looked toward the ICU doors one more time. "Yes, thank you," she said softly. "I'm ready."

"There's no reason for you to be walking alone in a parking lot at night as long as I'm here." He said it not as a suggestion, but as a certainty. "No reason at all."

Sam lifted his brows at that, glancing sideways at Kendra to see if she caught it too.

He turned his head slightly toward her and mouthed, *That's how it starts,* punctuating it with a mischievous little smile.

Kendra let out the first real smile she'd had all night and hugged him lightly around the waist… a small, instinctive gesture that drew them closer for a moment. A tiny sign that she was coming back to herself.

With that moment passing gently between them, Charlene and Raymond began moving down the corridor side by side, their footsteps in soft rhythm on the floor. When they walked through the sliding glass doors into the lobby and then out under the covered drive, the cool, damp air brushed against Charlene's face, waking her just enough to keep going.

"Feels strange," she said quietly as they crossed the lot. "A night like this… the uncertainty, the waiting, the prayers. Somehow, I still feel that God was right there with us, helping us just hold on and keep it together."

Raymond nodded slowly. "He did, and He still is," he replied. "I guess sometimes He just wants to let us know in His own way that He *is* God."

She let out a tired smile and nodded in agreement. "Can't argue with that, Raymond. Wow, that was pretty deep."

When they reached her Jeep, he stopped beside her, not rushing her, not moving away either. She unlocked the door, and after he opened it for her, she slipped inside, rolling the window down all the way.

Raymond leaned in slightly so he could see her face, rain misting across his. "Get some rest when you can. Pastor's still in the Lord's hands. And so are you."

"Thank you, Raymond," she said, her voice quiet and tired, but sincere.

"Text me when you get home, alright? Just need to know that you safely made it."

The softness and concern in his tone caught her off guard. The warm feeling that rose within her was one she didn't have the energy to pursue.

"I will."

He stepped back to allow her to leave and watched as she pulled out of the space and eased toward the exit, her taillights glowing red in the wet darkness. Only when her car disappeared beyond the edge of the lot did he turn back toward the hospital doors. As he walked towards his Humvee limo, he quietly reflected on the few souls still inside…those who still had to get through the rest of the night.

Sam and Kendra had followed closely behind Charlene and Raymond from the ICU hallway. The elevator ride was so quiet on the way down to the main hospital floor that the soft music ended up filling the silence between them. Charlene and Kendra both leaned against the walls, their exhaustion etched into their faces and eyes. Raymond and Sam kept watchful eyes on them, exchanging only quiet, knowing glances with every floor's descent. By the time the elevator reached the main floor, they all let out slight grunts just to coax their tired bodies back into motion.

When they reached the atrium and the main entrance, they waved their last goodbyes, and Raymond and Charlene walked together to her car.

Sam looked at Kendra softly. "Just wait right here, and I'll bring the truck around, okay?" He paused, not entirely sure he liked the idea of leaving her alone even for a few minutes.

Kendra looked up, hoping to catch his eyes. "Hey… thanks, but you know, I think I'll walk with you. This night air will wake me up a little, and I could use some fresh air."

Sam nodded with that wide, kind-eyed smile she had grown so accustomed to. He reached out for her, and she reached back for him. They walked through the parking lot side by side, hand in hand.

Her grip told him exactly what he needed to know. She trusted him, in spite of everything she was going through. They glanced at each other now and then, speaking without ever saying a word. And with every step, she seemed to gather a little more strength.

At the truck, Sam opened the door for her and helped her slide in. He reached for the seatbelt, but she placed her hand over his.

"I've got it," she said gently.

He smiled softly. "Alright."

When he rounded the truck and got in, he sat for a moment with his hands on the wheel, staring out the windshield as if gathering his thoughts.

"Kendra," he began quietly, "it's a little after three in the morning. Your parents are asleep, and if I take you home now and walk you inside, they're going to wake up. And they'll know something is wrong. You don't need that right now… and they don't need that. To be honest…" He sighed softly. "I don't need that either."

He glanced at her before continuing. "I think I should take you to my place. The ocean view is calming, and I can keep an eye on you, and we both can get some much-needed rest. And whatever questions come afterward, we'll face them then… together. You can take the bedroom. I'll take the couch. Fair enough?"

She couldn't argue with his reasoning. He was being direct, respectful, and caring. He was being Sam.

Kendra nodded. "I knew you were going to say that."

He met her eyes. "And you knew I was right."

She released a tired breath; not quite a laugh, but close.

"Yeah. I did."

As the truck moved out onto the wet road, Kendra sat back, letting her muscles relax. Her eyes drifted half-closed from the kind of exhaustion that only quietly surrenders to the safety she felt beside him.

Sam steered carefully around scattered limbs and broken branches left behind by the storm. Puddles shimmered across the asphalt, some deep enough for the tires to send soft ripples outward as he eased through them. A few intersections held pockets of shallow flooding, but nothing he couldn't navigate. Beside him, Kendra drifted deeper into sleep, her head resting lightly against the window. Sam didn't disturb her. Each time he paused at a stop sign or light, he turned his head slightly to cast a brief glance at her. He felt his heart melting just to look on the quiet peace finally settling over her.

A quiet prayer rose in him, simple and sincere. *Thank You, Lord… for giving her the rest that she needs.*

When he pulled into his parking space, he could see beyond the waterfront that the sea had become calm again. He turned off the engine and sat there for a moment, exhaustion finally catching up with him in the stillness. The long day and the long night had taken their toll on him — physically, emotionally, and spiritually… and only now, in the tranquility of the waterfront, did he finally feel the full weight of it.

He reached over gently and touched her forearm.

"Kendra… hey. We're home."

She stirred slowly, blinking as sleep released its hold.

"Already?"

He nodded. "Yeah. Come on. Let's get you inside."

Sam slipped out his side a little more weary than when he'd stepped in and walked around to open Kendra's door to help her down. Both were a little unsteady at first, but Sam quickly recovered and steadied her with a gentle touch to her back. The walk to his condo was only a few steps away, and they both released a sigh of relief the second the opened door revealed a warm, softly lit room overlooking the quiet waterfront… a view so still and peaceful that it seemed to calm them the moment they were inside. The marina lights scattered across the water like reflections of distant stars, the whole scene resting in a stillness that almost felt sacred.

Kendra paused, taking it in.

Sam moved closer beside her, his own exhaustion finally making its presence known.

"You made it through," he said, still focusing on the view in front of them.

"*We* made it through," she responded, turning her gaze to him.

They drifted toward each other almost unconsciously, drawn by a need for reassurance rather than words. They embraced gently, using the last bit of energy they had left.

He pulled her into a tired, tender embrace… the kind meant to bring someone close enough to share heartbeats. They stayed like that long enough for the last of the tension to leave her body.

"Goodnight, Sam," she whispered.

He pressed a soft kiss to her forehead.

"Goodnight, baby."

They separated reluctantly, each weighed down by exhaustion but comforted by the other's nearness. Kendra made her way to the bedroom and barely managed to slip between the covers before sleep overtook her completely.

Sam quietly closed the door behind her and grabbed a pillow. He turned off the lamp and started a slow, relaxing jazz tune on the stereo, but not loud enough to awaken Kendra. He stretched out on the couch, pulling a blanket over himself without much care. Before the first full jazz note played, sleep claimed him too.

As they both slept away the weight of the day, the night seemed to exhale with them.

The storm had passed, leaving behind a town washed in a dim, sapphire pre-dawn glow. Inside the ICU of Harmony Grove Harbor Hospital, the night had never truly grown quiet. The circular unit pulsed with a steady undercurrent of activity; soft-spoken voices at the nurses' station in the center ring, the rhythmic beeping of monitors, the low hum of machines tracking each fragile breath.

Nurses moved between rooms with intentional purpose, slipping through the inner curtain entrances as they checked vitals, adjusted lines, changed dressings, and updated charts. Even the slightest change in a monitor's beep drew quick eyes to the central screens, where each patient's vitals were displayed in continuous vigilance.

Even at this hour, the air carried a sustained intensity; an acute awareness that lives were being held in the balance here, moment by moment.

Inside Pastor Nathaniel Thompson's ICU room, a weary Leah remained watchful and hopeful at her husband's bedside; her hand frequently touching his. She had managed a few short naps here and there, but between naps there were whispered prayers, some silent, spoken only from the heart. With every scripture read and every tear shed, she had found unwavering strength from somewhere deep inside that only God and she could name.

He had lain motionless during the night; the only sign that life still fought within him was the rhythmic rise and fall of his chest. Bandages covered the wounds to his abdomen and medicines to ease his pain, prevent infection, and provide hydration were delivered through multiple IV lines.

Leah awakened once again and sat up, taking a moment to remember where she was. She quickly moved to check on Nathaniel. She touched his face and gently stroked his cheek.

"Baby, it's morning… I love you," she whispered.

And then it happened so quickly that she wasn't sure she had seen what she thought she saw. His eyelids fluttered for a few seconds before they partially opened, then closed again and fell still.

A nurse who had walked in just in time to see Pastor Thompson's rapid eye movements offered a sympathetic smile. The look on Leah's face did not go unnoticed.

"Mrs. Thompson," she said softly, rechecking the monitors, "his vitals have been stable for the last few hours. That's a good sign. And yes, what you saw *is* a good sign. He could be coming out of unconsciousness sooner than we anticipated."

Leah nodded, a slight twinkle appearing in her eyes… a sign that God was moving.

"Is it too soon to know more?" she asked.

The nurse paused, choosing her words carefully. "The doctor will do another assessment this morning. And I have noted the eye movement. But stability is what we're looking for in these first hours. And he's now holding steady."

Leah closed her eyes, exhaling a grateful breath.

"Thank You, Lord…" she murmured.

The nurse touched her shoulder. "Can I bring you anything? Coffee? Water? I've seen you here since my shift started, and you haven't eaten anything. It's important that you take care of yourself so that you can take care of him. I can have the cafeteria send something up to the unit for you if you don't want to leave him."

"Thank you," Leah said softly. "I just need to stay with him."

The nurse nodded and left quietly, leaving Leah alone with the soft beeping of the monitors and the steady heartbeat of the man she loved… fighting his way back to her.

Leah leaned over his bed and spoke directly into his ear.

"You're strong, Nathaniel," she whispered. "Stronger than what this storm did to you. And I do believe that God is not done with you yet."

Leah reached for his hand once more… and she felt his hand gently tighten around hers.

"Nathaniel…?" she said softly.

His eyelids fluttered faster now and then his eyes opened more fully this time before closing again.

Leah skipped a breath, and gently touched his face.

"I see you," she said, "And I'll be right here until you come back to me."

And for the first time since this whole ordeal began, Leah allowed herself to believe that he *was* coming back to her.

Outside the ICU window, the faintest line of morning light had begun to trace the horizon; gentle and subtle, just enough to promise that a gentler tomorrow was coming.

Chapter 16

A Morning of Mercy

The storm clouds had moved on from Harmony Grove Harbor hours ago, leaving behind fallen branches, slick mud-coated roads from minor flooding, and several downed palms. The stretch of Coastal Highway 17 where the multi-vehicle accident occurred remained closed as cleanup crews worked through the aftermath. In its fury, the storm had claimed seven lives, but twenty-seven survivors occupied rooms throughout Harmony Grove Harbor Regional Hospital… among them, Pastor Nathaniel Thompson.

Raymond Carter reached the ICU doors around nine, arriving just as physicians and surgeons were beginning their morning rounds. Some road closures and tangled traffic had pushed morning schedules back, but the corridors had eased into a calmer rhythm now; a welcome shift after the chaos of the night. Raymond paused for a moment, taking in the quiet and gathering himself before going inside. His main mission was to relieve Leah from her overnight vigil, but he already knew there would be pushback, if not a downright refusal to leave her husband's side.

A nurse inside the ICU saw him through the glass and pressed the door release, letting him in with a gentle nod. When he reached Pastor Thompson's room, he paused just outside as the medical team finished their examination and updated Leah, staying close enough to hear what was being said.

Their voices were low but clear.

"Vitals have been stable for several hours now... bleeding controlled... responsiveness is improving."

One of the physicians leaned closer, watching for subtle movement in Pastor Thompson's eyelids.

"He's regaining consciousness," she said, offering a practiced smile. "His wounds are already showing signs of healing, with no indications of infection. Let's go ahead and update his condition from critical to serious."

When the team left, Raymond eased inside the room and observed the slow, steady rhythm of Pastor Thompson's breathing. Leah looked up and smiled the moment she saw him enter, then hugged him tightly. The exhaustion in her eyes was unmistakable. Raymond motioned for her to sit in the same chair she had occupied through most of the night, then took another chair, positioning himself so he could look at her directly as he held her hands.

"Sister Thompson," Raymond said softly, "he's improving. You'll be better able to help him when he wakes up if you get some rest and take a moment to exhale."

She started to protest, but he shook his head and met her gaze with a firmer look.

"I've already arranged for one of my drivers to take you home. He's just outside the ICU doors and will escort you to the limo. I'll stay with Pastor until you come back... you have my word."

Leah hesitated only for a moment before her resolve gave way. She stood, kissed her husband's forehead, and whispered,

"I'll be back soon, love... Raymond will be with you while I'm gone."

With one last grateful look at Raymond, she quietly left the room and headed toward the ICU doors.

Kendra woke to a soft band of sunlight stretching across her face and pillow. Her body felt lighter, but her muscles ached from everything the night had demanded of her. She just lay there for a moment, enjoying the stillness and the quiet… something she felt she had not been able to do for far too long. She didn't hear movement outside the door, so she thought, "*Sam must still be sleeping.*"

Reluctantly, she forced herself out of bed and pulled a fresh change of clothes from her tote. Practiced military habits die hard... she never went anywhere unprepared. After a quick shower, she dressed then quietly opened the bedroom door.

As she passed the couch on her way to the kitchen, she paused, watching Sam sleep. Even in sleep, he stirred that familiar flutter in her heart. His breathing was slow and deep now, his expression unguarded in a way she rarely saw. It was almost as if he were sleeping away the cares of the world, at least for now.

In the kitchen, her movements were quiet, and she made a pot of coffee and found a packaged turnover heating it in the microwave as the coffee brewed. The smell filled the generous space with something warm and cozy. When the coffee was ready, she took a cup and tiptoed up the stairway leading to the rooftop deck, deciding not to wake Sam just yet. He needed the rest as much as she did.

Outside, the morning was cool and bright, the harbor spread out in a soft silver light. Kendra wrapped her hands around the warm mug and breathed in the quiet.

Sam woke to the faint smell of coffee drifting through the quiet space. He blinked groggily, sat up, and noticed the bedroom door standing open. When he walked inside and saw the wrinkled scrubs laid carefully across the bed and an open tote bag… but no Kendra, he smiled.

Of course she was up already.

He pulled on a T-shirt, wandered into the kitchen, and found the fresh pot of coffee waiting. He poured a cup, reheated a biscuit from the fridge, then climbed the stairs to the rooftop deck.

Kendra sat with her legs tucked under her, gazing out at the harbor. She looked peaceful... finally.

When she saw him, she smiled, and when he was close enough, he leaned down and kissed her good morning. He meant to pull away, but she held him there for a second longer.

"You and your ready-made meals," she teased softly. "I swear, Sam... you're one microwave meal away from becoming a bachelor legend."

He chuckled, easing down beside her. "Hey now... those biscuits are a bachelor's mainstay, unless, of course, you're volunteering to make breakfast for me every morning?"

"Be careful what you ask for." She raised both eyebrows and gave him a flirtatious smile.

They shared a hearty laugh and fell into easy conversation, letting the warmth of the sun and the comfort of each other settle around them.

Sam slid his chair closer and let his shoulder brush lightly against hers as they sipped their coffee in easy silence. After a moment, he exhaled slowly and glanced out toward the harbor.

"You know," he said quietly, "I don't scare easily... but last night?" He lowered his head slightly. "That storm hit so fast, and I kept thinking about what you were going through in that ER and trauma center. Then seeing you in the atrium by the window, in the state you were in… it… it shook me more than I expected."

Kendra looked over at him, her expression softening.

"I'm alright, Sam," she said gently.

"I know…I can see that…now," he replied, offering a small smile. "But walking with you through it last night... it reminded me how much I care. More than I think I realized before." He paused, rubbing the back of his neck as if embarrassed by the admission. "I guess I just needed to say that out loud."

Kendra's smile deepened, warm and sincere. "Thank you... that means a lot, and I felt it."

They fell quiet again, but the connection between them felt even stronger now; anchored by something spoken and equally understood.

Sam's phone vibrated against his pocket, breaking the stillness. He glanced at the screen.

"Raymond."

He answered and switched to speaker so Kendra could hear.

Raymond's voice carried a brightness neither of them had heard over the last few hours. "Good news... the doctors upgraded Pastor Thompson's condition. Critical to serious. He's stabilizing... and he's starting to come around."

Kendra closed her eyes, relief washing over her. Sam exhaled and pointed toward the sky, acknowledging the God who ruled above it. Their shoulders relaxed at the same time.

"Thank God…" Kendra whispered.

Sam nodded, meeting her gaze with a gentle smile. "Yeah… thank God."

After the call ended, Sam placed his phone on the table and let out a sigh.

"That's a blessing," he said.

Kendra nodded. "Yes, it is. And by the way, I called my parents earlier… just to let them know I was okay."

Sam's shoulders eased. "Good. I was going to ask if you'd had a chance to talk with them this morning."

She leaned back in her chair, closing her eyes as the morning sun warmed her face. “I think I just need a little quiet today.”

“Yeah,” he said softly. “Me too.”

Sam smiled and made his way down the steps. A few moments later, she headed downstairs as well; the sound of running water drifted from the bathroom, followed by a voice. A really good voice.

Sam wasn’t just humming. He was singing… rich, powerful, soulful, almost angelic, like he’d forgotten anyone else in the world could hear him.

Kendra paused, coffee cup halfway to her lips. “Wow… he can really sing,” she whispered to herself, shaking her head as if this discovery were something extraordinary.

When he reappeared, hair still damp, she folded her arms and raised an eyebrow.

“Why am I just now finding out that you can sing like that?”

Sam shrugged, reaching for the remote on the counter. “Everybody sings in the shower.”

“Not like that they don’t.”

He grinned. “Well, since you like my singing so much, why don’t we just relax with some jazz tunes, and I’ll sing to you until you get tired of listening to me.”

“Deal.”

So Kendra and Sam fell into a rhythm of gentle jazz and quiet laughter, letting the weight inside them slowly release its hold… as if the morning itself whispered grace to them. Whatever came next, they knew neither of them would face it alone.

And somewhere in the steady rhythm of the hospital, a weary heartbeat strengthened… answering the mercy the morning had brought.

By early evening, that same mercy lingered in the halls of the ICU. Leah returned to the ICU just as Raymond finished a slow stretch near the curtained entrance to Pastor Thompson's room, facing the large windows lining the hallway. He rolled his shoulders once and twisted gently at the waist, easing the stiffness from hours spent at Nathaniel's bedside. True to his word, he had not left the room.

Leah spotted Raymond as she walked down the corridor and gave a small wave, quickening her pace, anxious to know how Nathaniel had fared while she'd been gone. Raymond parted the curtain for her, and they entered the room together.

The lights were dimmed, casting the room in a soft glow. A slow jazz tune played quietly from Raymond's phone, giving the space a calming ambience. Leah instinctively glanced at the monitors, then at the familiar rise and fall of her husband's chest.

"How's he doing?" she asked softly. "Any change?"

Raymond lowered his voice. "I noticed a little movement off and on. Nothing dramatic… but different from earlier. The nurses said I should keep talking to him."

Leah nodded as she moved closer to the bed. She gently touched the side of Nathaniel's face and looked into his eyes as if she could will them to open. For a moment, she thought she heard the faintest sound of his voice, but maybe it was a groan.

"I'm back, Nathaniel," she whispered. "I couldn't stay away too long."

She was about to pull her hand back when she noticed his eyelids flutter. His lips parted slightly.

"Leah," he whispered, barely audible.

She leaned closer immediately, her hand finding his. "Nathaniel?"

His eyelids fluttered for a few seconds, then opened just enough for her to see his eyes as he turned slightly toward her voice. The effort tightened his brow. A faint smile touched his lips, followed by a soft grimace of pain.

"I missed you," he whispered.

He raised his hand just enough for Leah to notice, and she wrapped her hand around his.

"I'm here, baby."

Chapter 17

Reflections

By Saturday afternoon, the city had begun to settle into its familiar rhythm again. The storm had passed days ago, the air felt washed clean, and somehow the town seemed quieter now, as if it were catching its breath after holding it too long. Fear had loosened its grip, and now, Sam, Kendra, and Charlene allowed themselves to simply be.

On Sam's rooftop deck, smooth jazz flowed through small speakers near its edges. A calmness drifted through the air that was soft enough to blend with the sounds of the city below. Kendra allowed herself to sink into one of four plush deck lounges, her sunglasses resting loosely on her nose. It was warm for an autumn day, and the warmth of the sun eased away the last of tension that had lingered.

Charlene sat nearby, content to be silent, reclining her lounge back further to watch clouds move lazily across the sky. The urgency for motion had paused for now. Sam, too, rested easily, taking the lounge next to Kendra with no desire to move.

The only conversation between them was the rhythmic movement of their feet and occasionally fingers to the beat of the music. The three of them, comfortable enough with each other in the quietness; nothing pressing, nothing demanded, nothing expected.

When a notification chimed softly on Sam's phone, he glanced at the screen and tapped once, unlocking the front door remotely. Moments later, Raymond emerged onto the rooftop, his face showing the familiar etchings of fatigue, softened now by something else…relief.

Raymond delivered the news gently, without ceremony. Pastor Thompson had been moved out of the ICU earlier that morning and into a private room. Access to windows and sunlight, along with less monitoring, would offer a calmer, less intense atmosphere. The doctors' updates were optimistic; measured and careful, yet hopeful. Recovery would take time, patience, and strength, but they believed the worst had passed.

When Raymond finished, Kendra exhaled slowly, her shoulders relaxing as if she'd been carrying more than she realized. Sam sat up and sat sideways, lifting his eyes toward the sky for a long moment, his gratitude evident in the simple pressing of his hands together in silent praise. Charlene sat up and bowed her head, arms outstretched, eyes closed.

Raymond, not wanting to break the silence, turned away and placed one hand over his heart, drawing in a deep breath. When the moment passed, he took the remaining lounge and soon drifted into sleep beside them.

The music continued to play, unbothered, as if time itself had paused just for them. Below them, the city moved on. Above them, the sky held space for what had been lost… and for what had been spared.

Saturday gave way to Sunday the way it always did in Harmony Grove Harbor…quietly and faithfully. But this Sunday, the voice of the bell returned to Main Street Baptist Church, ringing out again after years of silence.

By midmorning, the church was already welcoming its first worshippers. A steady stream of cars filled the lot unceremoniously, followed by the gentle clicks and thuds of car doors opening and shutting. Familiar voices offering warm greetings filled the air as they made their way toward the sanctuary.

Inside, greetings with hugs and handshakes and even some waves across aisles of pews continued as the worship hour approached. People spoke in lowered tones, though not always out of reverence. News travels quickly at Main Street Baptist, and almost everyone was aware of Pastor Thompson's injuries and the long recovery anticipated ahead. His absence was spoken of in quiet conversations, and some huddled in small groups to exchange updates they'd already heard twice. More than one prayer that morning had been spoken for Pastor Thompson and Leah, still at the hospital.

Even beyond quiet conversations, there was an unmistakable somberness. The absence of their shepherd was felt, even as they entered the place of worship. The spirit of the congregation wasn't dampened, but softened, as if the morning was urging them to tread more gently, and to love more intensely.

With the final ring of the bell for this Sunday, the congregation quietly prepared for worship, pew by pew, family by family. Worship time had come to Main Street Baptist Church.

The familiar rhythms of Sunday morning worship were taking hold. In attendance this Sunday sat an extended family… those who had carried one another through seasons of joy and sorrow, and moments both ordinary and remarkable: Sam Whitaker, Kendra Williams, Charlene Matthews, and Raymond Carter. Their presence was quiet and unassuming, each of them keenly aware that simply being there together was a gift.

This Sunday, Sam chose a pew closer to the front of the sanctuary, unusually close to the choir. Noticeably quieter than normal for him, he guided Kendra down the aisle and stepped aside, allowing her to take her seat before settling into the end seat himself. It was an intentional choice, one that felt less like confidence and more like purpose. As they settled in their seats next to each other, Kendra's hand gently brushed his. Her parents sat a few rows behind them, watching with the kind of love and tenderness that comes from having prayed through the night for both of them more than once.

The worship service followed its normal order; scriptures were read, prayers were offered, hymns were sung. Sam quietly rose from his seat just as the choir prepared to sing before the sermon and joined them. The choir director graciously acknowledged him and motioned for Sam to take the microphone near the center of the choir. The musicians started and Sam started to sing… his voice anointed, and rich.. delivering a simple message in song: *See What the Lord Has Done.* This was Sam's personal testimony. It bore witness to where he had been, what he had come through, and where he now stood. It was not done by his own strength, but only by the grace and mercy of a faithful and loving God.

The truth in the words of the song, along with the power in the voice of the man delivering it, brought the congregation to its feet. Tears began to flow freely, hands raised in acknowledgment of what the Lord has done. Sam's and Kendra's parents stood with the rest of the congregation, tears visible on their faces. But it was Kendra who understood the deeper meaning behind this song. For the few moments when their eyes met, both recognized their shared journey… one of restoration and healing that God was still carrying them through.

When the song ended, there was reverent applause. Even as Sam took his seat, many worshippers remained standing, their hearts and souls full, reminded once more of the faithfulness of God.

Afterward, an associate pastor approached the pulpit and observed a congregation still wrapped in sincere praise and worship. He declared that God had spoken, and that the sermon had already been preached. Shortly after, the final song was sung, the benediction was given, and the worship service ended.

The congregation slowly spilled out into the parking lot, conversations light and unhurried, the warmth of the service lingering in quiet laughter and easy goodbyes. Sam, Kendra, Charlene, and Raymond stood together for a few moments longer… reluctant to rush away just yet.

Just above them, clouds had begun to stir, threatening to change an otherwise beautiful Sunday morning. They stirred just enough to cause them to look up. But when Charlene looked up, just slightly in the direction of the church's bell, she saw it. Slowly and almost deliberately the clouds were forming into a familiar pattern in the sky. She held her breath for just a moment and then she smiled, a simple smile of recognition and confirmation.

Sam noticed first. Then Kendra. They followed her gaze, and they understood. Words were not necessary.

Raymond looked from one face to another, sensing something had passed between them, even if he didn't quite see it himself.

When they looked back at each other, they gave their final goodbyes with hugs and quiet waves, they parted ways, each carrying something different; yet all lifted by the same grace that was still carrying them through.

And higher above Main Street Baptist Church, and Harmony Grove Harbor, the sunlight blessed them with its face once more…faithfully.

Epilogue

Sam slowed a few steps before stopping at the glass storefront that reflected more sky than street. He stood there for just a moment, one hand reaching for the door. He took in a couple of deep breaths before opening it.

A little silver bell chimed softly as he walked inside.

Warm light spilled across polished counters and silver velvet trays. Somewhere behind the glass, a friendly salesperson looked up and smiled.

"Good morning. What can I help you with?"

Sam met her eyes, sure and resolved.

"I'm looking for an engagement ring."

"Do you have something in mind?"

Sam nodded.

"Yes. I do."

He glanced down at the cases, not searching…just confirming what he already knew.

He had already found the one long before today.

A time to be born, and a time to die;
a time to plant, and a time to pluck up that which is planted;

A time to kill, and a time to heal;
a time to break down, and a time to build up;

A time to weep, and a time to laugh;
a time to mourn, and a time to dance;

A time to cast away stones, and a time to gather stones together
a time to embrace, and a time to refrain from embracing;

A time to get, and a time to lose;
a time to keep, and a time to cast away;

A time to rend, and a time to sew;
a time to keep silence, and a time to speak;

A time to love, and a time to hate;
a time of war, and a time of peace.

Ecclesiastes 3:2–8 (KJV)

Words from the Author

If this story stirred something in your heart, and you find yourself longing for the same faith, grace, and quiet assurance experienced by the characters in *Blessings from Above*, I want you to know that such peace is available to you as well. The prayer that follows is offered simply as an invitation—for anyone who feels led, in their own time, to take that step of faith.

Prayer of Salvation

Dear God, I come to You admitting that I am a sinner. I believe that Your Son, Jesus Christ, died on the cross for my sins, and that You raised Him from the dead on the third day. I accept Jesus as my Lord and Savior, and I repent of my sin. Thank You for Your gift of salvation.

In Jesus' name, Amen.

www.ingramcontent.com/pod-product-compliance
Lightning Source LLC
Chambersburg PA
CBHW030811310726
48980CB00006B/464/J

* 9 7 9 8 9 9 4 5 9 3 7 2 1 *